11 - 11 - 11

by

John Rachel

Published by
Literary Vagabond Books
Los Angeles • Osaka
literaryvagabond.com

11 - 11 - 11
(Third Edition)
Copyright © 2015
by John D Rachel

Print Book ISBN #978-0-692-59428-5

Cover Art by Muriel 'Kitty' Orton

11 - 11 - 11

by

John Rachel

Noah was turning 23 and desperate to get out of town. Pulnick, Missouri had forever been a hopelessly hayseed blemish on the anemic face of rural Bible-belt America. Always bland and soporific, it was now being invaded by white supremacist meth heads, visited by an unprecedented crime wave, exploited by spiritualists and local politicos, and driven to hysteria by paranoid rumors that the world would end on November 11th. Moreover, Noah's personal life was becoming more convoluted by the day. Everything seemed to conspire against his singular need to go somewhere where he could begin a new life and learn how to dream.

Acknowledgements

First, I'd wholeheartedly like to thank the fictional citizens of the fictional town of Pulnick for their unparalleled hospitality and valuable assistance during the writing of this book. For a place which doesn't exist and which therefore I've never been, I feel like I have lived there all my life and now have a second home to which I can comfortably return anytime.

I want to profoundly thank my best friend and constant companion Masumi Nishida for her encouragement and faith in me, and her magnificent role as teacher and guide in my discovering the wonders of Japan and Japanese culture.

For their inestimable contributions to my literary and intellectual development, and my current tentative grasp on reality, I wish to express my appreciation and awe to: Tom Robbins, Woody Allen, Kurt Vonnegut, Stanislaw Lem, Christopher Moore, Chuck Palahniuk, Charles Bukowski, Jerzy Kosinski, Bertrand Russell, Ludwig Wittgenstein, Neil Postman, and Jared Diamond.

For their continuing friendship and support, I extend my heartfelt gratitude to Judy Rachel, Randy Calligan, Mickey Eres Finn, Travis Rood, Ron Ruiz, Gilly Adkins, Russ Swider, Nicholas Penrake, Jeff J. Brown, Randolph Winters, and Alex Malherbe.

Lastly but certainly not leastly, for their belief in me and their unwavering enthusiasm, much gratitude and heartfelt wet willies go out to my untiring publisher Literary Vagabond Books, specifically the svelte and droll head of that organization, Sybil Fairbanks, and my new editor there, Evelyn Ishimoto, who despite never having bothered to learn English has done a marvelous job on this challenging book. Both of you are studies in and witness to the irrepressible power of the human imagination.

Table of Contents

Prologue

The world would finally end. For sure this time.
Not like all those other times.
Really.

Chapter One

Bambi Meets Godzilla

Noah was watching *Bambi Meets Godzilla* on YouTube.

He loved that little film. How many times had he seen it? Fifty? A hundred?

Almost the entire length of the three-minute film consisted of opening credits rolling over an idyllic animation of Bambi eating and frolicking in the forest. Gentle spring flute music playfully accompanied the chirping of birds. Finally the credits finish and to a thunderous, forest-shaking *kaboom!*, Godzilla's giant foot comes down and squashes the innocent little fawn. All we see is Godzilla's grizzly leg and Bambi's four tiny twig-like limbs sticking out from under the giant reptilian foot. The music and birds have stopped, and as the *kaboom!* trails off in a drawn-out tail of reverberation, **The End** fades up on the screen and the film is over.

What a perfect metaphor! thought Noah. Especially for life in this stinking town.

As many times as he had watched it, it never failed to put him in a great mood. Of course, the first twenty or thirty times left him rolling helplessly on the floor in convulsions of laughter. Now it just left him pleasantly amused. Buoyant. Hopeful.

He knew he wasn't alone. Like minds. Somewhere out there.

When the clip finished, he clicked on the *Today's Recommended Videos* link.

The Featured Video was called "11-11-11: The Pleiadians Warned Us!!"

What was this all about? Some fat loser with greasy hair flopping in his face offered a five minute rant based on alleged alien visitations from the Pleiades constellation. Filmed with a hand-held camera, it was replete with photos of flying saucers and very weird mathematical symbols scribbled on a white board. The presentation concluded with a wildly unhinged catalog of every imaginable catastrophe and collusion of spiritual forces, a cosmic fusillade of supernatural cataclysms all occurring exactly at 11:11 am on November 11, 2011.

Right.

What a pile of kaka!

11:11 am. What time zone, loser?

Jokers like this annoyed him. All of these prophets of doom, conspiracists, rapturists and various peddlers of paranoid poop — and that included gurus, televangelists and faith healers, even parish priests and local Bible-thumpers if they were mongering fear from their bully pulpits — really pissed him off.

Whether they believed their own nonsense or not, these lunatics went around spewing this ridiculous crap, scaring the hell out of people and actually getting paid for doing it, while real people like himself actually had to work for a living.

Speaking of which … he had a job to go to.

Noah threw on his work clothes. He didn't have to be at work for three more hours but this was a perfect day for riding. He hated it when he got sucked into the internet and wasted such beautiful weather geeking out.

With a wifebeater under his open work shirt, a pair of jeans tucked into his riding boots, and his backpack buckled on, Noah kick-started his 140 cc Kawasaki off-road bike. It fired up on the first try and he did a decent enough wheelie out of the garage under his tiny studio apartment. Without looking back, he knew his landlady was at her window cursing him and his errant youthful ways. She would go back to mumbling prayers for God's forgiveness and His blessing for her abominable existence here on Earth.

Pulnick was one of the three main city-towns along a corridor that ran diagonally through Monroe County, Missouri. Monroe City sat in the very northeast corner of the county, Paris was dead center, and Pulnick midway between them just north of the artificial lakes that were the recreational foundation for Mark Twain State Park. Pulnick's surrounding landscape was a mixture of farms, woodlands, and open fields, and showed both the growing and shrinking pains of development, successful and otherwise. The area bore witness to the ambivalence of a region of middle America which could not make up its mind whether to jump on the freight train of industrialization and modernization, or to just lean back as it had for many decades and watch the corn grow.

As the crow flies, Noah's job was exactly 18 miles east and slightly south of Pulnick. If he went straight across town on Main Street, hammered it along Highway 24, then took some back roads east around Mark Twain Recreation Area, he could be there in less than twenty five minutes. Frankly, this was a pretty boring way to go. He had done it way too many times.

Today he had the time and wanted a little variety and challenge. That either meant heading north on the county roads where he could open up his little screaming metal monster for some serious speed, or south of town past the Monroe County Industrial Park, out toward Swinkley Lake. The lake was surrounded by woods, and there were lots of hiking and biking trails. It was fairly hilly and if he could avoid the mud holes from the recent rains, he could do some great off-road riding.

Noah opted for speed. He banked a right on Dillinger, left on Smithers, then right on Gandolph, which turned into County Road 171 at the outskirts of town. Two more lights and a stop sign and he'd be looking at thirty miles of pedal-to-the-metal open road. He could pull around any cars and trucks without blinking.

Just as he was approaching the last four-way stop, he suddenly heard a strange sound. It was coming directly from his left and behind him. It sounded like a combination of the roar of a truck engine and the blast of air brakes.

Then nothing.

The Long Weekend

When Noah came to, he was inside of an ambulance. He heard the long shrill whine of a siren and as the fog partially cleared, he could see he was not alone. Next to him looking out the side window was a man wearing an antiseptic mask. He gently held a breathing apparatus over Noah's face. The man turned back and noticed that Noah was regaining consciousness.

"Darn good thing you were wearing a helmet."

"Wha …?"

"Don't try to talk. Just be calm. You were in an accident. We'll be at the hospital in a few minutes. You're going to be alright."

Noah went back under, off into whatever world of dreams or metaphysical suspension is the temporary hospice for a traumatized body.

Next thing he remembered was feeling like someone was shoving something down his throat. He gagged and it felt like he tried to struggle. He couldn't be sure. Again the blank screen and autonomous hum of nothingness descended on him. Everything dispersed in a dreamless void. Time stopped. Then …

Faintly he heard moaning. Who was it? When he licked his lips it stopped.

Noah felt a cool damp cloth on his face. It gently patted his forehead. Brushed over his eyelids. With some effort he was able to open his eyes. Everything was a blur. He heard a soft voice. A female.

"Mr. Tass."

"Where am I?" Which came out as 'Wuh uh ah?'

"You're at Monroe County General. The hospital. And this is the intensive care section. You're going to be fine. You've had a bad accident but you are going to be okay. Just rest."

He was going to be okay. That's what the lady said.

He just had to rest …

Bones

They moved Noah out of the Intensive Care Unit after three days. His attending physician was a real comedian.

"Chances are you'll live. But in case you don't, we're moving you into a regular room, so you don't muck up the outstanding record of ICU this year. So far, they're batting a thousand, if you don't count the people they dragged out into the hall before they drew their last breath."

Noah was in a semi-private room. The person in the next bed was about 127 years old and if he had regained consciousness at any point during Noah's stay there, no one seemed to notice. Noah had all of the privacy he could desire or handle.

Not that he could do very much.

Watch TV. Eat. Sleep. Watch TV. Eat. Sleep.

Even when he was awake, the pain medication floated him in the weightless cloud of a semi-conscious stupor. Considering the quality of the television programming, this was probably best.

Soap operas would segue into cooking shows into weather reports into heroics on the basketball court into crime scene investigations into talk shows. Somehow it made sense without making any sense at all.

Days went by. At first he couldn't count them. Then he started to recognize a definite pattern to the way things were done. How often they would take his blood pressure. How long it took for him to use up the contents of his IV bottle. Which nurses were on days, which ones on afternoons, who had the night shift. There was only one on nights. Her name was Eleanor.

Sometimes he would look out the window. The windows were sealed. One day he asked a nurse if maybe they could get some fresh air, but in the controlled environment of the hospital it wasn't allowed. Day after day, the weather continued to be beautiful. Great riding weather.

By the beginning of the second week, Noah was permitted — in fact he was encouraged — to get up and move around a bit. Slowly. Carefully. Always with a nurse at his side. And with his IV bottle and rack in tow. They told him that the more he moved around, without of course aggravating his injuries, the faster he would heal. It was important to work his muscles, flex his joints, get his blood flowing, and jack up his metabolism. All good for the body.

Moving around might have terrific things going for it. But unfortunately it hurt like hell.

He frankly could not believe how bad it hurt. What had he done to himself?

Exercise notwithstanding, most of the time that second week he still spent in bed.

Noah had seven broken bones. Three broken ribs. A broken collar bone. His left leg broken in two places. His right arm, down near the wrist. The good news was they were all clean breaks, none requiring surgery, truss rods, bolts, or screws.

He had also gotten pretty bruised up: His chest where he took the impact of his handlebars. His legs, feet and ankles which had whipped around and broadsided the grill of the 18-wheeler. His right arm and shoulder from the rear tire of his motorcycle as it landed on him.

Naturally, he had some scrapes and superficial gashes as well. His face, hands, knees and elbows had a number of abrasions and shallow cuts. But despite their gruesome appearance and blue puffy swelling, especially the first three days in ICU, none of these injuries were very serious and the doctor assured him he would have no scars. It could have been much worse.

Darn good thing he was wearing a helmet.

Noah never got straight in his mind all of the details of the accident. Partly this was because his mind still was not very clear. And partly it was because he frankly couldn't remember anything at all about what had happened that day. Not a thing. When the body is severely traumatized, the mind always protectively blocks any recall of the incident. That's what his doctor told him. That certainly seemed to be how it was. He couldn't remember leaving his apartment to go riding that day. He couldn't even remember breakfast. Or lunch. Nothing.

What they told him, however, was that a truck driver from out of town didn't realize that there was a four-way stop intersection on that stretch of road, got distracted by something inside the cab of his truck, then when he glanced back up immediately saw he was about to plow into one to four vehicles waiting their turn after stopping at the crossroads. He initially swerved into the oncoming lane but a school bus full of kids had just made a right turn onto the road. He cut his wheel hard back into his own lane, making the choice of lesser evils. That was when he nailed Noah, on his way to taking out two other vehicles.

Amazingly, no one else was seriously hurt. The drivers of the other two automobiles were a little shaken up, but even though their vehicles were totaled, they and the truck driver himself came through it virtually unscratched.

Noah got it all.

Bad luck and motorcycles.

Of course when you ride a bike you know the risks. But you rationalize. It won't happen to me. I'm a good driver. I'm a safe driver. I'm a lucky guy.

Bad luck and motorcycles.

It could have been worse. He could have been killed. He could have …

He was rowing a boat. The water was like oil, a thick shimmering pool of impenetrable black. The boat felt like it was being pulled, and regardless of how hard he rowed, it slipped sideways away from the shore. A girl at the other end smoked a cigarette and gazed off. She laughed as she turned to him. Her lips and hair were black but she had piercing blue eyes. *"Your friends told me this was how it would be."* He felt humiliated and was overwhelmed by a desperate need to defend himself. *"Honestly, I'm doing the best I can."* Then one of the oars slipped out of his hand and disappeared into the shimmering black lake.

He reached for it and banged his head on a length of tubular metal. It turned out to be the safety rail on his bed.

Noah was awake again. Painfully awake. He felt a small lump on his forehead.

The glare of the overhead florescent lights made him wince. He threw his arm over his face and tried to roll over.

He suddenly heard the acid-washed whine of his kid sister Gretchen.

"You look terrible!"

Noah's sister never was up for the Miss Congeniality Award and never would be, especially in her relationship with her brother. Whether prompted by envy or intimidation — she was three years younger and failed in every way Noah excelled — she always made it clear that she thought Noah was a loser and things could only get worse for him.

He didn't feel like fighting with her. Not now.

"I asked for my bandages to be in mauve with yellow and silver embroidery. Look at these. And what's with cosmetic surgery these days? I wanted a subtle sculpturing of my naturally beautiful chin, not this Jay Leno demolition bumper."

"You are so gay."

"Shhh." Noah pointed his bandaged thumb toward his 127 year old roommate. "Let's just keep it between the two of us. I think he's a homophobe."

Noah started to ask where his mom was. But then he saw her standing by the door.

"Hi mom. Gretchen here was just trying to lift my spirits. She always sees the bright side of things. That's why she's so popular."

His mother had an unlit cigarette in her mouth, the filter caked with red from her lips. She removed it with her white gloved hand and waved it in the air as she spoke.

"Ha. Just like your father, young lady. Always trying to be funny."

Gretchen chomped on her bubble gum and sneered.

"I thought dad was never funny."

"Sometimes. I think so ... I don't exactly remember."

"Then why did you say it?"

"Say what?"

The soft subtle electronic sounds of the medical monitoring equipment next to Noah's bed sounded like an industrial roar compared to the uncomfortable silence which now filled the room. The Tass family was clearly out of its element. Whatever that element was.

His mother stared at Noah like he was a stranger. She always had. But it was worse today. She seemed to be looking at a spot six inches above his head and three feet behind him.

He himself had been staring at her as a stranger since his father left. Since her coronation as Queen of Trailer Park Chic. That was fourteen years ago. A long time. And these days he definitely couldn't remember the good old mom that raised him. There she stood in a full-length fur coat. In the middle of spring. Layers of pearls. Layers of makeup. Earrings that looked like Christmas tree ornaments. Thick amber frame rhinestoned glasses. Old lady cleavage swabbed with an orange base powder that couldn't hide the age spots and moles. Lipstick like the Joker.

Menopause was a bitch.

She always looked both frightened and aloof. Her best days behind her but hoping no one else would notice. Not a chance.

She was 49 going on 99, a poster lady for the never-was-never-will-be. It was as if she carried a sign that said: *Ye who enter here abandon all hope.*

In some strange way, his mother and sister were two of a kind. There was obviously a contrast in individual style. They were after all separated by a gaping generation gap. His mother was Victorian pseudo-chic. His sister was Gothic ultra-geek.

But if you looked beyond the particular outrageous choices each made to mock herself and send a hazardous substance warning to the rest of the human race, essentially they were both doing the same thing. Tragically, that was putting a wide forbidding psychological moat around themselves, guaranteeing that no one could get close enough to get a good look and see how woeful and self-loathing they were. A barrier barring any help from the outside.

Noah never played head games with his mother but he loved baiting his sister.

"Hey, Gretch. You look pretty stunning today yourself. How are things at the coven?"

Gretchen dismissed him with a snarling aside to her cell phone which she was pointlessly checking for non-existent text messages. "So pathetic!"

"Come on now. Don't you two get started."

Mommy dearest. The peacemaker. Never deterred by her complete and total failure to keep them from tearing into one another at every available opportunity. Somewhere beneath his physical pain, Noah couldn't help but feel sorry for her.

"Aw, mom. It's just healthy sibling curiosity. I like to know what's going on with my lovely little sis. I was just going to ask if they had set a date for her exorcism yet."

"Noah! Enough. Be nice! I can see you're feeling much better than when they brought you in."

"I am I am! Doctor says I can run the marathon this weekend. Besides I am being nice."

"Well, then … be nicer."

A nurse walked into the scene of smoldering family warfare.

"Time to check his vitals. I'll just be a minute. You both can stay put, if you wish."

After taking his blood pressure and temperature, then annotating his chart, she started to leave but Noah stopped her.

"Eleanor! You haven't met my family."

"No, I missed out on that." She turned and flashed a beauty contestant grin, extending her hand to Noah's mother. "You're Noah's sister?"

"Why, thank you!" Giggle giggle. "But I'm his mother."

Noah couldn't believe it. His mom fell for that cheap bit of flattery.

"Well, Mrs. Tass. Noah is doing quite nicely. And this here …" She then started to offer her hand to Gretchen but since the girl was totally preoccupied with her cell phone, she skipped it and went into her oft-repeated but always enthusiastic official visitors spiel.

"Visiting hours are over shortly. It is very important that nothing upsets Noah and that he gets lots of rest. But you are certainly welcome to visit whenever you can. The comfort of family is very crucial to his full recovery. If you have any questions, please feel free to ask."

She then left to continue her rounds.

The comfort of family is very crucial. That was a good one! He liked Nurse Eleanor. Wickedly wry, understated sense of humor.

His mom and sister remained another ten minutes, most of it passed in the silence of a strained detente. Noah wondered if they intentionally came this late in visiting hours to avoid spending more time with him. Whatever the reason for their brevity, he was grateful.

His mom bent over to kiss him good-bye but rather than risk smearing the artlessly applied red gunk on her lips — which he assumed was lipstick though it could have been some designer calking compound available now in all shades of the rainbow — she stopped several inches short. She puckered and floated an air kiss toward his forehead.

"Get well, my boy. The world is an oyster."

"And I am the pearl."

"You *have* been listening all these years."

"Only because I am a sucker for metaphors. Thanks for coming, Mom."

Gretchen stood up and still staring zombie-like at the screen of her cell phone, headed toward the door. Noah's mom poked her in the back, prompting her to say something.

"Good-bye, loser. I think you should fuck Eleanor."

"Thanks, Gretch. Have a great evening with your vibrator."

Big Thoughts

Laying there recovering in the hospital, Noah had a lot of time to think. Time to take stock. To think about things he never usually stopped to think about.

Nearly being flattened by a 52-ton truck can definitely prompt a person to try to gain a new perspective on life.

It now seemed *extremely* important to figure out what was important. Establish some priorities. Ask the big questions. Like ...

What did it all mean?

Okay. Maybe that was too big. He needed to scale it down a bit.

How about ...

Is there a God?

Hmm. Probably not. Anyway. Who cares?

Next ...

Is there an afterlife?

Probably. Too bad when you died you weren't around to enjoy it.

Ha ha ha ha.

Will good triumph over evil?

In practical terms, not a very useful question but easy enough to answer.

Answer: Only if Hollywood writes the script.

Hmm. That wasn't even funny.

Noah could see he was not making much progress.

He needed to be more specific, to think in terms of something more directly applicable to him and his current situation.

Okay …

If life is a journey, where exactly was he at?

Aha! This was doable. This was a dog he could hunt!

Plus it was a very important question. A profound question. A relevant question. One with real meat and gristle.

It was certainly something he should think long and hard about.

Unfortunately, it only took about six seconds and no effort whatsoever to answer.

He was nowhere.

He had been nowhere.

And was heading nowhere.

Worst of all, there were no prospects that anything would change.

Let's face it. He was the perennial hamster on a tread wheel. A one-trick pony going round and round in a circle. He was a fish in a very small bowl. No one ever even changed the water.

What a horribly depressing state of affairs! Only 23 years old and already at a dead end. Stuck in a cul-de-sac of blandness and monotony.

He had to wonder. How did this happen? What was it about all of the particular elements of his existence on Planet Earth which collectively managed to add up to one big fat pitiful zero? Zilch. Nil. Nix. Nada.

Hmm.

There was his job. He had been working at Walmart for almost two years now. Unloading trucks and opening boxes. Steady pay. Got along with everyone. Seemed in the performance of his duties to please management in general, his boss in particular. Okay. But? He had always thought of it as a temporary arrangement. He had just assumed the job would do until he came up with a better plan. But where was this plan going to come from? Would it miraculously drop out of the sky? Or would he find it in a box of Coco Crispies?

Score that a big zero.

Moving on.

There was his family.

What family?

Both his mother and sister were seriously damaged goods. His father had disappeared.

Another zero. Next …

Church?

He didn't go to church.

Zero.

How about sports?

Is drinking a sport? Bowling? No, that's a game. Realistically, the last time he did any sports was high school. That was over six years ago and even then he had only been a bench-warmer on a 2-wins-7-losses baseball team. As bad as the team was, he was worse. He would have been a better second base than a second baseman.

Zero.

Ah! There were his friends. And when he wasn't at work or tearing up asphalt with his bike, he was out doing something with his friends. The only thing he looked forward to in life.

Then again, they always did the same things. Said the same things. Laughed at the same jokes. Looked at the same girls.

Zero.

What's next? Of course!

Pulnick. His home town. Born and raised.

Immediately a huge black cloud descended over Noah. The same one that descended over him every time he stopped to think of the god-forsaken patch of the planet where he lived.

What was a town? Some would say the past. The history. The heritage.

But for a young man like him, forget about it. It was the present and the future.

Let the old people who got together and yakked away about the good old days, and formed committees to try to preserve the golden symbols of better and simpler times, pine away all they wanted. When you're 23 and you still have your whole life ahead of you, it's what you see right now and what you might see in the very immediate future that counts for everything.

Pulnick? What could he honestly say about Pulnick? Honestly.

That was easy.

Pulnick had nothing to offer now and no hope for the future. It was an abysmal little place in an abysmal area of an abysmal state.

Missouri! Whoever named the damn thing just couldn't spell.

How about M-I-S-E-R-Y? That made more sense.

Pulnick? A bunch of deadbeats and hicks.

They should rename it Voidville.

Or maybe Black Hole.

Or The Abyss.

Or just leave the name blank on the map.

Alright! Finally he had his answer. Noah had nailed the problem.

Pulnick was the problem.

Randomly and cruelly located in the center of flat, lifeless, boring, dreary, barely alive Monroe County, Missouri, it was a stone's throw to another stone's throw. The center of oblivion. A nearly impossible leap to anything that was anything.

Barren. Forgettable. Forgotten.

It was no wonder that even Noah's earliest memories embraced one common theme. Thinking back over almost twenty years, he recalled this one particular recurring thought — actually more of a scream than a thought.

Get me outta here!

Yes! At last …

The lights came on!

The writing was on the wall.

No more thinking about it.
No more contemplating and analyzing.
No more empty brooding or muddled daydreams.
He would miss his friends. But so what?
He knew what he needed to do.
Time for real action.

He made himself a solemn promise. By this time next year — maybe next month! — he'd be gone. As far away from Pulnick, as far away from Missouri, as far away from this dreary life as he could be.

His new battle cry ...
Go! Go! Go!

The Usual Suspects

Yes. He would miss his friends. That was understandable.

It's very easy to have friends in a small town. Everybody knows everybody. People didn't bounce around the way they did in big cities. Some families in Pulnick went back four, five, six generations. Even back to the founding of the original settlement in the 1850s. Mobility in this part of the U.S. was measured in feet, rather than miles. People were no more likely to cross the state line than to move to the southern hemisphere or the International Space Station.

At bare minimum, kids stuck around all the way from kindergarten through high school. Then only a handful went away for college — there were three easily commutable community colleges in the area — and most of those who did attend a major university somewhere else, ended up coming back to Pulnick or one of the nearby towns, after getting their degree.

College wasn't an option for Noah. He had the grades but lacked the money. Which was pretty much the case for everyone he knew. At least the money part. With only one exception, everyone in his high school graduating class stayed put right there in Pulnick, the town which was home for their parents and grandparents.

As a result, Noah could think of quite a number of individuals — twenty maybe thirty — who he had known the majority of his life and would consider pretty decent friends. Kids he had grown up with, had at one time or another done stuff with, and was to this day comfortable with. He still ran into them, especially on weekends, would give them a high five and maybe a chest bump (the guys), or a hug and a butt tweak (the girls), and would know pretty much all there was to know about what was happening in their lives at any given time. Living in a small town made this degree of familiarity both a requirement and an inevitability.

But of all of these, there were three guys in particular who he would say he was really close to, who he completely trusted, who he could turn to and count on, if he ever got into trouble or really needed help in a crisis.

Jeff Duncan had been his best friend forever. They went to school together right from kindergarten, riding the same yellow bus. Then the summer vacation after second grade they started hanging out practically every day. Baseball was the common bond. Every afternoon, except when it rained, they would be at the Parks & Recreation baseball field for a scrub game. By third grade they were inseparable. That was about the time everyone started calling Jeff 'Jiffy' or 'Jiff'. Apparently his mother only knew how to make one kind of sandwich, Jif peanut butter on tasteless and nutritionally void plain white bread. Jeff tried unsuccessfully almost every day to trade with one of the other kids, attempting some occasional relief from the daily monotony of one peanut butter sandwich and an apple. It never varied, nor did anyone's response to the propose exchange.

"Not a chance, Jiffy Boy!"

Jiffy and Noah had been through it all together. When they were nine, they both quit Cub Scouts to become full-time cowboys. Noah remembered how they were ridiculed when they tried to organize a posse to protect the town from marauding bands of Mexican hooligans and bandits, expected to invade any day. No one would join them. The other boys said they were stupid, and instead opted to become astronauts, having it on good authority that NASA would be calling them soon for an all-boy mission to Mars.

Noah also used to help Jiff on his paper route, delivering every Saturday morning the *'News to chase away the blues"* in the form of Pulnick Platitudes & Pleasantries, perhaps the worst small town paper in America. The PP&P was an institution which had its roots in the early years of the Great Depression, and was created as an antidote to the abundant negativity in the world. It only printed good news, stories which would warm the hearts and hopefully bring smiles to its readers, especially in times of trouble and need. Jiff and everyone his age considered it an embarrassment, and naturally he was humiliated at having to deliver it every week to its several hundred loyal subscribers. But his mom was one of the regular contributors to its stream of Pollyannaish drivel, and she insisted he take the job. As often as he could, Jiffy found some excuse for not being available Saturday morning — baseball practice, a Cub Scouts workshop, imaginary choir rehearsal — and Noah filled in for him. Noah could care less what the paper said. It provided him with some much-needed extra spending money.

It was Jiffy that introduced Noah to his second all-time best friend. This was in the third grade.

Albert Jenkins — the kids all called him Jinx — had moved to Pulnick from the big city, St. Louis. At first, everyone thought he was stuck up but he actually was just very shy — at least at first. Eventually, he started talking more and actively playing with the other kids, such that by the end of the school year he was one of the most popular in third grade. Jinx was the only one to ever trade sandwiches with Jiffy, and though it was only once, they became good buddies.

Noah, Jiff and Jinx went through the annual sports cycle together — football, basketball, track, finally baseball — and it was Jinx who always came out on top in their fierce but friendly rivalry. He was a gifted athlete and by the time he reached high school, despite being both boastful and completely tactless, he was universally admired for his prowess as a running back on the football field, and his take-no-prisoners aggressiveness at basketball. Jinx was barely 5' 6" tall but incredibly powerful, so instead of going over or around, he just barreled *through* his opponents. They scattered like bowling pins.

The cheerleading squad even had a special cheer for him ...

We're gonna beat 'em
That's what we thinks
'Cuz there ain't no stoppin'
Our one and only Jinx

His most famous play was the final football game of the season his senior year, one which secured him a permanent place in the chronicle of local legends. He received a pitch from the quarterback on the opponent's 18 yard line, proceeded to run completely the wrong way, both the opposing team and his own in hot pursuit, all the way to his own goal line. Then he reversed directions and plowed straight up the center of the field, sending everyone attempting to tackle him flying, each toppled player ending up in a writhing fetal clump on the turf. With only 14 seconds on the clock, he scored the game's winning touchdown. His own team, yelling and still in hot pursuit, caught up with him in the end zone, hoisting him high aloft in ecstatic celebration, then paraded the crazed hunky hero before the wildly cheering home team fans.

Jinx was married now. In fact Noah had been his best man. He made it official with his pregnant high school sweetheart, a girl named Gina he had been following around like a puppy dog from the day he first talked to her at an after-game dance their freshman year. On the heels of the shotgun baby, which arrived the summer after they graduated from high school and two months after the wedding, she kept spitting out babies and they now had four kids, all under seven years of age.

This should have meant that Noah would never see Jinx, his being tied down to family life and a mortgage. But as fate would have it, he now spent more time with Jinx than his wife did. They worked together five, sometimes six days a week, not only for the same employer, but in the same department. This was the receiving and stocking department at Walmart.

Noah and Jinx were practically opposites in every respect. Noah was tall and wiry, graceful like a river heron. Jinx was short and stocky, built like a bulldog. He actually looked a bit like a bulldog and shared the canine's temperament. While Noah was more inclined to soothe and comfort when he spoke, Jinx barked and spat. Noah was soft-spoken and composed, Jinx short-tempered and impatient. Noah tended to put others at ease, Jinx without even trying was intimidating. His bulk and unkindly face, coupled with the potential for serious bodily harm bottled up in his charged muscular frame, put everyone around him on notice, even though being threatening was the usually the furthest thing from his mind.

Maybe the contrast and resulting tension fueled their friendship. They certainly were never at a loss for things to talk and argue about. Religion was a biggie. Jinx was a member in good standing with the unquestioning flock at his Baptist church. Noah a declared atheist. Baseball was another. Jinx was a to-the-death St. Louis Cardinals fan. Noah, for reasons he would not divulge, had glommed onto the Boston Red Sox. Jinx refused to speak to Noah for two months at the beginning of their senior year, when Boston trounced St. Louis four games in a row to win the 2004 World Series.

They had had only one serious fight. It was in their junior year and came on the heels of some ribbing Noah was throwing Jinx's way about how Gina had Jinx wrapped around her little finger. 'Pussy whipped' was the phrase that finally sent the fists flying. What should have been a first round knockout by Jinx, ended up a full-length split decision. Jinx won the physical bout but Noah won the psychological battle and was still laughing when Jinx pinned him to the ground, sat on Noah's arms and demanded an apology. Two weeks later, Noah reiterated that he had only been joshing but apologized. They were back to being buds again.

Noah had one other close friend who went back as far as memory would take him. This was Phillip Roswell, aka Zipper. Zipper had gotten his nickname from spending several years, beginning shortly after his initial potty training and extending well into elementary school, with his fly open. At first he was politely reminded, 'Hey Phil. Your fly is open.' Or, 'You need to zip up.' But it became such a constant theme in all of his appearances in public, soon the other kids would just giggle and resort to shorthand, merely saying, 'Zipper.' Eventually, this became the standard for greeting him, lasting beyond the day in sixth grade when he finally started remembering to zip up his pants, right to the present.

Noah for some reason never bothered to call him Zipper, nor frankly did he really take him very seriously, despite the fact they spent a lot of time together. He just called him Phil, plain and simple, and hung out with him when their paths crossed, which happened to be pretty often. Phil was never someone Noah actively sought out, at least during their school years. Basically theirs was a friendship by default, born out of convenience and circumstance, rather than built on common interests. Phil's family lived next door — actually on the adjacent farm property — and that proximity meant that he and Noah were thrown together almost every day into the hopper of life. They rode to and from school together, then on the weekends often quietly explored the surrounding fields, creeks and streams. More frequently than not, they ended up playing in the same pick-up baseball and football games in town on an empty lot that had been marked off for some impromptu sports action.

They typically had very little to say to one another. Phil was quiet by nature and Noah not much interested in what came out of Phil's mouth when something did, things which tended to be rooted in whatever was Phil's obscure preoccupation of the moment. It was a constantly evolving menu of unconnected oddities.

For example …

Phil went through a phase when he was ten, of being obsessed with the Unabomber. It was never clear how this had come about or where he got his information. But for about two months, he might have been regarded as the world expert on all things Una and bomber. Dangerously, this fascination ended up embracing the design and construction of small explosive and incendiary devices. The climactic culmination of the two months was the field testing of a pipe bomb. Phil came over one Saturday morning and requested Noah's assistance in a "scientific matter". With nothing else to do, Noah accompanied Phil and watched him set the device on top of a tree stump in the corner of Gil Coulter's corn field. Gil made his living growing the stuff and since it was September, his hundred twenty acres were well along and only a few weeks from harvest. Not this year. When the pipe bomb exploded it sent a shower of molten sparks a few yards in every direction. A freak wind fanned some initially fairly harmless fires, which the two boys tried to stomp out. Within minutes, these few innocent smolderings had turned into a major conflagration. A wall of flames nearly twelve feet high swept across the field and turned Coulter's entire season's planting into a black cindered moonscape.

The boys escaped unharmed. They did make a last-ditch effort to limit the damage by running as quickly as they could to Phil's house and making an anonymous phone call to the fire department. But it was too little too late. No one ever found out who or what had caused the fire. Fortunately, Coulter was a savvy businessman and his insurance company paid up.

Another time — this was when they were twelve and Phil was convinced he was going to be the youngest driver to ever win the Grand Prix de France and would go crazy if he had to wait until he was sixteen to start driving a car — Phil gathered up not only Noah, but Jinx, Jiffy, and a girl from their class, Liz Sharona, for a drive in the country. They were all just leaving the school grounds when Phil pulled up in his step-mother Mabel's 1983 Chrysler La Baron Town & Country station wagon, looking all proud and slightly demented.

"Jump in. Let's go for a ride!"

They did. Phil proved to be a more than competent driver. He had apparently been practicing quite often over the last couple weeks. Whenever Mabel got a ride to work with one of her fellow employees at Mark Twain Solid Waste Management District Headquarters, he hopped behind the wheel. Today she wasn't due back home until 5:30. They could safely be out driving around for at least two more hours.

"Hey! There are no keys in the ignition."

"I hot-wired it. It was easy."

They stopped in at the Buckman's convenience store out on Highway 24 to stock up on corn nuts, ice cream bars, marshmallow treats, and sodas. They must have looked pretty odd. After all, it is not typical to see a station wagon full of 12-year olds, by themselves, on a party cruise in a family station wagon.

But there really was no one there to notice, other than the clerk on duty. He was either bored out of his mind or weak from all of the festering pimples which had taken up residence on his face. He just took their money and never looked up from the cash register or the counter, as he rocked autistically from one foot to the other.

The hooping, hollering and giggling in the early stages of their adventure had calmed considerably by the time Zipper pulled the car into the long driveway leading up to his house. But they were still in very high spirits.

At least they were until they saw Mabel.

Phil slammed on the brakes bringing the Chrysler to an abrupt stop, as he spotted his mountainous step-mom standing dead center in the drive, hands on her hips, with a look on her face that could have made Saddam Hussein shrivel in horror.

They were caught red-handed. She apparently had come home early, found her car missing, noticed her son also missing, and put two-and-two together. Now there she stood, taking up a large chunk of the horizon, ready to mete out some serious punishment to whoever had made off with her car without her permission, knowing full well who that was.

They sat there transfixed. Silent. She likewise stood there solid, steadfast, immovable, but far enough away she most likely could not see who was in the car with her son. Jinx was the first to say something.

"Looks like a family matter to me. No use in the rest of us getting involved."

This was the cue for Phil's companions to bail. The passenger doors flew open. Jinx, Jiff, Noah, and a very frightened looking Liz, slipped out and half-slithered, half-scurried directly into the bushes which lined the long narrow driveway. They dispersed and left poor Phil there to face the thunder on his own. As they made their way back to the road, they assuaged their feelings of guilt by agreeing among themselves that were the situation reversed, Zipper would have done the same thing. And he would have. That's just the way it was.

Phil ended up grounded for a while and no one saw a sign of him outside of school for over two months. When he finally started to show up, everyone acted like nothing had happened. Nothing much had. Just another event which came and went, growing up in Pulnick.

With Friends Like These

Jiff. Jinx. Phil.

His best friends. The guys who went so far back in memory Noah couldn't remember them not being in his life. Considering the state of his family life over the years, Jiff, Jinx and Phil were in some ways more family to him than his mom and his sister.

He was there for them and likewise, they for him.

True to form, within hours of the accident they each showed up at the hospital. This was unbeknownst to Noah, of course, since immediately after arriving he was so heavily sedated, a team of sumo wrestlers could have used him as a hackie sack and he wouldn't have known it. But his best buds were most definitely there, managing to bully the doctors and charm the nurses enough to get some sort of prognosis on him, finally only leaving when they were satisfied that he was going to be alright and their unwelcome and disruptive assistance in matters of his care would not be necessary.

Later when Noah was conscious and making daily progress towards complete recovery, they each independently visited him.

Jeff stopped by on a Tuesday.

"Dude! You're looking good!"

"Jiff!"

"What's with these nurses? This is the ugliest bunch of scags I've ever seen. Are any of these Florence Nightingales under 50? Is this supposed to make you want to live?"

"What can I say? And this is the A Team. You should see the others. It's something out of *Dawn of the Dead*. With one exception. Her name is Eleanor and—"

"Listen, man. I've got something serious to tell you. I hate to bail on you in a time of need. But I came to say good-bye."

"What? You're joking, right? What are you talking about?"

"You know that chick Margie … Margie Guster? Well, she's a month late and doing this guilt dance on my skull. I know that look she's flashin' me. She's got big plans for the Jiff. Dollar signs in her eyes. Like I have any money."

"I told you she was trouble. What were you thinkin', man?"

"I don't even remember bonking her! And the truth is, I know for sure at least five guys who have been spiking her. Half the town's playing volley ball in her twat."

"Well, did you or didn't you? Ugly as she is, I'd think you'd remember."

"She says I would if I hadn't been so drunk. I really don't know. I think she might be just gaming all of us. The little slut!"

"So what's this got to do with saying good-bye?"

"I joined up, man! The U. S. Army! I'm out of here Friday. This here dude is off to Fort Jackson, South Carolina for Basic Combat Training. It happens to be where they also send 99% of the female recruits."

"This is crazy. Then what?"

"I'll go to Iran or Korea or Clusterfuckistan or wherever the hell else we're fighting wars and … and whatever. It'll be an adventure!"

"It'll be an adventure till you get blown up. Or beheaded."

"I'll be fine. Luck of the Irish and all that."

"I'm going to miss you, Jeff."

"Wait! I got it. When you get these casts off, why don't you sign up too? We'll see the world. Shoot some towel heads and commies. Fuck our way across the third rock!"

"Not a chance, my friend. Not a chance. I'm thinking about getting out of here, but on my own terms. I can't see myself in uniform, man. No way.

Absolutely no way."

On Wednesday it was Jinx's turn to come by with more bad news.

However, as a married man of seven years, his perspective on the sex appeal of the hospital staff was a little different.

"Man, these nurses rock! Can I get a bed here?"

"Just drive your station wagon into a tree and I'm sure it can be arranged."

"How is it hangin'?"

"Like a chicken with a broken neck. Jiff came by yesterday. Did he tell you what's going down? He's splitting. Flying the coop. Running from the law."

"He's in trouble with the law?"

"Well, not exactly. But that sea lion Margie with the cellulite ass is talking a paternity situation. Jiffy is sure he has nothing to do with it but isn't going to hang around to find out. Check this out. He's signed up with Uncle Sam. Combat soldier. Can you believe that?"

"As long as the enemy wears lipstick, he'll kick ass as a soldier!"

"I can't say I follow your logic but I get your drift. How's everything at Wally's?"

"Uh … there's a problem there, Noah."

Jinx reached into his back pocket and pulled out a letter. He handed it to Noah.

"I didn't read it but I know what it says. Assholes!"

Noah had been relieved of his duties at work. Given the boot!

"This can't be for real. Laid off for lack of work? What's going on?"

"Of course it's bogus! Cutting back my ass. They gave me more hours and told me I had to train some new yahoo from Hannibal. Some kid with a face that looks like cold pizza."

"Man, this sucks. I guess the only time I'll see you now is if your wife takes me off her shit list and lets me watch you trim the hedges."

"She just thinks you're not the best influence for me right now. It's not you in particular. It's just because you're single. Then there's the whole motorcycle thing. If it's any consolation, she feels the same way about Jiff and just about everybody else. Unless they're married with children and a lawn tractor."

"Well, the motorcycle is history. And so is Jiff. Now I don't even get to see your sorry ass."

"I feel ya, dude. Life sucks and then you die."

"And it probably keeps on sucking."

"Yep. Same ol' same ol'."

Last but not least, Phil came in right at the tail end of visiting hours on Thursday. He was carrying flowers in one hand and a paper bag in the other.

"How is it?"

"The rumor that I keep repeating myself is ridiculous. The rumor that I keep repeating myself is ridiculous."

"Ha ha ha ha. That's pretty funny."

"So how you doin'? So how you doin'?"

"Okay. Okay. Listen. I gotta ask you something. Did your whole life pass in front of you? You know. When you had the accident."

"It was strange. No. Actually, mine didn't. But someone else's did. I think it might have been Marilyn Manson's."

"Are you serious?"

"Did he invent acrylic nails? The nine-inch long ones."

"You're so damaged. But that's old news. You had me going, though. Marilyn Manson. Good one. Ha ha ha."

"How are things at Merkel? Did they make you CEO?"

"No. In fact, I'm MIA. At least for a couple weeks. They lost part of a contract. I took a voluntary leave just to get out of there for a while."

"You mean you lost your job? Is it permanent?"

"No no! Not at all. We've got more work than we can handle. I've been working like 50 hours a week. But one of their regular customers put a temporary hold on things. Overstocked. Or maybe the economy is hurting them. No big deal. It'll pass. I could have just moved over to another section but, man, I needed a break. Factory work can get to you."

"I lost my job. Walmart canned me. Bastards. They kick you when you're down."

"Hey! You should apply over at Merkel. Seriously. They're getting busier by the minute. Someone told me they're going to be hiring at least twenty more people. Very soon."

"Right. Looking like this. Do they have a handicapped ramp at their employment office?"

"Gotcha. You probably should heal first. The casts are a red flag. But as soon as you get them off, you gotta get your ass over there. I'll put in a good word for you. Promise."

"I'll think about it. Thanks, Phil. You're the best."

"How's your sister?"

Phil had a thing for Gretchen. It went way back. All the way to high school. Which made it very weird for Noah at the time. When Phil first brought it up, Gretchen was only twelve. From the looks of it, she hadn't even reached puberty.

"Vampirella? She's the same as always. I thought you were over that."

"Hey! I'm just asking. She's not my type."

"She's not anyone's type. Unless the guy is a serial killer."

"How's your mom?"

"Phil. Zipper. Please. Cut with the cheesy small talk. My family needs an exorcism. You know that."

"So, when are you getting outta here?"

"I don't rightly know. Everything still hurts. They say I start physical therapy on Monday. After that, I guess I start training for the 2012 Olympics."

A nurse popped her head in the door. "Excuse me. Visiting hours are over."

"I guess I better go."

"I guess you better go."

"Need anything? I can come back maybe tomorrow. Want a six-pack of Corona?"

"Tempting. Maybe not the best idea."

Phil didn't come back.

If fact, none of them did. It was strange.

He did get a card in the mail from Jiff. He sent it right as he was leaving for boot camp. Someone had snapped a Polaroid of him with his arm around an army guy. Must have been at the bus station. It was included with a supposedly funny *Get Well* greeting card. It featured a huge-titted nurse squeezing her breast, and a guy on the floor trying to catch the milk that was shooting out of it in his mouth. The caption read *"Hope they are nursing you to health ..."*

Lame. Who comes up with such stupidity?

In any case, it was obvious Jiffy was out of the picture for a while.

Jinx, of course, had a lot on his plate. Job. Kids. Wife. And apparently Noah was somewhere at the top of his wife's no fly list. Jinx definitely had an excuse for not coming by. But the fact that Phil never made it back or even called seemed really odd. He had made it sound like he would be making another visit the very next day. But not a word.

When Noah finally got out of the hospital, it became apparent that the guy was completely avoiding him. Noah never heard from him. Really strange. Even though Noah had his own place and they were no longer neighbors, before the accident they still saw one another at least once a week. Phil had his own trail bike — actually he got it before Noah got his — so they would often meet up somewhere and go riding together. Noah couldn't think of a single weekend in the last year or so when they hadn't hooked up sometimes both Saturday and Sunday — even in the dead of winter — spent the afternoon riding, then either put away a few beers at a local club or gone to a party.

What was going on eventually became crystal clear.

Phil had not given up on Gretchen at all. In fact, he apparently decided to take advantage of Noah's hospitalization to seriously woo her. Phil knew that Noah would not merely disapprove, but would harass and ridicule him to keep them apart. The accident was the right ticket at the right time for Phil. It meant that Noah would be out of circulation for a while, providing the perfect opportunity for him to apply a full courtship press on her.

For whatever reason, this time it worked. After all these years, he and Gretchen did start spending time together. A lot of time. At least that's what Noah in due course starting hearing. Phil and Gretchen were seen together so often that, whether it was a signed and sealed deal or not, everyone seemed to think they were an item.

There was another reason Phil was avoiding Noah, one that Noah wouldn't find out about until much later. Phil, of course, had a long history of odd and sometimes dangerous pursuits. Recent years it seemed this had tapered off, that the passing of adolescence meant that the novelty of pipe bombs, cult rituals, transgender porn, time travel, and the like, had waned. Apparently not. Phil had somehow gotten sucked into a cult thing Noah would be hearing more and more about. Something that Gretchen was involved in as well.

In any case, Phil's romantic involvement with his wretched sister by itself was sufficient to cause some serious strain in their friendship. Combined with a new whacky obsession with voodoo or metaphysics or whatever it was, could pretty much be a lethal blow. It was probably smart of Phil to keep his distance. At least for the time being.

Noah would miss him. Maybe kind of.

Or then again, maybe not at all. After all, he was leaving.

Chapter Two

June 3 ...

The Big Box

When Walmart came to the Pulnick area in 2006, the community was unevenly divided about it. The clear majority bought the corporate PR line and believed that it would mean jobs, economic growth, and a bright new future for the community.

Others — generally those with more secure employment and a slight edge in education and political/social awareness — warned that it would completely destroy the frayed fabric of the community and deplete Pulnick of its already tenuous economic vitality. They were right.

Not long after the "big box" opened, local retail businesses throughout the region were wiped out. Pulnick's legacy stores, some that went back generations, were driven into the red and had no choice but to shutter their doors.

There had been a barber shop. The spinning candy-stripe pole sat idle. Now looking through the front windows, the place appeared to be storage space for a mattress company, which had no posted hours of business and never seemed to be open anyway.

The five-and-dime had become some sort of antique mall, which at least had the potential to offer an item-by-item flea market for the town's history. Unfortunately, the only real antiques were the five or six ladies who manned their booths full of worthless junk, hideous old clothes, and broken household appliances. Stuff that even the Salvation Army Store in nearby Fennersville wouldn't touch.

Three home-style restaurants had for years happily thrived. The most popular had been Fat City, a meat and fries place where in better days gastronomical gut bombs were consumed by the hundreds. Every spring it sponsored a pork-and-beef-barbecue street festival, which brought in people from five counties. They claimed the smoke from the barbecue pits drifted all the way to mainland China. The other two eateries were Gilda's Home-style Cooking and Mark Twain's Pudding & Pie, which despite the name had made the best fresh bread for counties around, seven days a week. Now all three were out of business.

A hardware store, a walk-in vet clinic, two beauty salons, a sewing supplies and yarn shop, a Bible book store, a collectibles consignment shop, and a genuine country-style haberdasher, were all likewise out of business. Several still had their last words of apologies and regret posted in their now empty and unattended storefront windows.

The only exception was Fuller's Apothecary. Mr. Fuller mysteriously seemed content running his business at a loss, or had some unknown source of income which kept the place afloat. Whichever it was, the old-fashion drugstore held its own and opened its doors at 312 North Main Street, 7 am till 6 pm every day except Sunday. Fuller had expanded beyond medicinal needs and did a fairly brisk business in candies and frozen treats, though hardly enough to compensate for the loss of his entire prescription business to the mega-drugstore contained inside Walmart.

Even with Fuller's still in business, what charm the town might at one time have claimed had steadily eroded, as all along Main Street the paint pealed, the signs faded, the limestone discolored and dissolved, and the building bricks became dark and dingy with dirt and decay. The store front windows were either boarded up, unwashed and dusty, or randomly pitted as targets for occasional drive-by slingshot practice.

This is not to say there was no vehicular or pedestrian activity on Main Street. Despite the lack of traditional commerce, Main Street still had its peak moments, early morning and late afternoon from regular daily thru-traffic, and more spectacularly from special civic events — holiday parades, public award ceremonies, fundraisers, a couple annual flea markets, and a Christmas pageant.

But this was all just frosting and a thin layer at that. The cake was gone. 99% of the economic activity of Pulnick — at least the consumer economy — now transpired in the big ugly box and the new stores around its huge blacktop parking lot on the outskirts of Center, an even smaller town east of Pulnick over in adjacent Ralls County, 18 miles as the sparrow flies. On balance, Walmart's subjugation of eastern Monroe and western Ralls counties represented a net economic loss. Far more people lost their means of subsistence than obtained employment with the mega-store. Far more money was sucked out of the local economy than was put back in. Walmarts across the country turned healthy profits and the $1.15 saved on a hair dryer or the $2.12 on a packet of underwear had to come from somewhere. A big chunk of it was the paltry wages it paid.

Worse than the economic drain was the sense of personal betrayal. Small towns run on trust, generous deeds, respect for others, personal relationships, and values that put community and its citizens first. Mega-corporations are driven exclusively by profit. People are just another quantifiable data point on a spreadsheet. It was a painful lesson for the people of Pulnick, collectively and individually.

Noah, of course, still while in the hospital, had been given a layoff notification by Walmart, effectively immediately. He found it impossible to grasp. His boss Ernie, just two days before his motorcycle accident, had promised to request a merit raise for him, so impressed was he by Noah's performance and flawless attendance record — Noah had never taken a single sick day or requested any personal time off. It was inconceivable that they had booted him. Why? What was their basis for letting him go? The notice said lack of work. What a joke! As Jinx had related, they already had some pus-faced loser from St. Louis doing his job. There was no lack of work. And Noah was the right man for the job. It wasn't fair. In fact it sucked.

He decided to tackle the problem head on.

Noah reported back for work three weeks after being discharged from the hospital. As the result of an ankle brace, he still limped a bit. But generally he was on a fast track to complete recovery, healing well and feeling good. He was confident he could do his job no problem. After all, it was 60% clerical and the other 40% fairly light lifting. He felt optimistic about the situation, as he approached the employee's entrance at the rear of the huge building.

What could they say if he just showed up?

He found out.

"You are to leave the property immediately or we will call the sheriff and have you removed."

Hmm. That didn't go well.

Not well at all.

Girl in a Blue Dress

To regroup after his banishment from Walmart, Noah headed over to Hannibal. He had to borrow his mom's car, since he hadn't yet decided what to do for transportation after his motorcycle had been totaled. He was leery about getting another bike right way. There was no doubt in his mind that eventually he'd ride again, but for now it was too soon. He still had two casts and an ankle brace. His scars were a bright scintillating pink. And every few days he would end up with a splitting headache. His painkillers didn't seem to have any effect. For now, it would be an automobile. He even buckled his seatbelt.

Hannibal was about twenty miles up the road from Center. He'd be there in under thirty minutes.

The little city of nearly 18,000 was famous, of course, as the boyhood home of Mark Twain and the very town that was the inspiration and fictional setting for Twain's most famous books, *The Adventures of Tom Sawyer* and *Adventures of Huckleberry Finn*.

It was a decent place to hang out. Naturally it had more than its share of tourists traps — which Noah hated with a passion — but unlike Pulnick at least it had a functioning main street. There were a couple local restaurants he liked. Hannibal also had Hilltop Cycles, the shop where he bought his Kawasaki off-road bike, and a YMCA with a swimming pool, racquetball courts, a gym, Nautilus equipment, and weightlifting gear. Noah had been a regular at the Y, coming by at least twice a week for a general workout, and Thursday evenings for his martial arts class. Of course, that would be on hold for a while. Today he would stop by, let them know that he was still alive, maybe check out some of the babes who worked out during the day. He never got there daytime hours, so it was probably a completely fresh crop.

Noah topped off the speed limit on State Highway 19 and pulled into New London, the halfway point in his journey, in less than thirteen minutes. From here he'd swing north on 61, on into Hannibal.

As he was leaving the New London town limits, he spotted a billboard that must have gone up fairly recently. It was quite an eye-grabbing but totally bizarre scene, featuring a very beautiful young girl in a billowing blue dress. She was sitting on the ground, her dress spread about her, centered on a lush, brilliantly green lawn which extended indefinitely in every direction. She was looking up and smiling into the face of Jesus, who was standing on what looked like a flying saucer, hovering directly in front of her. Jesus had a silly come-to-daddy grin on his face, and had His arms stretched out before Him, beseeching the girl to join Him on His Jesus spaceship. Strange as all this was, it was the look on the girl's face which stole the show. It was both demure and flirtatious, coy and coquettish—more what one would expect to see on the face of a young lady being asked out on her first date by someone she had a massive crush on, than that of a girl beholding the Son of God. At the same time, her eyes weren't so much sexually or romantically charged, as they were just plain vacant. Dull-witted. Lights off. The girl didn't look like a deer caught in the headlights. She looked like a brain-dead deer. In fact, Noah decided that despite her eye-catching superficial beauty, this was hands down the dumbest looking female he had ever seen in his life.

Appearing at the top of this scene of enchanted surrender and doltish gullibility, seeming to flow out of the huge halo which surrounded the head of Jesus like gases escaping the sun, was a simple message born by a billowing white cloud.

The end is near.
Jesus will return to take
his children home . . .

11 - 11 - 11

Noah slammed on the brakes. Hold on here! 11-11-11? Why did that sound so infuriatingly familiar. November 11, 2011 ...

He couldn't immediately make a connection. But it sure reminded him of something.

He decided to go about his business for now. Maybe it would eventually pop into his head. Or after he got back home, he could check it out on the internet. God bless Google!

There was no one at the YMCA he knew. The day shift. All different people. There were only three girls working out. They were on the treadmills. It looked like the hippopotamus ballet scene from Disney's animated *Nutcracker Suite*. He left and headed up the road. Mysteriously, Hilltop Cycles was closed for the day. No reason given. Just the 'Closed - Come Back and See Us Again' sign in the window. Then he stopped at Kidder's — a mom and pop restaurant which he had been to more times than he could count — and they served him what ranked as the absolute worst meal of his life. Apparently Mrs. Kidder was off sick, so they had some new kid filling in who apparently learned cooking at a vulcanizing plant. What was supposed to be a hamburger but could have passed for a hockey puck, sat on a bun which was so greasy it fell apart on the plate before Noah even picked it up. The French fries were petrified. The lemonade tasted like vinegar and aspartame. When in disgust, Noah started to get up to leave, he realized that his nose was bleeding. The meal had made him hemorrhage and he hadn't even touched it!

Not a good day.

Kicked out of Walmart. Grossed out at the YMCA. Struck out at Hilltop motorcycle shop. Now he had to make the drive home hungry and bleeding, drop-kicked in the gullet and head butted in the face by some high school drop out. He should have stayed home in bed.

And oh yes! How could he forget? There was the girl in the blue dress with seducer Jesus — the bizarre 11-11-11 billboard thing.

What was that all about?

Very weird ...

Björn Agynn

Björn Agynn was coming to Monroe County. The itinerant peddler of a potpourri of end-of-the-world metaphysical hocus pocus, a hodge podge of fundamentalist Christian babble, numerology, New Age physics, astrology, Kabbalah, juju, voodoo, Candy Land cosmology, and astral projection, would be making a very special appearance right here in Noah's backyard. The big event was scheduled for Wednesday September 28th, on the sprawling grounds adjacent to the historic Rockcliffe Mansion in Hannibal.

This is what Noah found out in connection with the girl-in-a-blue-dress billboard, when he started poking around the internet. Not that the high priest of rapture and ruin made it very easy. Apparently Mr. Agynn was using some post-modern advertising psychology. His approach seemed to be one of building curiosity and intrigue around his appearance here in the Bible Belt by initially only making enigmatic allusions to the arrival of End Times, allegedly on 11-11-11. The billboard Noah saw was the first of a series of teasers which would pop up in the area over the coming weeks.

Noah also figured out why the reference to 11-11-11 sounded familiar. It finally came back to him that just before the accident with his motorcycle — in fact earlier that day — he had briefly watched a video about 11-11-11. It wasn't Björn Agynn but some other wing nut who lived in Switzerland. The guy was a farmer who claimed for the past thirty years to have been meeting regularly with a race of super beings from a planetary system based in the Pleiades constellation. He had ridden in their space craft, had hundreds of pictures and movies of little wobbling saucers landing on his property, had developed close friendships with several of them, and though he didn't specifically mention it, probably had had them over for schnapps shooters and a round of croquet. In any case, this bonehead now railed against the "newcomers", guys like Björn who had only recently hopped on *his* message of doom and gloom, now that the date was fast approaching. He labeled them all a bunch of opportunistic frauds, who had essentially stolen his message, repackaged it, and now were out to make a fast buck. He said he'd been talking about 11-11-11 since the early 80s. And as far as he was concerned, the discussion of the cosmological line in the sand had gotten way off track. It had nothing to do with the Bible, the Mayans, harmonic convergence, harmonic divergence, karma, dharma or any of that pseudo-spiritual claptrap. It was simple mathematics. Well . . . maybe not *that* simple, but mathematics all the same. Certainly not the Magic 8-Ball and Ouija board stuff that those others were floating. He asserted that applying the trans-derivative hyper-dimensional calculus commonly used on their home planet to determine specific dates and times for cosmological benchmarks, the Pleiadians had been warning us all along that we needed to get out act together here on Earth by the 11-11-11 deadline or else.

Or else what? Here is where Noah's memory got a little fuzzy. He knew some bad things were supposed to happen but couldn't remember what. Now he couldn't even locate that particular video on YouTube. It apparently had been pulled.

Why did all of these guys rant? The Swiss farmer looked pretty short. Maybe he had been bullied in school.

Of course, Noah didn't know if Björn Agynn ranted or not. The super guru was keeping a low profile, long on mystery, short on everything else. Noah did find one picture of him, posted by some blogger. It was just a snapshot but the guy did appear to be rather handsome. And he towered over the several people who were gathered around him. So either Mr. Agynn was quite tall or he tended to hang out with leprechauns.

Also missing on the web was anything resembling a biography of the man. Björn did have his own internet site, simple and scant as it was. His name and the contact information listed there suggested that he was Scandinavian. Swedish? But where he was originally from and in which country he was now physically based was unclear. Also conspicuously absent was even the usual basic data. Things people would want to know. Did he have a degree in divinity studies? Philosophy? Had he even attended university? How old was he? Was he married? Family? How long had he been a metaphysical teacher? How long had he been preaching the 11-11-11 message? Was Björn Agynn even his real name? *That* seemed kind of dubious.

What his website did offer was a calendar, listing his appearances across the globe over the coming months approaching the Divine Day of Destiny — as he referred to it — and a glimpse into his spiritual and personal musings. What a story those told! A few select passages …

"We shall 11 at a time submit to the Lord as sheep to slaughter."

"Humans had 11 fingers before the Great Flood. Right-handed people had six fingers on their right hand and left-handed people had six on their left."

"Buddha took 11 roads to find 11 masters in order to discover and declare his 11 Principles as the ultimate guide to 11

Reincarnations of the Ascending Spirit."

"The 11th Commandment says that God's love is a cauldron of fire and His children shall melt the heavens and the Earth with eternal flames of His passion and all races of man will become a clear molasses of flesh and spirit."

"The Twin Towers of the World Trade Center were an 11, numerical chopsticks burning under the fingernails of the Devil. Isn't history just fetid sashimi and the melting glaciers the soy sauce of our drowning ambitions?"

"I have always been fascinated with my hands and feet. As a boy I spent hours studying them, as if they were something apart from me. Now I know that I have the hands of Christ and the feet of Buddha. This is a great blessing."

"There are 1,111 fun-loving spirit guides, playful angels called Midwayers, who are constantly alerting us to 11-11 things in our lives. Everything from seeing 11:11 on our digital clocks and cell phones to significant events taking place on the 11th day of the month is their way of reminding us what's coming."

"The 11th Gate of Heaven will open up for 49 minutes at 11:11 on November 11, 2011, releasing something from another world into our earthly realm.

"The Earth will have 11 suns after the Divine Day of Destiny."

His itinerary, to put it mildly, was impressive — not to mention strange and inexplicable.

June 18: Seoul, South Korea
June 21: Changmai, Thailand
June 22: Manilla, Philippines

July 2: Roswell, NM (USA)
July 3: Pierre, SD (USA)
July 10: Fullerton, CA (USA)
July 11: Tupelo, MS (USA)
July 14: Havana, Cuba
July 17: Helsinki, Finland
July 20: Konstanz, Germany
July 22: Lotz, Poland
July 23: Stuttgart, Germany
July 29: Boise, ID (USA)
July 30: Santa Fe, NM (USA)
July 31: Traverse City, MI (USA)

Aug 3: Augusta, GA (USA)

Aug 5: Saskatoon, Sakatchewan (Canada)
Aug 8: Sedona, AZ (USA)
Aug 17: Cannes, France
Aug 19: Cardiff, Wales
Aug 23: Istanbul, Turkey
Aug 26: Sophia, Bulgaria
Aug 27: Valencia, Spain
Aug 28: Barcelona, Spain
Aug 30: Rabat, Morocco
Aug 31: Cairo, Egypt

Sept 3: Vladivostok, Russia
Sept 6: Miyazaki, Japan
Sept 8: Okinawa, Japan
Sept 11: Chengdu, China
Sept 14: Florence, Italy
Sept 15: Antwerp, Belgium
Sept 16: Holstebro, Denmark
Sept 19: Salzburg, Austria
Sept 24: Montgomery, AL (USA)
Sept 25: Louisville, KY (USA)
Sept 26: Chillicothe, OH (USA)
Sept 28: Hannibal, MO (USA)
Sept 30: Milwaukee, WI (USA)

Oct 1: Washington, DC (USA)
Oct 4: Addis Abab, Ethiopia
Oct 6: Lusaka, Zambia
Oct 12: Reykjavik, Iceland
Oct 15: Montreal, Quebec (Canada)
Oct 19: Grand Rapids, MI (USA)
Oct 26: Abilene, TX (USA)

Nov 4: [TBA]
Nov 6: Mesa, AZ (USA)
Nov 9: Bellevue, WA (USA)
Nov 10: New York, NY (USA)
Nov 11: Racine, WI (USA)

There seemed to be no logical trajectory, discernible plan, or hierarchy of importance to the order and the choices of places he would appear. No explanation was even given for his final destination, Racine, WI — why he would be there on 11-11-11 and what we should expect. Was this the point of departure for the Rapture? Maybe his appearance on the Bill O'Reilly show the day before might shed some last-minute light on this. This Fox TV interview apparently was considered the highlight of Mr. Agynn's sweep across the globe, since it was touted on a sidebar to every one of his web pages.

The obvious question was why this self-proclaimed spiritual sage, who extolled his certain knowledge of the future of the Universe and the ultimate destiny of the human species, would even bother coming to Monroe County. Or any place in ultra-Christian Missouri, for that matter. Noah couldn't imagine a less likely place to preach anything but the traditional gospel. This after all was a fortress for the Bible Belt. People here couldn't spell Buddha or Taoism. New Age was how old you were on your birthday. Monroe County and Pulnick might not have a monopoly on all of the ignorant hicks in America, but it definitely had its share.

Which reminded him of what he really should be focusing on right now. Not playing detective on weird billboards or tracking down tent show spiritualists. But getting the hell out of Dodge before it was too late. Before this town sucked the last drop of life blood out of him. That was what he had decided in the hospital. That was what he needed to be thinking about.

That and that alone.

Frankly, the more he considered his present circumstance — no job, hapless family, disappearing friends — the more convinced Noah became of both the timeliness and urgency of his departure.

No doubt about it.

The sooner the better.

The Great Escape

Noah made a list. He didn't need much. He'd be living on the road for a while, so the less the better. But he had to be organized to make it work.

He stopped at the bank withdrew all but $10 from his savings account. Next morning, he got an early start and drove to St. Louis, figuring he needed the breadth and depth of big city shopping if he were to get this done right. He had heard about the sprawling, ultimate shopping experience of the St. Louis Mills Outlet Mall in suburban Hazelwood. It sounded perfect.

The place was all it had been cracked up to be and he could have spent several days there. But his list of required items was short and to the point. Not that he stuck with the original list. In fact, as he wandered from one shop to the next, he became overwhelmed with the options. With his head whirling, at the end of the day he left with three bags full of exactly what he thought he should have for his travels.

Of course, he got a healthy size backpack. And a plastic raincoat with an American flag adorning the rear. A hot and cold steel thermos. Leather gloves with the fingertips cut out. Two pen lights and an official Swiss Army Knife. An insect-repelling headband. A 3-pack of instant-drying antibacterial underwear. Heavy-duty hiking boots and Dr. Scholl's Odor Eater insoles. Thermal body liners for cold weather. Two tank tops and a pair of breathable hiker's cut-off pants for warm weather. Heavy-duty toenail clippers.

There were, of course, a few optional but useful things. A luffa exfoliating back scrubber. Two Christopher Moore books, *Lamb: The Gospel According to Biff, Christ's Childhood Pal* and *Bloodsucking Fiends: A Love Story*. A pocket World Atlas. A diary and two sturdy pens. An electronic rhyming dictionary — in case he decided to start writing poetry. Sun block with anti-acne crème mixed in. A sampler pack of Swedish condoms. A combination jockstrap and travelers money belt that also would serve to bolster his bulge, given sufficient funding. Jasmine-scented wet naps. A skull buster key holder which accommodated an optional vial of pepper spray. A 4 GB USB memory stick. Finally, UV-blocking arm chaps.

Noah returned to Pulnick that evening, exhausted from looking at so much stuff, most of it irrelevant to him under any circumstances. He was satisfied that he had what he needed to get rolling and anything else which came up in his travels he would be able to find along the way.

He slept well. Though excited at the prospect of beginning his new adventure very soon, he was also content in the knowledge that life's worst was behind him. It could only get better.

Next day, after he caught up on a few remaining personal errands — paying a handful of bills that had piled up and picking up enough groceries to get him by the next 48 hours before he officially hit the road — Noah returned his mom's car. When he walked into the kitchen, she was slumped over a cup of Lipton tea crying.

"I brought your car back."

"You can have it. I have breast cancer."

"Breast cancer? Won't you need it to drive to the hospital? Or buy a new bra?"

Noah tried not to sound totally casual, flippant, or brutally insensitive about his mom's newly discovered disfiguring, potentially life-threatening disease. But it was nearly impossible. He had been through this so many times.

Diabetes. Muscular sclerosis. Congestive heart failure. Eczema. Retinal detachment. Fybromyalgia. Brain tumors. Typhoid fever. Spinal meningitis. Irritable bowel syndrome. At one point she was convinced she had contracted AIDS from a toilet seat at Saturday night bingo. There was the time when she went to the doctor convinced she had Parkinson's disease. The shaking of her hands was magically cured when he got her to stop drinking fourteen cups of coffee a day.

She started to whimper. Then she just sighed.

"It's too far along. There's nothing anyone can do."

"How did you find out, Mom?"

"My nipples got hard."

He was sorry he had asked.

Truth was, his mom might be the healthiest person in the world. Or at least in Pulnick. She did have one ailment. And it was purely psychological.

Psychosomatic disorder. All her illnesses for the past 17 years were products of her own disturbed mind. She was a world-class hypochondriac.

Her pathological obsession with everything that could go wrong with her health began right after Noah started first grade, and continued unabated right up till today's alleged onset of breast cancer. Noah — and everyone around her including her family doctor and even several specialists she had been referred to in St. Louis — was helpless in disrupting the continuing evolution of her neurosis. One imagined ailment followed another. She was becoming a one-woman encyclopedia of human afflictions, often displaying the actual symptoms of whatever was allegedly destroying her body at the time. All of it in her mind.

So today Noah just humored her. He knew she didn't have breast cancer.

And he was right.

What she would be diagnosed with when she went in for the umpteenth time to the county hospital was not breast cancer. It was ovarian cancer.

This time for real.

Of course, Noah's mom didn't believe them. Ironically this time around, she passed up a perfect opportunity to immerse herself in the misery of an actual disease. She put up a huge fuss at her follow-up appointment with the gynecological oncologist she had been referred to, told him he was crazy, and refused to come in for more thorough tests, necessary for a recommended program of treatment, which would probably argue for immediate surgery.

Noah got the call from the referring doctor the morning after the unfortunate confrontation.

"Dr. Norville here. Can I speak to Noah Tass, please?"

The doctor, who had been their family physician for a number of years, explained the situation to Noah and requested his intervention on his mother's behalf. Her condition was serious — how serious remained to be determined — and they needed to address it as soon as possible to prevent any possible further spread of the cancer.

Next day, Noah was back at the house.

"Mom, please. Listen to me. This is very important. You have to listen to the doctor and go in right away for treatment."

"I don't want them to cut off my breasts."

"Mom. This has nothing to do with your breasts. You don't have breast cancer. You have a problem with your ovaries."

After a lot of back and forth, she finally relented. The next step was her going in for an exploratory operation called a laparoscopy, to confirm the preliminary findings. She was admitted to Barnes Jewish Hospital in St. Louis early the following Thursday.

"I was so afraid."

"I am sure your doctor is one of the best in the field."

"But all these Jews. What if they thought I was German?"

The lab results were back by Saturday and she was scheduled for major surgery — removal of all suspect tissue and a complete hysterectomy the following Wednesday at 9:30 a.m.

On the day of the surgery, Noah sat in the waiting room until she came out of anesthesia, waited yet another two hours for the doctor to tell him everything went well and she was resting. When he came back the following day, his mom was fairly coherent. At least as coherent as she ever was.

"Now I'm a man."

"Come on, mom. It's not that drastic. You weren't planning on any more babies anyway, were you?"

"You never know. If Mr. Right came along …"

"You could adopt. Maybe a little Chinese or Guatemalan baby, eh?"

"Did you put gas in my car?"

"It uses gas? I've been putting fabric softener in the tank."

"Where's my fur coat? I had my fur coat with me when I came here. These Jew nurses—"

"Mom! Please stop it. Your coat is fine. I've been feeding it every day. Yesterday I took it for a walk around the hospital grounds. It met a couple squirrels it knew from high school."

"Noah. Did I cause this? How did you end up so strange? Gretchen and I can't figure you out, no matter how hard we try."

"I'd love to be a fly on the wall for that discussion."

His mom's eyes started to tear up. It was obvious she didn't want to cry and she fought it. But her upper lip started to quiver.

"I … I … really appreciate your being here with me. I was so afraid. I am so afraid. What's going to happen to me?"

"The doctor says the surgery went well. You're going to be fine, Mom."

"Noah. I couldn't do this without you … without your help."

He had trouble processing that one, since he hadn't done anything.

"You … well … I just … thanks for being such a good boy. You know. You're here … and well. Um … your sister. Well … you know what I mean."

"Yeah. I know what you mean."

It was a long drive back home. More than two-and-a-half hours. But it seemed like days.

Once he got thirty or forty miles outside of the St. Louis, traffic was light. He watched the countryside, the farms, the fields, the small towns roll past him like huge panoramic scrolls on each side of Highway 61. Beautiful but bland. Stark and simple. The vast void of Missouri. Each house, each farm, each vehicle, each face a story without a storyline.

What now? He hadn't really had time to think since the crisis hit. It was only two weeks ago that he had gotten the call from Dr. Norville. Everything had stopped. And? He didn't want to be callous. But either his mom would be alright or she wouldn't. It was in the hands of the doctors and the Grim Reaper. There was really nothing he could do to affect the outcome.

He stopped at Casey's General Store in Perry. In twenty minutes or so and he'd be home. He picked up a six-pack and a can of Pringles. A new flavor. Thai curry and lime.

The beer was lukewarm when he slumped down in the overstuffed chair in the corner of his little flat. It had no flavor. The chips dissolved in his mouth with chemical predictability. He barely had to chew.

It started to get dark. He switched on the lamp on the stand next to his chair.

Noah's backpack sat in the corner of his studio apartment where he left it three weeks ago.

So much for getting out of this godforsaken town.

Slow Bullets

Noah never watched TV. But he was addicted to videos on the internet. Documentaries. An occasional music video, if it was a band he really liked. But mostly just random stuff. Crazy, interesting stuff. Anything to take him out of Pulnick, out of Missouri, away from the sameness, the boredom, the ennui, the numbness, the sleepwalking of life in Monroe County.

It wasn't difficult to find them. There were so many phenomenal sources of strange, wonderful, haunting, grotesque, thought-provoking, inspiring, exalting, hideous, chilling, bizarre, perverse, thrilling, frightening, informative, random, funny, and heartbreaking videos, mini-movies and even epic independent film productions, all posted online. In one sitting you could end up with emotional whiplash riding the roller coaster of human tragedy and comedy. YouTube.com had just about everything, wimp.com an eclectic mix, comegetyousome.com cool fights and martial arts, videovat.com the strange and paranormal, and liquidice.co.uk delivered weird advertisements.

But www.engr.colostate.edu/~dga/high_speed_video/ and its vast selection of slow motion videos was Noah's favorite site.

He spent one full evening watching a water droplet bouncing on a super hydrophobic carbon nanotube array. Another watching rain collect on a spider web. There appeared to be no limit to the fascination of scientists with the balletic grace of hydrodynamic phenomena. Drops of water into oil. Drops of oil into water. Red paint into a pool of yellow paint. Yellow paint into a pool of black. Rainbows spreading over thin shimmering films of soapy water.

He explored the object obliteration and ballistics collection.

There was something almost meditative — Noah hesitated to use the term 'spiritual' — about watching the seemingly endless selection of things shattering, splitting, disintegrating, and exploding. Things splattering, bouncing, bounding, ricocheting. Objects smashed, shot, hammered, quartered, obliterated, annihilated, powdered, zapped, nuked, melted, vaporized.

There was a series just on bullets. Bullets going through glass. Bullets going through cans. Through butter and cheese, fruits and vegetables, Jell-O and ice. Through books and pressboard. Aluminum siding, sheet rock, ceramic tiles. A submarine sandwich, carton of milk, bottle of ketchup, bread dough. A card table, rocking chair, bookcase, mattress, pillow, television screen. A deck of cards, Ballerina Barbie, a Gundam Titan action figure, Mr. Potato Head, an Easter egg. A small tree trunk, a beach ball, thermos bottle, artillery shell casing, a fish tank full of tropical fish, a preserved pig's brain. Even bullets in head-on collisions with other bullets.

Slow bullets. Well, actually very fast bullets slowed down through high-speed filming, so that every nuance of their devastating effect could be seen and savored. Noah was mesmerized.

Late one Friday evening — actually it was Saturday morning only an hour before sunrise — he had one of those epiphanies that only come late at night after hours of imposed solitude.

It occurred to Noah that there were no slow bullets in his life. There was no object, person, force, or emotion which could be fired into the core of his being and reach the center.

And by the way, what was at the center? Was it his soul, his essence, a point of zero gravity suspended in the interlocking sinew of his corporeal self, that somehow delineated and defined him? Was it a unique bit of mathematics which didn't subscribe to any formula or formulation that we mere human beings could comprehend?

Was it infinity? Was it zero?

By the time the sun came up, the very idea had exhausted him. He could no longer think.

He fell into a deep chasm of unconsciousness, a sleep which to his body felt like death.

To his mind, it was the perpetuation of a profound, fateful and ultimately necessary journey.

Huge pillars of hypnagogic stone thrust upwards out of the chaos of the earth beneath him. Artifices of dignified and profound structures soon surrounded him in every direction, giant temples honoring the great and eternal concepts and constructs of the human mind.

At the end of a long plaza stood the greatest temple of them all. Columns soared grandly upwards as if to support the base of the sky itself. Across the architrave were grandly written: Truth, Beauty, Good, Knowledge, Divinity, Perfection.

He walked with purpose through the portico of this, the most profound and magnificent temple of all time. Directly in front of him in the very center of the grand atrium sat a single crystalline lens mounted on a simple gold pedestal.

From any and all angles and points of view, the lens beckoned him. He could not resist. Nor did he want to resist. This was precisely what he had been looking for …

A portal to the center of the human soul. His human soul.

Noah stepped up and leaned forward, his right eye almost touching the cold surface of the beckoning optical object, which seemed hard like a diamond but still shimmered on the surface, with the continuous melting and rippling fractals of an internal light.

He could see it now. He now knew with certainty, what he already knew and had always known — what everyone knows but spends their whole lives trying to deny.

At the center of every human being is an impregnable core of loneliness.

A black hole of perfect impenetrable solitude.

That … is the human soul.

A few hours later, Noah woke up at his computer with the reddened cheek of his limp face in a puddle of his own drool.

He got up and poured a bowl of breakfast cereal but then remembered he had no milk.

He sat back down at his computer and made a simple banner.

He saved it as his new desktop image.

Home is where you park your loneliness.

Chapter Three

June 25 ...

The Day Michael Jackson Died

Noah could never tell his friends. He couldn't tell anybody.

He loved Michael Jackson.

The day Michael Jackson died — June 25, 2009 — Noah turned 21.

It was true. Michael Jackson died right on his birthday.

Noah would never forget that day.

How could he?

After all, he had just officially become a man. With full gambling and drinking privileges. Why now, he could even buy a gun, and in most states rent a car.

Despite that, it ranked — at least so far — as the single worst day of his life.

Noah remembered the first time he saw a Michael Jackson video. He was just going on four years old and was flipping through TV channels. They had just gotten cable service — probably the last people on the planet to finally get it — and he landed on MTV. It was 1992 early in February, and his mother was in the other room nursing his new baby sister.

There on the screen with more magic and wonder than a hundred Disney characters could garner, was this beautiful, mysterious, mesmerizing dancer-singer-storyteller-magician who glided and skipped, shimmied and shook, twisted and twirled in ways which didn't seem humanly possible. He sang like no one else, looked like no one else, danced like no one else, and performed with a passion and intensity matched by no one else. The video was *Billy Jean*.

Noah had no idea what the song was about but he was hooked. From that moment till the very present, his obsession with Michael was set. It was a part of him. It was a part of his life. It was his secret from the world. It was his private passion.

He watched Michael Jackson's movies — *The Wiz, Captain EO*, and *Moonwalker*.

He caught songs and performances which had occurred long before he was even born or when he was just a toddler — *Rockin' Robin, Dancing Machine, Ben, I'll Be There, Shake Your Body (Down To The Ground), Don't Stop 'til You Get Enough, Wanna Be Startin' Somethin', Thriller, The Way You Make Me Feel, Bad, Man In The Mirror*.

After school, whenever he could, Noah sat in front of the TV waiting for an MJ video to come on, hoping that he could get through it without either his mother or Gretchen coming into the room, which would prompt him to immediately change the station.

It was difficult. He was constantly ridiculed by his mom for watching any television at all. She would wrestle the remote from him. Then when Noah left the room she'd sit glued to the tube watching the Home Shopping Network or one of the tabloid talk shows like Jerry Springer, or a few years later, shock jock Howard Stern.

Either that or his sister would horn in. She always played her little girl trump card to demand either the Disney Channel or Nickelodeon, and always got her way.

But by sheer determination and sometimes keeping some very late hours, Noah managed to follow Michael through the glory and the hysteria of the 90s, all of the incredible fame and idol worship that followed him everywhere. He captured on VHS all of the best live performance concert footage, and the scores of music videos which made Michael the megastar he was. Hidden away safely his room were video tapes of Michael's Bad Tour shows at Wembley Stadium in London, the HIStory Tour performances at Weserstadion in Bremen, Germany, and the mega-productions *We Are The World*, *Thriller*, *Smooth Criminal*, and *Jam*.

His two favorite songs were *Bad* and *Human Nature*. He liked *Bad* because it kicked ass. He loved *Human Nature* because it had a great message and a melody that touched the deepest part of his soul. When Michael soared into the high falsetto of the bridge, Noah felt cradled in the arms of a sad angel that whispered in his ear promises of an end to the days of hopelessness. It always made him cry. He cried from a place so deep inside, he felt his tears were escaping from a region of his soul still unknown even to him.

This was all very hard for Noah to admit to himself, much less understand. These feelings would have been labeled "sissy" and "powder puff" by his father — way back when he had a father — and "queer" or "fagboy" by his friends.

But the feelings, the explosive joy and the heartfelt tears that erupted when he listened to Michael Jackson's music, were real. Certainly more real than the tough nonchalance, the poseur cool, and all of the macho affectations which had been imposed on him and expected of him his entire life in conservative Bible Belt Missouri.

Four months after Michael Jackson's death, the film *This Is It* was released. On opening night, Noah snuck into a theater in St. Louis to see it. He was among the first in the entire nation to see the movie about the creation of and rehearsals for what was billed as the most spectacular concert tour in pop music history, a production which was halted when Michael was found at home in bed, dead from an overdose of a surgical anesthetic.

Noah now owned the DVD of *This Is It* and when he could emotionally handle it — maybe once or occasionally twice a month — sat transfixed and desolate, watching some of the last film footage of his fallen hero, as Michael rehearsed and performed the entire range of songs and dance numbers from way back in his days with the Jackson Five right up to the present. There was a lot of footage of Michael not just dancing and singing, but working out all of the details of the show with the choreographers, dancers, musicians, background vocalists, the director, special effects and costume people, everybody involved. It was like being right there in the huge rehearsal sound stage with him. It both stunned and sickened Noah. Michael at age fifty danced and sang better than ever, rehearsals were exhilarating to behold, and the concert looked like it was going to live up to the extremely high expectations and hype surrounding it.

When Michael Jackson died, to Noah it felt like he had lost his best friend. It was that personal connection which haunted Noah to this day, and which made watching *This Is It* such sweet torment.

In some twisted, ironic way, Michael Jackson even now, two years after his death, was still so *present*. More present than most of his contemporaries who were still alive. More present in death than many could hope to be in life.

That night of Michael's death — that one fateful birthday — was like no other in his life. He was so completely paralyzed with grief. But it was a grief he couldn't share with anyone.

Naturally, he was obligated to go out and party like there's no tomorrow. Universal rule. Law of the land. Unbreakable tradition. Who knew? It might even be in the Bible.

His friends definitely wouldn't take 'no' for an answer.

There would be no holds barred, no expense spared. The usual suspects would see to that. Not that they particularly cared whether he had fun or not. Actually, it was just like a wedding. His birthday bash was for everyone around him. Meaning, it was their excuse this one particular night to get shit faced, puke all over themselves, and then talk about it until the next time they got shit faced and puked all over themselves.

Noah desperately tried to get out of it. Fat chance.

"This is your b-day, dude!!" You can't sit home and play with your pud. You absolutely have to come with us. We've got it all figured out."

That was the incredibly articulate and persuasive Eddie Scott, Pulnick's version of Mr. All American and erstwhile captain of the Calvin Coolidge H.S. wrestling team. Now he was a used car salesman in Hannibal. They — meaning Jinx, Jiffy, Zipper, Eddie, and Ted Buckner (another used car salesman Noah didn't even know) — had him cornered in what passed as a sports bar in nearby Paris. He was in such a daze he couldn't even remember how he got there. But there he was with jaws flapping at him, beers being set down in front of him, hands whapping him on the back, whoops, hollers and birthday battle cries careening from every direction.

So Noah went along and tried to put on a happy face. The fact was, he was dying inside. He couldn't believe it. The King of Pop was gone. Impossible. Was it all a bad dream?

Already pretty drunk — and it was only 6:30 in the evening — they decided to take him bowling, normally one of his favorite dudes-hanging-out pastimes. They piled into an SUV Eddie apparently had borrowed from the used car lot where he worked, and headed for the Pal Bowl over in Palmyra. It took them over an hour-and-a-half to drive the 43 miles. Though it was almost impossible, since it merely required staying on two main highways, they kept getting lost. Their navigational sense was not at all aided by the beer stops they made in Stoutsville, Monroe City, then Hunnewell, the last of which was completely in the wrong direction on Highway 36.

They didn't even finish bowling one game. After arguing with the cashier over how much they had to pay for each only bowling seven frames, they pointed their Chevy Trailblazer to the outskirts of Hannibal to do some go-carting. The owner of City Limits Scooters & Go Kart, based on a quick assessment of their level of intoxication, turned them right around and pointed them back out the way they came in. They refused to go, demanding time on the track. They finally left under the very real threat that the owner if he had to would call the sheriff.

They then swerved their way to Injun Joe Campgrounds, conveniently right down the street, which had a miniature golf course. Injun Joe was no stranger to drink and the boys put away another two cases of Pabst Blue Ribbon, before finally dragging themselves to the 9th hole of the course. Fortunately, it was a slow night and there were no other players, because they spent almost an hour on that last hole. None of them managed to put the ball in the cup. They stopped counting after twenty or so strokes, since no one could remember how to count.

The drive home was punctuated by many stops. To piss. To vomit. To chase a terrified stray dog across a field. More pissing. More vomiting.

Noah still doesn't remember how he got home.

Next day he woke up at noon beside his bed. He had a golf ball in his left pocket.

Rarely did he watch television anymore. But that day he tuned in to CNN on his little black and white set and confirmed the news about Michael Jackson's death, an event that massive amounts of beer could not somehow erase from the sinister ongoing laugh track of current events.

That was two years ago. Two years that could have been an eternity.

Now it was June 25, 2011. Michael Jackson dead two years. Noah Tass two years older.

Not a bit wiser, as far as he could determine.

Maybe less. Stasis did that to you.

Noah's cell phone rang. It startled him. It hardly ever did.

"I've got a party to take you to."

Joanna Pillsbury. A girl he knew but wished he didn't.

"What's the occasion?" Thinking maybe someone remembered his birthday.

"The usual. Except the high schoolers are still celebrating graduation. Maybe you could get some young pussy tonight."

Joanna had so much class. She was a card-carrying member of a group of five girls, two to three years younger than Noah, known to everyone who knew them as the Super Skanks. Actually very good looking girls who had managed to avoid the Missouri cow bloat disease which inflated most Monroe County girls into bovine blimps. Lookers that they were, this bunch was so full of themselves, and generally so slutty, foul-mouthed, and lacking even the slightest hint of feminine charm, Noah did his best to avoid them.

"Wow. Did you say junior high? I love *really* young pussy, you know."

The irony in his voice would be lost on her. Since she was usually so involved in ginning up whatever next nugget of truth and beauty would come out of her mouth, she never listened to anyone else.

"You can't fuck me tonight."

After last time — desperation sex about a year ago born out of extreme horniness and several too many drinks — that had definitely not occurred to Noah. It had felt like necrophilia. She looked like she was doing a crossword puzzle in her head. Except as far as he knew, there were no crossword puzzles which only used words with three letters or less.

"You're breaking my heart."

"I'm breaking your balls, silly boy!"

Uh-oh. Maybe she had designs on him after all. He really wanted to go out. But no car. No cycle.

"You should probably wear latex gloves. My herpes look like sliced chili peppers floating in mayonnaise. I have to wear a diaper."

"You're so cute. I'll pick you up in twenty. Wear your best wifebeater."

As soon as they arrived at the party, Joanna ran off to look for her friends. He was immensely relieved. Holding up a conversation with her required Herculean strength and patience. He didn't have a gun with him on the ride from his studio apartment to the party, or he would have been tempted to put her out of her misery. In doing so he would have made a profound contribution toward decontaminating the gene pool.

The party was a ways out of town on CR486, on the sprawling farm of Stephanie Sharona, who for some reason went by Liz. Liz's parents were quite well-to-do and their affluence was reflected on every square inch of their 319 acre estate. Technically it was a working farm but the land lay fallow this year, as it had for the past ten years. It still made money. Even though the agricultural earnings only provided a meager portion of their total income, they came entirely from the father's astute maneuvering on the lucrative toll ways of U. S. government subsidies. This year they were being paid to not grow corn. But as good stewards of the land, they annually rotated their crops to take full advantage of a variety of programs compensating them for a whole range of grains and vegetables they never grew.

Tonight was supposed to be a rave. Liz's parents were out of town — they were gone nine weeks out of ten and this weekend were in Aruba, gambling and scuba diving. Tonight's event was just one of many such happenings which would take place here over the summer.

It was the ideal setting for a rave or any other mass gathering. The five-bedroom house had plenty of rooms for privacy — perfect for random coupling and doing dope. The functional areas of the grounds included two barns, four equipment sheds — which unlike most farms had wet bars —

spectator stands and a staging area for horses they didn't own, much less ever compete or show, two gazebos, three picnic areas each with five large tables. In the center of it all, there was a huge marble fountain with a replica of the Discus Thrower — everyone used the fountain as a swimming pool and wasted girls would simulate oral sex with the Olympian when their alcohol level and the desire for cheap laughs dictated. Finally, stretching from the front of the house, there was a long driveway visible all the way out to the main access road, giving the partiers ample visual warning for the extremely rare occasions when the inept local sheriff patrol might decide to make a surprise visit.

To call tonight's event a rave was a bit of a stretch. Like everything that happened in Pulnick, this would be a feeble copycat of what was and had been happening in the rest of the world for the past twenty years.

Missing were almost all of the standard elements. No MDMA or acid, and certainly none of the more recent designer drugs like the 2Cs, Atomic Fever, B2, Salvia or Bromine Dragonfly. The main drug of choice was of course alcohol, sometimes in its purest form as everclear. Second was marijuana. Occasionally someone would come by some tranquilizers. Either human or animal would do. As staples of substance abuse, these were of course all downers. To compensate, in the current spirit of Red Bull cocktails and Four Loko, it had increasingly become popular the last couple years to balance the beam by throwing some speedy ingredients into the mix. These included amphetamines, Ritalin and, whenever anyone could afford it, cocaine. Crack had pretty much come and gone.

The most obvious thing absent from tonight's rave-lite event was anything that even remotely resembled dancing. Of course, considering the music this was no surprise. Missing was the four-on-the-floor thump thump and hypnotic rhythms of acid house, dub, trip hop, techno, and drum and bass. Instead, playing over the stacks of JBL speakers on either side of a DJ-wannabe was speed metal and thrash. Metallica, Megadeth, Sepultura, Death Angel, Evil Dead, Pantera, Uncle Slam, Suicidal Tendencies, Anvil, Voivod. It was a mind-numbing aural assault at decibel levels which crushed the bones of the inner ear, and caused a sympathetic vibratory buzzing inside the head. The sonic blitz combined the musicality of a chainsaw and the agony of a dentist's drill tearing into every sensory nerve from the neck up.

At least that's how it felt to Noah.

Heavy metal.

All anger. No melody. Thunderous pounding. No groove. A relentless siege.

All of the subtlety and sophistication of a sawed-off shotgun being fired in your face.

Occasionally someone would leap out into the mostly vacant area in front of the DJ's stage which had been set aside for dancing, start writhing, convulsing, and maybe playing air guitar. Typically it was some wasted guy with mangy horse mane hair, his eyes rolling and mouth twisting, his tongue in its own epileptic struggle to escape the mad prison of torment that was the dude's face, his movement largely indistinguishable from a grand mal seizure.

It was revolting. But no one really seemed to notice.

Noah hated everything about tonight.

Of course he was the lone wolf on all of this. As far as everyone else here was concerned, tonight's "rave" was the latest and the greatest. Besides, any excuse for getting totally fucked up would do just fine. All in all, raving in Pulnick was more about stumbling and falling down than getting high and celebrating. The sticky points of what a rave actually was or should be, could and would be disregarded.

As Noah approached one of the wet bars, at this point himself desperate for anything to smother his senses with a thick layer of anesthetic unguent, Liz Sharona intercepted him. She put her hands around his neck and started to sway in time with the music. He instinctively put his own hands firmly on her waist, not to pull her closer but to keep her at bay. She was the perennial cock-tease temptress. But the word on the street was that she was also the town's Typhoid Mary for both chlamydia and the clap. He doubted the rumors but frankly, even if she was one of the foxier girls in this pathetic town, her head trips weren't worth the happy ending that might or might not result from a hook-up. She was a money girl who was too used to everything coming her way and only her way.

"So, lovely Liz. Where are the folks this time? Ibiza? Rio? Paris? Or maybe they're in Rio *with* Paris."

"Dutch Antilles, my broken boy. When do the casts come off?"

"Don't exactly know. Maybe three or four more weeks. Except the one on my penis is permanent."

"Really? You have a—"

Their profound exchange was interrupted by Chrissie Barker, one of the Super Skanks.

"Liz! Hurry! We're bottling!"

Liz caught Noah completely off guard and planted a wet palpating roto-rooting kiss on his immobile lips. He gagged as she managed to stick her tongue halfway down his esophagus. Mercifully it ended as quickly as it started.

"Later, dude. There's more where that came from."

Fearing that was true, Noah made a mental note to keep as much distance from her as he could for the rest of the party. She was gone for now, skipping along in a manner that only cheerleaders and twenty-somethings who had not outgrown their early adolescence could.

Bottling.

Also known as deep throating.

This was one of those completely mindless party games the participating girls and gawking guys never seemed to tire of. It was a contest to determine which girl could shove the neck of a Corona Beer bottle furthest down her throat and keep it there the longest without gagging. Maybe it was so popular because it left so little to the imagination. Guys looking on would typically at some point not so very discretely grind the heal of their hand into their crotch.

He stood there for a moment to watch. Liz grabbed the bottle next. She shoved it so far down her throat, Noah started to gag himself, an empathetic reflex. She had no such problem. She pushed it in and out of her throat like she was clearing a plugged sink. Her baton twirler smile never wavered. He wondered if she had been practicing on a baton.

"Go girl!" Squeals of delight all around. "But what a waste. There are no guys in this town who can come close to that."

She should know. That was Megan. Behind her back, everyone called her Glory Hole.

Noah grabbed a beer and headed in the opposite direction.

He really hated being here. But at the same time he didn't. There was this other feeling he always had at these parties, he could never figure out. Like tonight. This sense of anticipation. As if some adventure lurked on the dismal and predictable horizon that was Pulnick.

It was puzzling. This anxious feeling. As if something amazing and different were going to happen. As if some person other than the usual inbred stock of Pulnickians was magically going to appear and interrupt the monotonous slide show of faces that repeated itself ad infinitum. As if someone was actually going to say something original and interesting and not just repeat the hackneyed monosyllabic pseudo-hip phrases and sound bites aped from their favorite TV programs, then from one another.

Noah decided the grinding expectant gnaw in his stomach and loins must be physiological. He must be hyperthyroid. Or maybe his ocean of sperm was splashing over the internal levees. That was it. It was testosterone toxicity. He was drowning in hormones!

Alright. Get a grip, Noah!

There was no reason for optimism.

No way was he going to get laid. And that was that.

Considering what was available here, that was the only way it could be.

He continued to walk around the grounds. Most of the party goers were casually mingling, or lingering with either a drink or a joint in hand, sometimes both. There were maybe eighty or ninety there. Evenly split guys and gals. It was still early. People would be coming and going.

From his blithe but thorough assessment of the scene, it looked like the usual cattle call. Anyone new would have stood out like a koala bear in a tulip garden.

Out of the shadows, Margie Guster suddenly appeared with none other than Rich Flanagan in tow. This was a little surprising, since little Rich had been declaring since grade school that he was going to be a Catholic priest. Here he was with mega-slut Margie, the chick who had threatened his friend Jiff with a maternity situation, prompting his sudden and spontaneous departure from Pulnick into the welcoming arms of Uncle Sam.

If she was pregnant there was no way of telling. She was one of these fat slobs who would go the whole term without ever showing, spit out the eight pounds of protoplasm, and still look exactly the same. Ready for another meal at McDonalds.

"I hear you have a bun in the oven."

"What?"

"It's a good feeling."

"You don't look so good. What the fuck are you talking about?"

Rich just looked away. He was such a wimp. He would make a good priest.

Noah made a dramatic sweeping motion with his head, looked left, looked right, then behind him, as if to take in everyone present. Then he leaned in within inches of Margie's face.

"It's a good feeling knowing I am the only guy here who could not possibly be responsible for that fetus you claim to be carrying around like it's someone's IOU."

"Fuck you, twerp!"

She led Rich away. Surprising she didn't have a leash on him. Rich just sulked, moon-eyed like a puppy dog. It wouldn't be wild speculation to reckon that Rich felt ashamed that he was not enough of a man to stand up to Noah for insulting his girl. Ever so briefly as they were walking away, Rich glanced back but avoided looking Noah in the eyes.

Okay. That's good news for Jiff. Looks like the paternity matter had been decided and had been glommed on that pathetic sucker. Noah wondered if he should send Jiff a post card. Maybe he could skip all that Army nonsense after all.

Then again. What was Noah thinking? Skip the Army and then what? Come back here and be bored shitless in this dead end hellhole. The truth of the matter was, Jiff had the right idea. The only thing Noah could hold against him was that he managed to get out of Pulnick first.

Noah grabbed another beer. Actually two. The creeping haze of inebriation further darkened his mood. He kept fabricating generally nonsensical mental commentaries on each little scene and drama as it unfolded around him. His disposition continued its gradual glide down down down into the doldrums.

What the fuck was he doing here? Was this any way to spend a birthday? Was he just feeling sorry for himself? Then again, why shouldn't he feel sorry for himself?

Two hands clamped on his shoulders. Fight or flight? He turned around ready for action.

It was Jessie Grier. It was summer. And the guy was wearing a leather jacket.

He had graduated two years before Noah. Truth was, since his less-than-spectacular performance one summer — no one had the courage to tell him how bad he was — with the Hannibal Thespian Art Ensemble, a predictably horrible local community theater group, in the lead role in *Grease* as Danny Zuko, Jessie had never once been seen in public *not* wearing a leather jacket. He would probably be buried in this very same leather jacket.

"So dickhead, looks like you met your match. What was her name?"

What was he talking about? The guy never made any sense.

"What …?" Suddenly Noah got it. The casts. Jessie, incredibly clever star of stage was implying that Noah had gotten his ass kicked by some girl. Wow. Jessie was so funny.

"Ever watch Ultimate Fighting on TV? Her name is Diana The Destroyer. Actually, I bit off both of her nipples and she was counted out just before she bled to death. She didn't do this. I did this trying to open a can of honey-baked ham after the fight."

"There you go! You funny fuck you! And I don't just mean your face."

The leather jacket wasn't Jessie's only trademark. For as long as Noah could remember, the guy had a toothpick in his mouth. It used to just rest casual and cool in one or the other corner of Jessie's mouth. Switching it from one side to the other itself was allegedly a stunning show of manliness and sexual allure. Tonight was different. Way different. Tonight the toothpick was being thrashed about, rolled end-to-end, somersaulted in the midst of a lip-biting, masticating frenzy. At the same time, his jaws clenched and unclenched, in some uncontrollable isotonic paroxysm.

"Are you alright, Jessie? How's the acting?"

Suddenly Noah found himself on the ground. Jessie stood over him. Rage filled his face.

Just as suddenly, Jessie was reaching down offering Noah his hand to help him get up, smiling no less from ear to ear.

"Ha ha ha ha. Just fuckin' with you. Hope I didn't break anything. Or I guess I mean, RE-break anything. Ha ha ha."

Noah got back to his feet. Jessie was whapping him on the back. Actually whapping him on the shoulder with the cast. Each whap sent a jolt of pain through Noah's entire body.

Like the laughing-crying theater masks, Jessie's face suddenly went from laughter to agony.

"It's not easy, dude! It's not easy being me. So suck my dick, eh! Yo, hang loose. Get me? Remember, No-ah-ah-ah. You skinny motherfucker! I'm here for you. Beer or bail. I'm always here for you."

Then he was gone. As he strutted away, he grabbed some girl by the waist, threw her up over his shoulder and carried her for at least twenty feet, while she laughed and squealed and pretended to beg him to put her down. You could tell she was loving it.

And so it went.

Back to the bar. Two more.

Two giddy girls ran by him. One was slugging down wine from a bottle she held in her hand, while the other girl yelped about some guy they had apparently just spotted. "That's the one! With the hairy ass!" Maybe these were the high schoolers Joanna had promised.

Then, as if the entire world had shifted into an alternative reality, something really strange happened. Right in the midst of the psychotic roar of *Angel of Death* by Slayer, Michael Jackson's *Smooth Criminal* started playing. First it played along with the speed metal song, then when the DJ-wannabe properly cross-faded the tracks, *Smooth Criminal* played by itself. It was obviously intentional. The DJ — Roger, that was this pathetic wimp's name Noah seemed to recall — went on fiddling with the knobs of his music workstation as if nothing unusual had happened.

A smile flickered ever so briefly across Noah's face, though he quickly suppressed it. There was so much immediate turmoil it was inconceivable that anyone had noticed. A big bright smile was, of course, his normal reflex whenever he heard anything by Michael Jackson. But tonight it also stemmed from the hilarity of the outrageous incongruity. From the absurdity of such a completely anomalous piece of music being inserted into the firestorm of metal anthems which were typically the only thing ever heard around these parts, certainly the only type of music ever played at one of these parties.

A few girls actually perked up and rushed the dance area in front of the small stage.

But simultaneously the hoots and catcalls started.

"Hey! What's that shit!"
"Kill the motherfucking DJ."
"Hey asshole, put Slayer back on!"
"Turn off that pussy music. Rock 'n roll!!"

Then some kid walked directly in front of one stack of speaker cabinets, yelled at the top of his lungs, "No queer nigger music! No fucking nigger music!" He proceeded to throw a full 40 ounce bottle of King Cobra malt liquor through one of the unprotected woofers. It was a solid shot and the speaker immediately started flapping and sputtering with a horrible blatting sound.

In order to prevent the onset of a riot, but more to the point, to keep any more of his expensive equipment from being destroyed, the DJ immediately switched the song to *Overkill* by Motörhead. Then he walked over to the column of speakers to inspect the damage, and unplugged the cabinet issuing the offensive animal cry distortion. It wouldn't be missed, since he had seven more speaker boxes on this side of the stage alone, pumping out over 3500 watts.

The crowd seemed appeased. The catcallers stopped catcalling. The grumblers stopped grumbling. Everybody drifted back into the seemingly random patterns of mixing and milling. The music roared on at deafening and mind-numbing levels of complete cacophony and total chaos.

It was close to midnight, still early as these parties typically went.

Two more beers.

Everything now looked like a very bad movie on a tawdry tattered screen.

He could only hear the mocking voice of the narrator in his head.

What's the point?
Will somebody tell me!
What exactly is the fucking point?

He was on his eighth beer. The party showed no signs of slowing down, but Noah decided he had had enough. He was fading fast and not feeling very good. He decided to leave. It then occurred to him he had no contingency plan for getting home. He had been avoiding Joanna all evening, so successfully that he hadn't seen a sign of her since he watched her giving head to a Corona bottle.

Suddenly a wave of manic electricity moved through the entire crowd like an undulating sheet of summer lightning. It was triggered by a single word.

Fight!!

No one usually knew or cared why a fight started. It was like the morbid fascination people had with accidents on the highway. Noah fortunately was unconscious at the scene of his own motorcycle accident or he would have been appalled at the number of people who craned their necks and stooped over him, drawn by the spectacle of his near dismemberment. He was thus spared seeing in their eyes the silent speculation and the bets being exchanged telepathically as to whether this kid was going to kick the bucket before he reached the hospital. At a party fight, certainly at the outset no one really cared who was involved. The elation at seeing some serious carnage trumped any actual concern for the participants, the exceptions maybe being a girl friend or best buddy.

The fight was at the far end of the party perimeter, next to and slightly in front of one of the gazebos. The crowd moved like stampeding buffaloes. Noah didn't drag but he didn't run either and by the time he got there, it was all but over.

A huge hulk of a man — most definitely a stranger to these parts — was in the final stage of turning his victim's face into a pulpy stump of raw meat. Using both his fists and the heel of his boot, like a wild beast he was pounding and stomping the motionless person on the ground. No one was going to try to stop the hulk. The guy would have been right at home in WrestleMania. His 250 lb frame towered somewhere around six-foot-four. His muscles bulged and glistened, his tattoos, piercings and brutality warning anyone who thought of approaching that they were entering the zone of their own senseless and arbitrary death.

Noah recognized his victim. He didn't really know him but had seen him around town. This evening he was the drunken loudmouth who had decried the music of Michael Jackson and thrown the beer bottle through one of the P. A. speaker cones.

Maybe hulk man had a soft spot in his heart for Michael Jackson?

Right. Not funny.

It was obvious the guy was just an evil motherfucker who enjoyed inflicting pain on others, and didn't need a reason. Noah certainly wasn't about to initiate a one-man investigation into the nuances of what had totally pissed off this brute and pitched him into a homicidal rage.

Speaking of homicide, Noah wondered if the kid was dead. He wasn't moving. Without question, the beating he had just taken would have vanquished the life signs of better men. Someone needed to get the kid to ER as soon as possible. He was bleeding pretty badly.

As brute man swaggered away, Noah got an even greater shock.

There was his sister, Gretchen. She had moved out of the shadows from behind the gazebo and started walking away with hulk man. Not exactly with him, but alongside. Definitely in the same general direction. They passed under a pole-mounted flood light giving Noah a better look. He was far more startled by what he now saw, than he was by the barbaric beating he had just witnessed.

She looked terrible. But terrible didn't begin to describe it. She was gaunt. Sickly. Emaciated. Skeletal. Her skin was a yellowish-gray and looked lifeless like dried fish meat. She didn't stagger but did seem to move with an unsteadiness. An uncertainty. Even so, she wasn't listless. In fact, she seemed kind of jaggy and nervous. But there was a gelatinous palsy about her whole bearing. She was a wreck.

What the hell had happened to her?

How long had it been? The last time he saw her was her visit to see him in the hospital. She looked completely normal then. Just as she always had. Not overweight but still with some baby fat. A soft roundness in her face, a little extra padding on her slight frame.

That was a month-and-a-half ago.

Now she looked like an anorexic zombie.

Did she have leukemia? AIDS?

She was gone now. She had disappeared into the shadows with hulk man. But just as she passed into the darkness, Noah caught a brief glimpse of another figure he knew all too well.

His next door neighbor and erstwhile friend. Phil Roswell aka Zipper.

Also not looking very healthy.

Noah got his ride home two hours later. In the Skankmobile. But he lucked out. Two of the girls were so wasted they were comatose, another was busy sucking the nipples of a local truck driver — a Super Skank fuck buddy that they passed around like a tube of lipstick — and the driver, Joanna Pillsbury, who had given him a ride to the party, was obviously going home with the drunk sitting next to her, whose name Noah could never remember because he had no reason to. The guy was feeling her up with both hands and licking her neck. Hopefully he had a condom with him.

Noah walked up the flight of stairs to his tiny flat and flipped on the overhead light.

The second anniversary of Michael Jackson's death and Noah's twenty-third birthday were now in the history books. And neither were mentioned or given passing thought all evening by anyone else at the rave.

There's no place like home.

No place like Hell.

As Normal As It Gets

June left spring standing at the station and hurtled forward into the sticky swelter of summer.

Noah was uncomfortable on a number of levels — beyond the temperatures in the high 90s.

There was his mom's ovarian cancer, his sister's new cadaverous condition, his lack of a job, and his growing impatience with how long it was taking his body to heal from the motorcycle accident, though his doctors constantly assured him that he was mending fast and would be back to normal soon.

Noah's mom had been out of the hospital for just over a week now. What a relief that was. He had gone to visit her almost every day in her semi-private hospital room. To St. Louis and back was a five hour round trip.

The doctors put on their optimistic faces but the reality was that the outcome of the operation was inconclusive. It was wait and see, hope for the best, but plan for the worst.

Not much Noah could do on that for now. He visited her at home every few days, lent his moral support, and listened to incoherent ramblings about her inevitable fate which ran the gamut from almost immediate death, to licking the "Big C" and living to be a hundred. To be supportive, he mimicked the doctors' hollow but pleasant-sounding reassurances, based on the unwritten Hippocratic dictum that when positive data is lacking, resort to plausible fairy tales.

On a purely personal level, what he was primarily looking forward to was getting rid of his damn, sweaty, itchy, confining, and ultimately humiliating casts. The good news for him was that the orthopedic doctors promised his splint and casts would be off next week. Maybe he could get back to a more familiar routine, the most important elements of which would be to find a job and start making some money again.

Of course, transportation was an issue. To hold down a job, he would have to deal with that. He could only borrow him mom's car so much. He left it with her the day after he brought her home from the hospital and could use it now and again, but basically was walking and hitching rides to get around.

Why was life so complicated?

Then there was Gretchen.

His sister. His fucking pain-in-the-ass sister.

He really wished he could care less. But he couldn't. There was no love lost there. But for his mom's sake, he had to care. He had to pay attention. He had to do something.

"She only came around once the whole time."

The whole time Noah's mom was referring to was the time of her hospitalization and now her recovery time here at home. To date that totaled about three weeks. His mom didn't appear angry but was certainly concerned and, though she tried to conceal it, hurt.

"She's lost a lot of weight. Have you seen her tattoo?"

Noah had only gotten a very brief glimpse of Gretchen at the party, and the light was poor. He hadn't seen a tattoo. He surely would have noticed.

"What tattoo?"

"It says 11-11-11. That's all. You know, the date."

"Yeah yeah yeah. The date. Did she say why? What it was about?"

"She said God is her new pimp daddy. She's gotten very potty-mouthed. Then she just laughed. That was it."

"Where is she living? I've got to talk to her."

"She moved out while you were in the hospital. She won't tell her own mom. Well … it's not that she won't tell me. She just changes the subject. Maybe it's kind of a game."

"Right, mom. That's it. She's playing hide-and-seek."

His mom went back to making bread dough. Which looked pretty strange since she was wearing what almost appeared to be a formal evening gown and fake diamond butterfly hair pins attached to her dramatically coiffed hair.

"How are things at Harriet's?"

"They changed the name to Bacchanal Beauty & Nails. I don't like it anymore. They've become so political. They're sponsoring a youth rodeo in Moberly."

Something was seriously wrong with his mother. But basically it was pretty harmless.

Something was seriously wrong with Gretchen. But it was far from harmless.

Gretchen was running with a bad crowd. From appearances anyway.

And his two-faced friend Phil was mixed up in it somehow.

It was confusing at best. A dangerous game at worst.

The young guy beat up in the fight at the party?

Noah heard he was DOA at the hospital.

At least he didn't spoil the perfect record of ICU at Monroe County Hospital by having the impertinence and ill manners to die there on the premises.

A New Breed of Entrepreneur

Their work ethic, not unlike their Givenchy and Brioni-suited counterparts on Wall Street, was driven by the dictum that profit should be maximized by securing market share — preferably a monopoly — at any cost, and at any one else's expense.

There was a huge difference in style, however. Instead of contracts, they used clubs and chains. Instead of buyouts, they used bullying. They didn't bury their competition with a marketing plan and entrepreneurial flair. They buried them with a shovel and dirt. They didn't lick 'em or join 'em. They eliminated them. Destroyed them. Killed them.

With this new breed of entrepreneur, all of the sophisticated methodologies and intricate tools of enterprise were displaced by a single instrument of negotiation and deal making — the sawed-off shotgun, either strapped to a leg or mounted in the cabs of their GMC Sierra 2500s or their Ford F-350s.

They kept things simple. They had only one product line. And it was highly illegal.

Methamphetamine.

This was the Arian Brothers of Texas.

A new breed alright. One that played by one set of rules. Their own.

Meth. Crystal. Crank. Speed. Whizz. Billy. Phet.

By any name it spelled trouble. Trouble for anyone who tried it. Trouble for anyone addicted to it. Trouble for any and all communities where it took up residence, either in the form of producers — meth labs — or in the form of sellers — pushers — of the most addictive, destructive illicit drug ever.

Everything good and bad and somewhere in between eventually made it to Pulnick.

It was always just a matter of time.

The Arian Brothers of Texas.

They had arrived in Monroe County. They made a cameo appearance at the rave party just outside of Pulnick. And gave a preview of things to come.

Only last year they had showed up in the outlying areas of Joplin, Springfield and Lebanon. News reports and editorials started appearing in the Jefferson City News Tribune and the Kansas City Star, followed by coverage on network television affiliates, about the latest crisis in suburban and rural Missouri, a scourge unlike anything that the relatively bucolic state had ever seen in its nearly 190 year existence.

It had originally spread like an unstoppable plague across Texas then quickly moved up through the Panhandle into Oklahoma, across into Arkansas, and now were rolling like a black cloud of poison gas, north into Kansas and Missouri. As they rolled in, young people died in droves, communities disintegrated, people cowered in fear, and local law enforcement found themselves in a losing war.

A new breed of entrepreneur. A vicious terrorist army.

It wasn't just the drug, horrible enough on its own terms, which caused the nightmare.

Magnifying their social toxicity many times over was their other agenda. The ABT were white supremacists in the purest and most pernicious sense. They simply and openly believed that all non-white people were not human at all, but filthy inferior animals, vermin, a disease.

This meant catastrophe for the large numbers of people of color in the regions where they now operated. Black people who populated the urban areas. Browns who had immigrated legally and otherwise to work the fields of the rural counties. Blacks and browns, who, though it was politically incorrect to stereotype them as such but still statistically accurate, tended in higher percentages to be involved in the existing drug trade in the regions — typically marijuana and cocaine. The ABT weren't going to work with these established networks. They on principle and racist conviction would eradicate them. And they did. Without remorse or mercy. They slaughtered them the way a household pest exterminator might deal with unwanted cockroaches and termites.

The warning shot had been fired in Pulnick.

Though it wasn't prompted by venomous racial loathing, the ABT dealt with potential white competition just as brutally. No one was safe. No one they didn't like, anyway.

The beating and killing of the Michael Jackson hater at the party was an example of how little the ABT valued human life. It turned out that the brute just didn't like the kid's looks. That was the only reason he killed him. As far as he was concerned, it was the only reason he needed. Plus he just felt like it at the time. It was his way of amusing himself. To fight the boredom. Just something to pass the time until he got around to the real purpose of his visit.

Brute man was a slightly less furry version of King Kong. Huge bull neck, head shaped more like a block than a ball, a massive frame covered with pro-wrestling slabs of highly annealed meat, muscles pumped and ready, perpetually twitching, just aching for some action. He looked like a one-man infantry. His uniform, however, communicated a huge and random appetite for destruction. He was covered with tattoos. From tasteless to offensive seemed to be the range: several swastikas, a girl with her legs spread wide to display her pubic region, several 'Fucks' and one 'Motherfucker', an 'All niggers die' manifesto, an equation that declared 'Kikes=disease', and an assortment of daggers, skulls and crossbones, bullet bands, barbed wire, and various demons and snakes. He was also adorned with several ounces of metal, including masonry nails through his eyebrows, a nose ring, thick rings through his upper lip and both ears, and iron spike wrist and bicep bands.

If image is everything, then this brutal monster — and any others like him who might follow and take up residence in Pulnick — was one of the nine circles of Dante's Hell.

As ugly and fearsome as he was, it was awe-inspiring to behold the enormity of his charisma. Like a lot of his cohorts back in Texas, he possessed a powerful personal magnetic force that pulled the innocent and unsuspecting to his side. These were typically the usual slackers who would immediately and heedlessly glom onto anything or anyone they perceived as the next big thing, so as to get a jump on everyone else. Hulk man was big, and he was definitely a thing — more thing than human. And sure enough, several of Pulnick's edgier young denizens had already joined his flock. It took no time at all for their curiosity and craving for some form of prestige and posturing — twisted as it might be — to overcome their trepidation.

Phil aka Zipper and the attached Gretchen were among his first recruits. Others like Jessie Grier, Chuck Ristoria, and Skank girls Chrissie Barker and Joanna Pillsbury would soon follow. These hangers-on would suck up to the mighty Trojan Horse, awed by his devil-may-care arrogance, blatant disregard for convention, fearless daring, take-no-prisoner bravado, his nihilistic abandon, and total embrace of anarchy. Everyone in and around Pulnick just dabbled. This man pulled out all of the stops.

One thing could certainly be said of the Aryan Brothers of Texas.

They scrupulously adhered to truth in advertising.

It was easy see the writing on the wall.

Too bad no one was looking.

Noah couldn't find his sister but he did find a job.

It turned out much easier than he had expected.

He got his broken bone enclosures off the Thursday before the coming July 4th holiday weekend. Early Friday morning he headed out in his mom's car and handed in only two job applications. One was at Quinn Farm Supply, a feed and equipment store in Monroe City. Then remembering Phil's recommendation, he headed out to Merkel Industries, conveniently closer to where he lived. Phil apparently was not exaggerating when he said Merkel was hiring because after two relatively brief interviews, one with the head of Personnel and another with a shop foreman, he was told to report Tuesday for work. Of course, he'd have to undergo a pro forma medical exam to make sure he had life signs and no obvious physical impediments to doing what was described as light labor.

He would be working the day shift, and the pay was decent at $15.75 per hour to start. Stopping to think about it, the pay was excellent compared to the $0.00 per hour he was earning right now.

Noah felt good. Real good. Maybe things were turning around for him. It was only noon and in a few short hours he had solved a major problem, and still had the rest of the day and a holiday weekend to chill out, have some fun, and get himself psyched for his new career as a member of the "Merkel Industries family", as the HR manager proudly called it.

He had never worked in a factory before but Merkel had an excellent reputation around the region. He heard that a few years ago, some organizer had come from out of town and tried to rally existing Merkel employees to form a union, but they told the guy to buzz off. They told him they had it good and didn't need a union to be charging them dues for what they already had accomplished on their own.

The lunch whistle blew just as Noah was handing his new employee forms to the Human Resources receptionist — a real doll maybe 24 or 25, who he hadn't seen around town before. He then gave a final glad-hand to the Personnel guy he had just interviewed with, as the older gentleman slipped past for his midday meal.

"Thanks so much, Mr. uh ..."

"Gladstone. You're welcome. Tuesday. 7:30 am sharp. Don't blow off any fingers this weekend or we'll change our minds."

"Blow off ... oh right. The 4th. Fireworks. Got it."

By the time Noah got back out to the parking lot, many of the employees were on their way to lunch. Merkel had a cafeteria but as he was later to learn, since it didn't serve beer, several of the guys from the manufacturing section shot down to a local bar on their lunch break.

As he approached his mom's Chevy Caprice, he couldn't help but hear the scream and rumble of a Slayer song — it sounded like *Blood Red* in the swirling muck of the distortion — filtering through the dusty air of the parking lot. As he got closer, he realized it was coming from an Oldsmobile Delta 88 parked next to him. It was a classic — a '71 or '72 — and was decked out with mag wheels and rear fender skirts, a fake air scoop on the engine hood, a racing-style spoiler on the trunk lid, and a tattered ill-fitting black vinyl bra across the front. The Olds was sitting so low Noah doubted it could clear a pair of gym sneakers. Whether this was intentional or just the result of broken springs was anyone's guess.

As he walked up to his driver-side door, Noah discretely tried to peek into the other vehicle, then stood there fumbling around trying to find the appropriate key on his mother's fluffy pink key holder — why did she have over fifty keys?

The guy on the passenger side of the Olds rolled his window down halfway. Someone lowered the volume of the music just enough for Noah to hear him.

"Nice key chain. You get hired?"

"I did. I start on Tuesday."

"Don't feel too special. As long as you can stand up and your heart is beating, they give you a job here."

He seemed kind of giggly. He was fat and munching on a king-size Snickers Bar.

The guy then offered Noah a hit off the humungous joint in his other hand.

Noah looked around nervously to see if any of the office people he had just interviewed with could see him. He didn't want to blow this job by appearing to be doing dope in the parking lot. Before he could even decline the offer, someone in the back seat spoke up.

"Don't give him that shit, you dumb fuck!" This new guy squeezed his face into the open window. It was quite a face. This dude was an albino. Puffy pinkish-purplish skin adorned with tufts of cumulous cloud curly white hair and wispy white eyebrows.

"Make sure you stay clean for the next few days. Their physical is a joke. But it's their excuse to get you to pee into a cup and test you for nasty chemicals. Merkel knows that drugs are real bad news when it comes to safety. And I hear there are some serious stoners already working there."

Roars of laughter from the four guys in the car. The cigar-size joint made the rounds and smoke billowed out of the partially lowered passenger-side window like the car's seats were on fire.

"That's right, dude! You can't be too careful!"

More raucous laughter.

The driver now leaned over. He was a stark contrast to the other two. Long combed hair. Stubble chic growth on his angular face. Very lean and muscular. He had an air of authority. A no-bullshit kind of a guy.

"We're all working in Building 4. That's probably where you'll start. Stay cool. We'll see you around."

The passenger window rolled back up. The volume of the music quadrupled to its original eardrum-shattering level. Noah climbed into his mom's car and pulled out of the lot.

Well, it looked like there were some interesting times ahead.

Those guys in the Olds were certainly happy to be working at Merkel.
Or maybe they were just ... happy.

Pulpit Fiction

Just as Noah was about to ring up his mother to tell her the good news about his new job, his phone rang. She was calling him.

"Hey, mom. Are you psychic or what? I was just going to call you."

"I've been better. But I appreciate your asking."

What?

"So you're still hurting? How long are the doctors saying you'll take to heal up?"

"I shouldn't complain. I am just grateful that someone listened to me. I could have died."

She was taking the credit for discovering her ovarian cancer? She might be his mom and surely he had been through many years of this nonsensical banter. But to be blunt about it, he could never quite get used to the way her brain functioned — or more accurately, failed to function.

"Yes, a darn good thing. Listen I—"

"Noah, I know you're going to hate this, but I want you to come to church with me Sunday."

This was new.

He was not aware that she *ever* went to church. Certainly as a family they had never gone, which probably provided the early underpinnings of what had evolved over the years into his full-blown, uncompromising atheism and hatred for institutional religion.

"I hear they have a Church of Elvis in St. Louis. I could handle that."

"There is a lecture and town hall meeting in Madison. It's at Salem First Baptist."

"Mom! You've got to be joking. That is the worst. The place is full of holy rollers!"

"It's a special evening. They have someone coming in to speak. I called Gretchen but she wouldn't say one way or the other. She kept changing the subject. She's been so weird lately."

"Gretchen? Weird? What a shocker."

It turned out that Gretchen showed up anyway. She came in about twenty minutes after the town hall meeting had already started. She was with Phil and they stood in the very back of the church, fidgeting and exchanging enigmatic looks and whispered asides.

She didn't appear all that much worse off than when he had last seen her, but the light was better here, so at least he got a better look. His general impression was still that her health was in serious jeopardy. She looked frail, undernourished and skittish. He also noticed there were some scabs on her forehead. Her hair looked unwashed and thin. Her scalp was showing.

About forty minutes into the evening's lecture, Noah glanced back to where Gretchen and Phil had been standing. They were gone. So much for trying to find out what was going on with her: How was she doing? Where was she living? Why had she been so scarce lately?

The meeting was the most tedious thing Noah had ever experienced in twenty-three years of unrelenting tedium. Out of courtesy, he tried to pay attention but it was a monumental challenge. It was like listening to the air pump motor on a fish tank.

The guest speaker was the "world-renowned" Dr. Theodore Clemus, a university professor of theology — they never said where — and reputedly an expert on end times and Biblical prophecy. His evident lack of public speaking skills was only surpassed by his supreme lack of anything coherent to say.

And this church! Noah couldn't imagine a more characterless or depressing setting for worship, prayer, a lecture, a public meeting, or even bingo. If the altar had consisted of a cheap folding card table, it wouldn't have been out of place. The lectern must have come from a garage sale. The entire interior was horribly shabby and howled like a hyperventilating banshee for serious structural repair and cosmetic restoration. The church had been built at the end of the 19th century and never undergone any upgrades. One plywood facing on the ceiling of the rectangular sanctum, was hanging precariously by a number of loose nails. It looked poised to drop on the heads of the congregants below if they so much as sneezed, or sang too loudly from their threadbare hymnals. Too much smoke and dust clung to all the interior surfaces to allow any reasonable guess as to the color of the last coat of paint. Now it was the hue of a weathered old boot. The carpet was so worn in spots it looked like burlap bags had been randomly thrown around the room. A couple stained glass windows depicting Jesus the Savior and Mother Mary were stained alright. Stained by so much muck that the portraitures could have been Jim Morrison as a beggar and Rupaul as the Flying Nun. Who could tell the difference?

This whole thing was dismal at best. Noah cursed himself for coming.

Dr. Clemus droned on. Everyone else seemed mesmerized. Noah was bored and confused. Not only did the guy make no sense, but he had as much charisma as a garden hose. What was the appeal here? Were the people of Monroe County that clueless?

Right ... he really didn't need to answer that.

Finally, two-thirds of the way through his lecture, Clemus actually mentioned a few things which made Noah pay attention. 11-11-11. The end was near. This was the date and it was for certain. November 11, 2011 was when it would all come to a head.

Alright!

Now we knew.

On good authority.

We'd all gotten the word.

Maybe if a person were completely uncritical and disconnected from logic and common sense — probably not that rare of a condition from what he was seeing of the crowd here tonight — it would be easy to buy into this nonsense, maybe even conclude that tonight's speaker was truly some amazingly gifted clairvoyant, a prophet, a seer with far-reaching and profound insights into God's plans for His humble little lambs here on Earth.

But if you had half a functioning brain ...

Noah turned around to get a good look at the expressions on the faces of the people behind him. It was disturbing. Sad. They all looked hypnotized. And frightened. Like the hypnotist had just told them that Attila the Hun was on his way to Monroe County and taking no prisoners. Or hydrogen bombs would be raining down on them like hailstones. Or the water they had been drinking for the past week was contaminated with a flesh-eating bacteria and they would within the next few days be turned into a puddle of pus.

The fear card.

Clemus was playing them like a bunch of terrified school children.

> *My Christian brethren. Just look around you. What do you see? Just turn on the TV? Every day. Day after day. The same things. Only more of it. And it keeps getting worse. Floods. Earthquakes. Global warming. Corruption. Crime. Hatred. Lies. Fornication.*

Fornication? Wait. Noah thought that was a good thing.

> *Ebola. Swine flu. Tuberculosis. AIDS.*

Right. Right. Disease. Bad.

> *Isaiah 24:20. 'The earth shall reel to and fro like a drunkard, and shall be removed like a cottage; and the transgression thereof shall be heavy upon it; and it shall fall, and not rise again.'*

Thump thump. It always came back to the old book of fairy tales.

> *And 2 Peter 3:10. 'But the day of the Lord will come as a thief in the night; in which the heavens shall pass away with a great noise, and the elements shall melt with fervent heat, the earth also and the works that are therein shall be burned up.'*

Did anyone bring any marshmallows?

> *Now listen to the words of Nostradamus ...*

Nostradamus?! How did he get in the picture?

... who in his divinely tuned prescience has accurately foretold of so many historical cataclysms. In Quatrain 9 44 Nostradamus explicitly warns us: 'All should leave Geneva. Saturn turns from gold to iron, the contrary positive ray will exterminate everything, and there will be signs in the sky before this.

Uh ... but we're not in Geneva. At least according to my map.

Again from the Holy Bible, Revelation 6:13 and 6:14 tells us 'And the stars of heaven fell unto the earth, even as a fig tree casteth her untimely figs, when she is shaken of a mighty wind. And the heaven departed as a scroll when it is rolled together; and every mountain and island were moved out of their places.'

I hate when that happens.

On September 11, 2001 courtesy of Islamic terrorists we were given a preview. A wake-up call, so to speak.

Blam!! The patriotism card! Military marches, holy hymns, medals and blaring bugles. 'Oh say can you see, by the dawn's early light ...'

9-11. 9 + 1 + 1 = 11. There are 11 letters in New York City. Many report that Jesus appeared 11 times after his crucifixion. In the mathematics of higher cosmology, there are 11 dimensions in the Universe. There are 1,111 angels called Midwayers living amongst us, right now here on Earth as I speak.

Would they all fit on the head of a pin?

In the Book of Luke, there are 11 parables that Jesus told during his ministry. September 11th is the 254th day of the year. 2 + 5 + 4 = 11. The final death toll for the attack on the twin towers was 2,801. 2 + 8 + 0 + 1 = 11. The President's plane is called Air Force One. "Air Force One" has 11 letters. "George W. Bush" consists of 11 letters. "Bill Clinton" has 11 letters. To call either Iran or Iraq, the area code is 119. 1 + 1 + 9 = 11. Mohammed, the divine prophet who founded Islam, died in 632 A.D. 6 + 3 + 2 = 11.

Any thoughts on this week's winning lottery numbers?

So it's not just Biblical prophesy. Though as the word of God, that is sufficient. The point is we see the signs from everywhere. We have been duly warned. And we must heed those warnings.

It always came down to fear and desperation. And the past ten years had produced no shortage of either fear and desperation. People were running scared. Running to they knew not where and scared of they knew not what.

Predictably desperation was at a high barometric reading tonight and fear was bending the needle on the voltage meter.

I call it the Dead Lincoln Effect. DLE for short. The night Lincoln was shot, for some reason the government's entire telegraph system was not functioning. So no one knew he had been assassinated. People went to bed and woke up thinking Abraham Lincoln was still their president.

This guy is priceless. Now he's introduced Abraham Lincoln into his convoluted logic. And the point is?

But consider this. If Lincoln's death had happened fifty years before, people around the country would not have known for weeks or months. News was carried on the backs of galloping horses, and while these steeds were driven hard across the mighty plains and mountain ranges, news traveled at a crawl. And now think about this. Had his murder happened centuries before ...

It would have been really amazing since Lincoln wasn't even born! Where was this going?

... it might have taken years for word of his death to travel across the vast unpopulated tracts of the planet, news which would have been met with doubt and confusion.

Doubt and confusion. Finally! Two words that belonged here.

The Dead Lincoln Effect. People isolated by distance. We too are in isolation. We are in cosmic exile in our little lonely corner of the Universe. You see, nothing can travel faster than the speed of light.

Aha! Einstein! This was like a celebrity guest panel.

News might travel fast but we are 26,000 light years from the center of our own galaxy. If some catastrophic event ever occurred there — and I'm not saying there has — we would not find out for 26,000 years.

Thank goodness for TiVo.

Something did happen a little further away. In our local group of galaxies, which includes among others our own Milky Way, Andromeda, Triangulum, and the Magellanic Clouds, there is one called NGC 205. It is 2,200,000 light years away and 11,000 light years in diameter. Or I should say it was. Because it is no longer. This galaxy was at the precise location of a cosmic event threshold, which is just fancy science talk for the border between our four-dimensional world and the infinite-dimensional world of the mind of God.

Noah had to hand it to the guy. He had carved out a very special niche for himself. It was highly doubtful that anyone would be stealing the Clemus unique brand of doomsday thunder. Or copying his trademark style of mumbling.

22,000,000 years ago God reconsidered. In a flash of thought, in the flawless infinity of his Divine Wisdom, he decided to redesign the human experiment, take it back to the drawing board, reboot the Universe.

Hold on! Are we talking Windows or Mac? Linux?

As God spoke in Isaiah 65:17, 'For, behold, I create new heavens and a new earth: and the former shall not be remembered, nor come into mind.'

Dr. Clemus took a deep breath. He looked around the room. The expression on his face for some reason made Noah think of George W. Bush reading "My Pet Goat" to a class of grade schoolers while people were leaping off the top floors of the World Trade Center.

Ladies and gentlemen. The world has already ended. We are merely the last to know.

He now introduced a pregnant pause, to make sure that the impact of the much-anticipated conclusion of his lecture would be powerfully felt and fully appreciated. Then he continued.

> *At 11:11 am on November 11th of this year of 2011, the Creator's message of universal redemption will arrive. The world as we know it has ended and we will finally stand illuminated in the perfect knowledge of truth. It will be as a searing sheet of white light, a vast energy field of God's love, which will exalt the True Believers and destroy those who have doubted Him. 11-11-11. Amen.*

Mercifully, the lecture had ended. There was a smattering of applause. The hundred or so people there, stunned by what they had heard and somnambulized by the anesthetic drone of Clemus' voice, clapped listlessly like advanced victims of cerebral palsy, an effect not unlike microwaving a ten-year old bag of soggy popcorn.

Dr. Clemus opened the floor for questions from the audience.

Three people stood up and proclaimed their love for Jesus. One said she hoped her yellow lab would get into Heaven, because if he couldn't she would miss him terribly. Then everyone shifted nervously in their seats as silence and vacant stares filled the ramshackle church.

Clemus thanked everyone for coming, declaring the official part of tonight's program over, but invited everyone to stay around for light refreshments, to mix and bounce their ideas off one another about what they had just heard. It was a noble attempt. The refreshments — cheese and crackers, pretzels, Lipton tea, and orange soda — were a hit but most everyone there was both shy by nature and inarticulate from bad nurturing. There was very little actual conversation taking place. A lot of throat clearing and some tentative murmurs.

The crowd dwindled quickly.

It was finally over.

Noah just sat there. He was speechless.

Unfortunately, his mother was not.

"It's good for us to get the truth about what's happening in the world."

Noah looked at his mother's earrings.

"Mom. Are those zircon?"

Chapter Four

July 4 …

Patriotism 101

"Whoa! There's Miss Poop Chute. And she's with Bucky McCall!"

"Who? What are you talking about?"

"When the crack you attack is the crack in the back."

"What's that supposed to mean?"

"Fuck! You are so clueless! Use your imagination, dude."

"God gave me an imagination so I could imagine anal sex?"

"You don't believe in God. But you do know what I'm talking about, eh?"

"How do you know she does that sort of thing anyway? Do you know this chick?"

"Everybody knows. If you don't believe me, just ask her. Go ahead. She'll tell you!"

Noah had gotten the call early that morning. July 4th. Well. Early for these guys. 10 a.m. The plan was to drive to Whiteman Air Force Base in Knob Noster. That was about 150 miles west of them, over in Johnson County, just seventy miles east-south-east of Kansas City. If one of them stayed reasonably sober, the drive should take about two-and-a-half hours.

They would be picking him up in about 45 minutes. A dude fest. Five all together.

While Noah was getting ready, his phone rang again. A telecommunications bonanza.

Unfortunately, it was Jinx and it was unfortunate because he would be turning down his old buddy's invitation. Jinx invited him over to spend the day with him and his family, and Noah had already said he'd be going to the air show. Which frankly sounded a whole helluva lot better than plunking himself down at a back yard barbecue with Jinx. His four kids running around screaming and generally being obnoxious. His cranky wife giving both him and Jinx dirty looks all day. He'd just have to take a rain check and hope it rained every day from now on.

"I'm really sorry, Jinx. I told these guys I'd be going with them. How's work?"

"It sucks, of course. What would you expect? It's no fun without you there. And this new pimple face kid who replaced you is an ass-licking company boy. Thinks he's going to go places there at Walmart. And he probably will. He's exactly what they want. A little fucking brown-nosing yes-man."

"No fun, eh?"

"I was really looking forward to seeing you. I negotiated a temporary cease fire with the old lady and it would've been cool. I don't think she would've tried

71

to kill you."

"Next time, dude. Next time."

His ride showed up a half-hour late. Typical.

"We had to make a beer run. Break Time was packed, man! You'd think they were giving the shit away."

"That's Pulnick for ya. The drunks even outnumber the cows."

For the day's outing it would be Noah; obnoxious Jessie Grier, the John Travolta celebrity impersonator; Rich Flanagan, the quiet kid that always wanted to be a priest, who Noah had just seen at the rave with putatively pregnant Margie Guster; Ryan Billingsley, a fellow maybe two years older that Noah didn't know except to have seen him around town now and then; and finally Jackson Madre, who Noah watched play short stop as he restlessly sat on the bench the one year he spent on Calvin Coolidge Jr.-Sr. High School's varsity baseball team.

For the first half of the drive, everyone was smiles but no one had much to say.

At the tail end of his fourth Pabst Blue Ribbon and about halfway to Knob Noster, Rich trained his sad bloodhound eyes on Noah, then tapped him on the shoulder with the bottle of beer in his hand.

"Hey, Noah. I gotta thank you, man."

"For what? Being the great human being I am?"

"Kinda. Until you made that bun-in-the-oven remark, I didn't know what Guster was up to, like why she was hanging all over me."

"You're not with her anymore?"

"Never was. She's a slut."

Noah handed Rich another beer from the cooler.

"So is it back to the priesthood for you?"

"Nah. Bad idea. Though I'd probably have a better chance getting regular ass from a nun than that slippery cunt Margie. Someone's got her knocked up, just like you said. Now her slimy been-there-done-that-done-everyone pussy is all over town. Till she gets some poor slob to marry her anyway. I pity the guy."

Jessie piped in.

"Any dumb fuck stupid enough to marry that worthless tub-of-lard bitch whore gets what he deserves."

Rich hoisted his beer for a toast.

"Down with worthless tub-of-lard bitch whores!"

It was expected of guys like Jessie but Noah found it kind of shocking to hear Rich talk this way. Obviously he was angry. But Noah had always known him as a soft-spoken, pious sort of chap. Other kids made fun of him behind his back, but Rich was so sweet in person, no one ever wanted to harass or embarrass him. So what if the guy wanted to be a priest. Whatever. Rich was regarded as a pleasant and tolerable oddity.

What had changed?

"What are you doing these days, Rich?"

"Chasing my tail, like everyone else. I work at Merkel for now."

"Really! I start there tomorrow."

"Cool. I'm in Building 2. When you get adjusted to the place, come on by. We'll do a doobie, and I'll take you to the Tin Monkey Cage."

"The what?"

"Tin Monkey Cage. I'll show you. It's pretty rad."

The exchange between Noah and Rich seemed to loosen everybody up. For the rest of the ride, everybody was jabbering away. Nothing in particular. Just the usual chucking and jiving.

"Guster is a two-bagger."

"What's a two-bagger?"

"You put one bag over her head and the other over your own head in case hers falls off."

That brought on a few chuckles. Enthusiasm was building a bit.

"Hey Jessie! You drive like an old lady. That pedal on the right is the accelerator."

"I used to love Henry Halder day."

"What are you talking about?"

"Henry Halder. The math teacher. I guess it was before your time. Like on Henry Halder day, everyone, even girls, dressed up just like the stupid dork. Plaid pants. Ugly fucking ties. Baggy striped shirts. Suspenders. He'd look around and notice something was strange but he was so fucking clueless he couldn't figure it out."

"What happened to him?"

"Dunno. Quit. Committed suicide. Became a clown and joined the circus. Beats me."

"The Cardinals are doomed. They traded away all their good players. Someone's smoking crack up in management."

"They were always doomed."

"Fuck you, Tass! Traitor!"

"Is that a police helicopter?"

"That's one of those medical transports. They've got a brain in a Styrofoam cooler on its way to Monroe County General."

"How do you know that, Madre? Unless you were the donor."

They arrived just after 1 pm. Under two hours. Jessie hadn't driven like an old lady at all. Unless it was the little old lady from Pasadena.

There was already a huge crowd. People had driven in from all around. It seemed like half of the population of nearby Kansas City was there.

Souvenir booths full of cheap Independence Day regalia, flags and plastic toys, alternated with food booths serving everything from fried chicken, pizza, hamburgers, hot dogs, sausages, French fries, chili, cheese steak sandwiches, greasy Americanized versions of ethnic foods, elephant ears, cotton candy, ice cream, donuts, and the latest craze, deep fried versions of all of the above, even deep fried candy bars and frozen butter sticks.

And of course beer. It was a hot day — high 80s low 90s — so the lines at the Coors and Anheuser-Busch booths never dwindled.

Ceremonies were already underway. Almost completely ignored by the crowd, some uniformed official was orating from a stage centrally located on the apron of the air field's main landing strip. The stage was decked out in red, white and blue, and filled with twenty-five or thirty other dignitaries seated in folding chairs behind him, at least pretending to be interested in what he had to say. His speech was occasionally interrupted by a smattering of polite applause. Another uniformed gentleman eventually replaced him but the general public basically went on doing what they were best at, gorging themselves on fast food and sucking down copious amounts of beer.

Since it was July 4th, there would be all of the usual Independence Day hoopla — speeches, parades, fireworks. But being held at the air force base meant the added bonus of a spectacular air show, featuring stunt pilots from the civilian sector and of course a proud and mighty display of the air superiority and firepower of a few of the Air Force's most awesome fighting machines.

It was a couple of hours before the air show began. For now Noah and the guys just strolled around, checking out the displays, booths and babes.

Only in Missouri could you travel halfway across the state and run into someone you knew from high school. Bucky McCall had been one year ahead of Noah, was the star both on the football field — pick for All-State running back both junior and senior years — and at the Y, having penetrated the defenses of many young girls and plunged deep into their end zone. One of the final victorious gold medal efforts in his ongoing vaginal Olympics had resulted his senior year in the pregnancy of Pulnick's lead cheerleader, followed by a hastily arranged wedding, and Noah had assumed, a whole new life of domesticity and relative anonymity.

But here was Bucky with another young lady, who apparently had quite a reputation of her own, one which kept her to this day in the spotlight. At least among the guys Noah was with.

"Alright. Let's assume you're right—"

"There ain't no assuming. The girl likes it in the ass!"

This was a hot issue! Jessie kept up his verbal crusade on the profoundly important topic. This was obviously something that he felt passionate about.

Noah tried not to laugh.

"Jessie. Who cares?"

"Have you ever fucked a girl in the ass?"

"No. Can't say I have. Have you?"

"Man! It's so nice and tight. There ain't no bumps and curves. It feels fucking fantastic! And the girl can't get knocked up. Where the fuck have you been all your life, dude!"

"Well, if it's that great, Billingsley here's got a poop chute. Why don't you fuck him?"

All of the other guys angrily registered their outrage, their faces mangled and distended in varying displays of disgust and nausea. Billingsley looked particularly infuriated that he had been singled out as the prey for Noah's homoerotic suggestion.

"Tass! I always thought you were a fucking poofter."

"Okay! Then how about a goat or dog or a sheep? They all have assholes. Nice and tight. No bumps and curves. Hey, with a sheep you could grab nicely onto all that wool and really be able to ram it home!"

Noah demonstrated. Grabbing two imaginary wooly clumps on opposite sides of an imaginary sheep and thrusting his hips forward in a humping motion, he threw his head back and started moaning.

"Ooh! Aah! Oh yes, baby!"

They really started yelling at him now. Other people around them started noticing and pointing. They had good reason to think that a fight among these five surly, probably quite inebriated young men was about to break out. They were shouting at one another, fists were clenching and unclenching. Beer — the most valuable single item under any circumstances — was splashing out of their plastic cups.

From the looks on their faces, Noah could see they were obviously missing the humor. Reading the situation accurately, Noah could see that even if they were his friends, he was pushing buttons that could get his ass kicked. He quickly threw up his hands and laughed.

"Hold on! Hold on! I'm just fucking with you guys! It's just a joke. Honest!"

The bellowing started mellowing a bit. Mere grumbling ensued. These guys didn't mind being "fucked with" but homo stuff was completely off limits. Sheep stuff was maybe okay. They all made jokes about lonely nights and visits to the barn. After all, this was farm country. Not that any of them would admit to any sheep encounters. But joking about it was at least within the realm of acceptability. However, implying even jokingly that they were queer was like declaring war.

Noah continued to try to smooth things over, by changing the subject somewhat.

"So what's the deal? I thought Mr. Gridiron Glory there was a picket fence family man. He knocked up Polly Perfect, didn't he?"

Jessie had all the answers.

"Maybe she won't let him fuck her in the ass!"

Everybody seemed to think that was insanely funny. But they laughed a little too hard, which was probably the rebound from all of the angry tension they had just been feeling. Adrenalin shock and bounce.

Noah laughed along too. Laughed on the outside anyway. Why the fuck had he agreed to come along? This was so typical. So lame.

And it was always the same.

Nothing ever changed.

Apparently Noah expected too much. Just because it was a major national holiday, just because they had actually gotten out of Pulnick and were some distance from home, just because they were attending a truly rare spectacle, a high-powered show of military ingenuity and daring, how could he think for a moment that the conversation would veer one degree from its usual course, or rise above its primal carnality even the slightest. Everything was inevitably about fucking and sucking. Either that or sucking and fucking.

Sure. He had done his share. Both the sucking and fucking. And the talking about it.

But he had grown out of it years ago. Right after high school.

Plus he had his limits. These guys obviously didn't share them. They could — and most likely the rest of their lives would — talk about *it* and nothing else. That was all they talked about the entire ride here. That was all they would talk about on the entire ride home.

Now what?

What were his options?

Before he could think about it, the entire sky filled with the thunderous roar of six F-16C Fighting Falcon fighter jets passing right over the heads of the oohing-aahing audience.

It was the world-acclaimed Air Force Thunderbird aerial demonstration team.

From the sheer power and proximity of these six technological wonders, capable of gravity-defying vertical climbs, supersonic speed, seemingly hair-pin turns, spectacular rolls and flips and countless other impossible to fathom maneuvers, people forgot to breathe. Literally. Several of the spectators fainted only minutes into the program.

Noah didn't faint but he did experience an exhilaration he had never experienced before.

Of course, he had watched countless video clips of these and other advanced fighting aircraft — some of them much more advanced, like the FA-18E Super Hornet, F-20 Tigershark, F-22A Raptor, the F-35 Stealth — while surfing the internet. But no video, certainly not one playing on a 17" monitor with sound coming through 2" desk speakers, could begin to capture even 1% of the sensations now assaulting him.

The program lasted about twenty minutes. Sometimes they flew and performed stunts using all six planes, sometimes four. Naturally, since they were moving at 600 MPH, they covered a lot of airspace and often were high in the cloudless Missouri sky. But every combination of aerial formation and interaction began and concluded with a breathtaking, body-shaking, eardrum-rattling flyover, which put them up so close, it felt like only a few yards separated the gigantic roaring birds from the spectators. On one pass, the heat of the engines could actually be felt on top of the already blazing heat of the summer sun.

Finally the Thunderbirds flew off over the horizon to Tinker AFB near Oklahoma City. They had performances there next week, then further west over at Altus AFB.

The military might portion of the show was not over yet. The announcement came on as soon as the thunderous roar of the six jets had subsided enough for the audience to hear.

Next, ladies and gentlemen, we have a very special treat for you. This is going to be brief and to the point, so I want to make sure everyone is paying attention. As you can see, in the center of the airfield directly in front of the viewing stand but a safe distance away, there has been constructed a four-story solid cement bunker. Take a good look at this now because in a few minutes it won't be there anymore.

Sure enough, a huge block of cement the size of an office building had been constructed — if 'constructed' was the right word for pouring several hundreds of tons of cement into a big rectangular mold — and sat there looking as vulnerable as a mountain range.

Now let me draw your attention to the skies directly to the east. Everyone look to your right. Ladies and gentlemen, let me present to you the most destructive flying gunship in the world, the Air Force's one and only A-10 Thunderbolt II.

An aircraft flying low and relatively slow — at least compared to the blinding speed of the F-16Cs they had just seen — was approaching the huge length of air strip, which stretched out at least a mile-and-a-half from the stands. The monster plane looked like a flying tank. While the F-16Cs had the darting grace and weightless ease of a leopard, the A-10 had the ominous presence and destructive promise of a charging rhinoceros. Its bulkiness was mainly a function of its thick armor plating, but it was the two oversized GE Turbofan engines sitting high and menacingly at the rear of the plane that unequivocally established its raging bull mettle.

As it got closer, it was easy to see what made this piece of war machinery so deadly. Mounted in the underside of the fuselage and projecting out of its nose was a 30 mm GAU-8/A Avenger Gatling gun-style cannon, capable of firing 3,900 rounds per minute. It was not firing jelly beans. It was sending 65 high-speed depleted Uranium armor-piercing chunks of explosive metal the size of Arnold Schwarzenegger's upper thigh each second. Each and every second! It had to be fired in bursts because the recoil was so powerful, sustained firing quickly reduced the air speed of the gunship below stall speed, which would result in the plane falling out of the sky.

The roar from the engines of the A-10 got louder and louder.

Compared to what happened next, those engines sounded like a whisper.

Bursts of 30 mm shells streaked from the front of the plane. 65 per second. Each firing was an explosion in its own right. On its own lethal terms. The thunderous rattling pounded off of everyone's chest like they were being hit by 65 Taiko drummers.

Clouds of dust instantly billowed up from the solid cement structure.

The bursts continued until the A-10 had passed the target building.

What building?

When the dust finally settled or blew away in the turbulence created by the passing of the aircraft, there was nothing left but a pile of rubble. Hundreds of tons of poured concrete had instantaneously been turned into gypsum confetti.

> *Yes, ladies and gentlemen. That was the awesome A-10 Thunderbolt II. Sorry you hunters. This piece of weaponry is not available to you eager sportsmen out there. (A few laughs from the audience.) Remember now, the show has just begun. We still have a spectacular lineup. Stick around for General Tso's Flying Chicken, Mister Rusty Winebeck, and the wing walking antics of Crazy Charlie Walker.*

There was a short intermission.

Then there would be the traditional nod to the barnstormers. These were the guys way back in the early days of flight who turned the airplane — at first bi-planes, then slow moving single-winged aircraft — into a flying vaudevillian stage, a floating platform for their slapstick clowning and generally silly antics. Robert Redford had made a movie about it back in 1975 called *The Great Waldo Pepper*.

With the extraordinary advances that had been made in the science of flight, no one was quite sure why these old timers in their relatively sluggish prop planes were still a staple in contemporary air shows. It was like seeing card tricks after David Copperfield had just made the Statue of Liberty disappear.

During the intermission, Noah was lost in thought about what he had just seen.

He was dazzled. Blown away. Awed and dumbstruck by the performance of the fly-boys.

Jessie had his own way of expressing his enthusiasm.

"This calls for another round of beers!"

On their way over to the Anheuser-Busch beer booth, Ryan and Jackson pointed out a girl in very tight short shorts and Rich went over and stood right behind her, holding his hands in front of his crotch like he was holding a baseball bat.

Jessie: "I'd like her tail to wag my dog."

Ryan: "Ooh yeah, baby! You rock my world!"

Jackson: "Oh my fucking God! That is so so sweet!"

Several older people around them looked at them with disgust.

The girl turned around. Rich quickly let one hand drop to his side and brought the other up to scratch his temple with his middle finger, and immediately started whistling innocently. The portrait of nonchalance, he looked up at nothing in particular in the cloudless sky, then strolled back to the other guys, who seemed only slightly amused by his antics.

As Rich rejoined them, Jessie tipped his empty cup up over his head and squinted into it with mock irritation.

"What the fuck! This shit must be evaporating."

They got another round — except for Noah who was better at nursing than guzzling — then continued to wander around, keeping keen but bloodshot eyes out for the finer fillets of female flesh.

When the short intermission was over, the civilian contingent of aerial pranksters tried to entertain the audience, but the military show was just too overwhelming of an act to follow. The wind had been knocked out of everyone by the Air Force Demonstration team. The remaining performances drew only a little drowsy applause and a few slack-jaw smiles from the gradually diminishing audience. The stands were two-thirds full when General Tso, looking like Confucius in an leather aviator hat, landed his badly rendered white and yellow paper mâche flying chicken, and only a third full when the Mister Rusty Winebeck pulled his smoking Curtiss Goshawk out of a death spiral, then flew over the stands upside down dropping little cellophane bags of gummy worms on everyone's heads.

The last performer, Crazy Charlie Walker, was half of a team, the Crazy Walker Brothers, who had wing-walked their way into the weary hearts of air show spectators for over a decade. Last year the partnership was torn asunder when Charlie's brother Manny took one step too many backwards, in his ongoing attempts to push the envelope of daring-do, and fell over six hundred feet to his death in front of an audience in Omaha, Nebraska. Apparently no longer grieving and undeterred by the inherently attendant risks of his chosen avocation, Charlie was back on the circuit this year as a solo artist. Noah wondered which way the expectations of the audience leaned. Were they here to see the remaining Walker brother survive the wing-walk, or here to see a repeat of the Omaha tragedy? Nothing like watching someone go splat on a cement runway to cap off a great Independence Day outing with the family.

Charlie Walker did his bit. He did his best. The audience craned their necks one last time, more curious than enthusiastic, shading their eyes from the sun which as the afternoon progressed had inconveniently dropped right down behind the sputtering aircraft, making him and his fragile old airplane a painful silhouette in the white hot sky.

When Charlie failed to plunge to his death, the landing of his backfiring, coughing antique — a real oldie-but-goodie Sopwith Camel that dated back to World War — was greeted with a lot of yawns, which no one made any effort to conceal, and token half-hearted applause. Though it was approaching 4:30, it was still unbearably hot and seeing someone stupid enough to stand on the wing of a struggling piece of aeronautical history, couldn't compete with the insouciance and ennui that had seeped into the sweaty pores of just about everyone still there, standing and sitting in the flat frying pan of the air field.

Jessie decided it was time to go home.

"Let's blow this pop stand."

He had just done a quick but highly rigorous 360 degree visual surveillance, an intense ocular scan which created the impression he was either lonely or homicidal, and concluded that all of the hot chicks — a purely subjective judgment skewed by inebriation and borderline sunstroke — had left. The others nodded their complacent assent, both at the suggestion they head back to Pulnick, and at the lack of decent candidates for lustful ogling.

Walking back to the car, Noah could not contain his excitement.

"What an amazing show! Maybe I should have joined the air force. But they probably have thousands of pilots who want to do that. You know, flying in these shows."

On the ride home he still carried on about it. His tongue was loose and excitement high.

"Man! When they headed at each other from four directions and passed in the middle with only inches to spare, I thought we were all in for it. If they had collided the fireball could have been seen from Tierra del Fuego. Incredible!"

His monologue landed on the numb ears of the other guys, who were dazed and dulled by having spent the afternoon in the brutally hot sun while putting away way too many beers. They were still drinking like drought victims. Empties littered the floor, around and under both the front and rear seats.

"Did you see the fire power of the guns on the A-10? That thing could turn a city block into a pile of dust in seconds!"

"Hey, Tass! Shut the fuck up. Your fucking voice is like fingernails on a chalkboard."

"Like you went to school?"

Noah had been considerably more moderate in the beer chugging department, but even he was on his eighth or ninth — or was it his tenth? Who was counting? He took a sip and continued his rambling torrent of plaudits.

"What a show! When they did that vertical barrel roll, then split off in four directions. Fucking amazing! It was so perfect. With the smoke trails! It looked like this gigantic flower opening up in the sky."

Finally someone else popped out of his coma and replied directly to what Noah was saying. It was Jessie — naturally — adding in his two cents.

"Yeah. That was really something alright. But you know what would even be better?"

Noah was startled to hear someone else offer an opinion. Everyone had been ignoring him or wanting him to shut up. He was certainly curious what Jessie thought could possibly be better.

"I'm listening. What, Jessie? What could possibly be better than that?"

"I'll tell you what. It would be to be in one of those fighter planes, do the vertical barrel roll, then split off in that perfect arcing climb, make those pretty flowers with the smoke trails ... *while* fucking Miss Poop Chute in the ass."

The $C_{10}H_{15}N$ Diet

This thing with his sister mystified him. Gretchen and their mom had been like two peas in a pod. Forever! Then right about the time of Noah's accident,

Gretchen started making herself scarce. It was shortly after that — literally a few weeks — that their mom had been diagnosed with the ovarian cancer and had gone under the knife for major surgery. If there was any time Noah would have thought that Gretchen would have been mooning around and sucking up the shared misery, it would have been then. Both of them were such drama queens, addicted to crisis and averse to permanent remedies.

But his mom had only seen Gretchen one time through that whole traumatic time of her life-threatening health situation. And that one time, Gretchen showed up looking haggard and thin, enigmatically sporting a new tattoo — her only tattoo — that read '11-11-11'. During the visit, Gretchen didn't have much to say, seemed distracted and more self-absorbed than usual — which itself was saying a lot! — stayed only a short while, and barely tuned in to the fact that her mom had just had a horrifying brush with death, and given the less than stellar survival rate of ovarian cancer victims, was still under a grave threat.

Noah had briefly spotted Gretchen at the rave party, and had to conclude she was now somehow mixed up with a bad crowd. She appeared to be with the killing animal that had publicly beaten a guy to death with less thought than you would give to deciding which chewing gum to buy. Noah confirmed his suspicions that his neighbor Phil was tied in with her in some capacity — pet? boyfriend? dom-slave submissive? — when he saw them together at Salem First Baptist Church.

It was one thing for her to take up with one of Noah's old friends. A completely different thing if she had fallen in with some bad elements from outside of town — and brute killer man was definitely bad news from somewhere else. Whatever was going on, she was most certainly doing a good job of making herself unavailable. Noah seriously needed to talk to her. Or at least get her to come home and talk to their mom.

All through this, Noah knew she couldn't have gone far. There was no 'far' in Monroe County, possibly no 'far' anywhere in the godforsaken state of Missouri. If she was around, Noah would find her.

Noah finally tracked Gretchen down. He had made some feeble threats, tried to pull a few favors, all to no avail, then by sheer dumb luck eventually got someone to tell him where she was holed up.

He finally dragged it out of Ralph Zender, a total loser and small-time drug dealer who dealt mostly in weed and pain pills. Though they went to high school together, Noah knew him more by reputation than personal interaction. Zender had dropped out at the end of his junior year and started his daily vigil just off of school grounds, where he peddled joints and tried to pick up girls. He was infamous for trying to get them to go back to his pad "for some serious partying". He had been in and out of jail at least three times that Noah knew of.

A couple of guys Noah was talking to at the Dugout Lounge in Monroe City told him that Zender got around more than anyone these days and he should ask him. Conveniently, Zender strolled into the bar about ten minutes later, pockets stuffed with fives and tens from several recent drug transactions.

The guy looked like a cross between a pimp and a cowboy.

Noah bought him a beer and described his sister. Zender was definitely already high on something. His face twitched. His hands shook. He couldn't stop looking around long enough to even glance at Noah. But apparently he was paying attention.

"Check out the old Cockrell place up in Clapper. But be careful. They're weird fuckers. Never seen anyone. They do business through the dog flap."

"Dog flap?"

"There's this little flap in the back door so the dog can come in and out."

"Got it. Dog flap."

"But they don't have a dog."

"Right. No dog."

Finally Zender looked directly at Noah. An acetylene look that could burn a hole in armor.

"They don't have a fucking dog, man! NO DOG!"

"I hear you. No dog. Thanks, Zender. You take care now."

Crazy fucker. Not surprising. He really should have finished high school.

There was an old farm house sitting on 84 acres of rich topsoil off of 487 just north of Clapper about four miles outside of town. It had once been home to the Cockrell family. They had put the property up for sale, and according the last rumors anyone around town had heard, had packed up and moved to the San Joaquin Valley northwest of Fresno, California to raise tomatoes and grapes. Noah and everyone else assumed the house was abandoned, since the property for whatever reason had never sold. Apparently it now had occupants.

If Zender was correct, it certainly wasn't a traditional family living there. Rather, the place was being squatted by a few drifters, and some of the Pulnick fringe elements — town youth who had become dropouts and deadbeats — which allegedly now included his vanishing sister.

Noah lost no time. Next day he was on his way to Clapper. If she was living there commune-style in that old farmhouse, abandoned and reclaimed by a bunch of losers for whatever purpose, he would get to the bottom of it.

Noah was using his mom's Chevy Caprice to get to and from work at his new job at Merkel, at least for a couple weeks until he could pick up a clunker of his own. He drove it to the farm and parked at the entrance gate of the dirt driveway, which led to a broad area between the barn and the front porch of the huge house. The area was shaded by two giant old maple trees. A rope-and-tire swing hung from one of the trees. Though the house itself was in gross disrepair — paint was peeling and several gutters were hanging — the overall impression was idyllic. It was a lovely place for a good Christian family to raise corn, cattle and children.

It was deathly quiet as he approached the huge porch, which wrapped around three sides of the house. Noah was not a nature buff, but even he couldn't help but notice the absence of any "natural" sounds. No crickets, no chirping birds. Not even any passing butterflies or moths.

As he got within maybe twenty yards of the front door, he noticed two other things.

First, the front door was boarded up tight, and the windows had been blocked off with sheets of plywood. The place looked like it had been turned into a bunker or a crypt. He circled the entire structure and confirmed that every window, both ground and second floor, had been masked off and there was no way to look inside.

The second thing he noticed was some strange chemical smell. He had no idea what it was or where it was coming from but it definitely was not any of the typical agricultural odors — manure, fertilizers, herbicides, insecticides — all the smells of Monroe County which he had grown up with and were familiar to everyone in the area.

He made another full circle around the house. No sign of life. No sign of anything.

If anyone was inside, they were either keeping very quiet or were very dead.

He stepped up the stairs to the porch, crossed the molding planks leading to the large barricaded front door, and started knocking. Knocking at first, then pounding loudly, in case someone was in a remote part of the immense house, the basement or attic.

"Go away, fucker! You're not wanted here."

It was definitely Gretchen's voice. He'd recognize that shrill adolescent whine anywhere. Even though she was turning twenty in a few months, either her larynx or her brain had stopped developing many years ago and her voice was still the grating whinge of early pubescent angst.

"I just want to talk."

"Go talk to someone who wants to talk to you."

"Come on, Gretchen. Mom is worried sick about you."

No response.

"Gretchen. If you won't let me in, just come out for a minute."

Silence.

"Gretchen! Stop this bullshit!"

Noah waited for several minutes. Nothing. Not only was there no reply, there was no sound whatever from behind the door. Either this house was built so solidly that it was completely soundproof, or nobody inside was even slightly moving.

Suddenly, something caught his eye, off to the right, in the periphery of his field of vision.

There she was. Momentarily anyhow.

She was maybe thirty feet away, several paces from the corner of the porch. Just standing there. Grinning with a sinister grin, anger, contempt and pain in her brow, one hand defiantly on her hip, the other flipping him off.

"There. Now you've seen me. Tell mom I hope she feels better."

"Why don't you—"

"Why don't you fuck off, Noah! Stay away!"

Then she scurried to the back of the house. It all happened too fast for

Noah to even react. There was no way he could catch her.

And no way at this point that he really wanted to.

Her rejection was total.

This definitely was not worth pursuing right now. It was obvious he wasn't going to accomplish anything today. At least he knew for better or worse where she was holed up.

Their encounter was brief, but one thing stood out.

She was really fucked up.

Noah had thought Gretchen looked pretty bad the last time he had seen her. But her appearance today made the Gretchen at Salem First Baptist look like the poster girl for a new line of health food products. It had only been a few weeks but she had lost even more weight. Probably lost more hair as well, though it was so filthy and tangled it was hard say. He could see open sores around her lips and on her neck. The worst of it was her skin. It didn't quite look like human skin. Not human skin that was alive.

What the hell had happened to her?

Noah went back to the car, discouraged but not completely without hope that he could and would figure out some way to get to her, and drove home. His head was spinning with many possibilities, but nothing made sense. She was fine. She disappeared. Now she was barricaded in an abandoned farm house. All that happened in two months.

He knew one thing.

She was mixed up in something.

And that something could only have a bad ending.

That evening, he spent a couple hours online and became convinced he had put it all together. God bless Google. The internet had just about everything on just about everything.

It all added up.

The weird chemical smell at the farm.

Gretchen's rapid physical deterioration.

The paranoiac fortification of the house.

There was only one logical conclusion.

They were running a meth lab there.

Somewhere on the premises they were cooking up $C_{10}H_{15}N$. The recipe was easy to find, fairly simple to execute. Though it was — to put it mildly — an extremely dangerous process.

One of the articles Noah read pointed out that meth was now considered the most addictive recreational drug out there. Far more addictive than cocaine or even heroin. Apparently, the very first introduction of methamphetamine into the bloodstream made immediate and dramatic changes in the brain's chemistry, such that it was theoretically possible for an addiction to the drug to occur from a single dose.

He read on. It just got worse.

The grip of the drug was nearly unbreakable. The impact was devastating and rapid.

Symptoms: Skin disease, paranoia, psychosis, vulnerability to opportunistic infections, loss of body fat, loss of muscle and bone mass, loss of hair, loss of teeth.

Gretchen was on the #1 most effective weight loss plan on the planet.

Guaranteed to shed away those excess pounds.

Then shed away life itself.

The $C_{10}H_{15}N$ diet.

Heavy Metal

They got the tin from China. Then they cut it, rolled it, pressed it, shaped it, twisted it, configuring it to the specifications of their customers. Mostly they produced corrugated panels and food cans. Those were the two big product lines, purely because that's what their three main customers needed — Hormel for their Spam and ham lines, Bartlett for everything from pears and walnuts to pork and beans, and United Sheet Metal Products for shipping containers, mobile homes, trucking enclosures, storage sheds big and small, and roofing.

From his first day on the job at Merkel Industries, though he was assigned to Bldg 4 as had been predicted by the dope heads in the parking lot the day he interviewed, Noah shuttled around all seven of the factory buildings, three which stored the raw sheets of tin in every conceivable size and thickness, and four where the metal was cut, shaped, punched, stamped, formed, welded, embossed, pressed, plated and packaged, in sum all of the processes necessary to produce a finished product. Except for Bldg 7, the warehouses were gargantuan structures the size of airplane hangers. Not that Bldg 7 was small. It sprawled over five acres but was only two stories high, while the others were five and six.

The company had been started in a barn by Thadeus Merkel, a blacksmith by trade who had the imagination and vision to conceive of how he could extend his simple metalworking skills to create a range of products useful for the home and places of business — kitchen and bathroom, garage and barn, factory and farm.

The firm was the longstanding pride of the state of Missouri, which had celebrated for nearly a century its innovation and expansion. At its peak throughout World War II, followed by the business and building boom of the fifties, Merkel Industries sprawled over the southern end of Shelby County and employed over 8000, nearly a third of the county's population. Of course, in the past fifty years a lot had changed in America's manufacturing sector. Now cheap labor across the globe had gutted its industrial capacity, resulting in significant and steady reduction nationwide in the durable trades workforce.

To remain competitive and profitable, Merkel had gradually downsized and become the relatively small but solid company it currently was. The labor union was long gone. The region certainly didn't substantially depend on it any longer for its bread and butter. But it had its place, its own secure and respected position in the community and among its sustainable set of loyal customers. It was still at the top of the list for most desirable places to get a job, both for the school dropouts and for those who made it all the way through Calvin Coolidge Jr.-Sr. High School who maybe had rudimentary job skills, but were not in a position to go to junior college or a vocational school to obtain specialized job training. It was the factory equivalent of pumping gas, working at McDonalds, or clerking at one of the convenience stores in the area.

In his daily rounds, Noah came in visual contact with practically all of the four hundred plus employees who worked at Merkel, mostly those in the manufacturing area, since he was constantly carting pallets of raw galvanized sheet metal to them, where it was processed into the requisite final configurations. But he also became familiar with a number of the office staff, because as a new hire, he was the one assigned to go to the engineering office and pick up the new orders, spec sheets and blue prints.

Even so, he really spent 95% of his time side by side with just four other guys, all close to his own age — the Full Metal Jack Its, as they affectionately called themselves. These were the four guys who purely by coincidence were in the car parked next to his, the day that he first interviewed with Merkel. The ones who spent their lunch hour in a cloud of marijuana smoke.

This mismatched, motley team, which now included Noah, manned the tractors, drove the fork lift trucks, maneuvered the hydraulic stackers, wielded the hand pallet movers, and operated the overhead cranes, to move hundreds of tons of metal every week across the thousands of square feet of factory floor space. They were renowned for their efficiency and effectiveness, but reviled for often being reckless and risky in the performance of their duties. Despite countless close calls, their track record was impeccable, unmarred by any embarrassing or potentially harmful accidents. Not that this offered any comfort to anyone else working there. Employees always scattered when one of the heavy duty Cat Lift trucks or medium size Raymonds came bearing down on them, carrying 40% more than the approved load capacity of the vehicle, engine whining as the huge stack of sheet metal or pallet of corrugated storage shed siding swayed like a circus clown's implausible stack of kitchen dishes.

Their antics had so entirely become the stuff of local legends that they had their own t-shirt. A young secretary in the front office with an artistic flair and a raging crush on one of them, designed it and had a number of the t-shirts made up. The front displayed a lift truck with its forks high in the air and King Kong on top beating his chest like he had conquered the world. The rear of the shirt said *The FMJIs Forever!*

The four guys that Noah was now teamed with had all been working at Merkel for some time, and among them had almost twenty years of seniority.

Tal "Blow Me" Caswell was the unofficial but undisputed leader of the pack. He was so nicknamed for the epithet which seemed to introduce or be somehow incorporated in his every utterance. Someone said that if Tal was orally serviced every time he used that particular phrase, by the end of a work shift, he'd be sucked so dry he would turn into a dusty, desiccated powder version of his self. *'Like blow me, dude. We gotta have five loads over to Bay 7 like ten minutes ago.' 'Hey, blow me. You still owe me five bucks from yesterday.' 'The Lakers? Right! Blow me. Their whory glory days have been over since Kobe got whacked for honey dipping that chick, you know, that Laker Girl.'*

Steve Toblinski was the strong silent type and a chain smoker. For a while the guys called him Mute, but since he never answered to it the nickname got dropped. A tall muscular facsimile of Heath Ledger, he could just sit in a restaurant or bar with a cigarette in his hand, never say a word, and within ten minutes have at least five girls competing for him. He never looked anyone directly in the eye, conducting the entirety of his human relationships in the periphery of his vision. He always appeared to be lost in thought, though no one was privy to the mysterious workings of his mind. He never really laughed out loud. In his moments of wild abandon, his handsome face might brighten momentarily in a tempered grin.

Freddy "Fat Fuck" Stangler was short, fat and giddy. His nickname did not seem to bother him, in fact he seemed amused by it, maybe even pleased, since it generated a certain pride in the acceptance it connoted. "Fat Fuck" was usually replaced by "F" in mixed company or just out of laziness. Between pepperoni sticks, candy bars, and other handfuls of junk food, he told jokes — cumulatively thousands of jokes — never to anyone's recollection repeating a single one. He seemed to be a walking encyclopedia of gags, one-liners, quips, humorous quotes, and funny stories with groaner punch lines. He always laughed first and laughed hardest.

Samuel "Ghost" Leek was an albino. Every hair on his body was white and his skin was a purplish pink and highly sensitive to the sun. During the summer he could get a sunburn just running from his car into the factory, so he always wore a wide-brim hat when he was outside. Though his albinism implied a fragility or vulnerability, the fact was he was incredibly strong and nearly indestructible. He often by himself did the real heavy lifting, or would be on one end of some huge load while three guys were on the other. He was understandable shy, since he looked like the photographic negative of a human being, but once engaged was the most personable and easy to get to know of the bunch.

Noah was the only one without a nickname. A few were tried along the way but nothing really stuck. Maybe it was because he was hard to define. No one could read him. He was a Teflon enigma. He always was right there in the thick of conversations but usually left everyone scratching their heads. Noah enjoyed propagating a moderately mirthful confusion. Not a particularly difficult thing to pull off with this new crowd.

The five of them were all around the same age, within five years of one another. Noah at 23 was the youngest, Steve the oldest at 28. They had all gone to the same high school — since there wasn't an alternative, what local boy hadn't? — but none had been in the same class.

They worked together well. They were a good team. They got the job done, whatever it was, quickly and efficiently. While they constantly vilified management, the usual stuff — not getting paid enough, their working conditions, the cowpiss-in-a-cup the vending machine passed off as coffee, the line bosses generally having their heads up inside a dark orifice — they obviously took pride in their work and relished what occasional praise came their way. It wasn't uncommon to see them wearing around town their navy blue work shirts with the Merkel Industries logo, even on their days off.

Noah was immediately accepted. There was no requirement that he jump through hoops to earn his place on the team. Everyone got along well, both on the job and later when they started inviting Noah to party with them. "Partying" could be anything — riding around, hitting a few bars, dropping in at some lame Pulnick party or get-together, going bowling or to a rodeo or some other local town event — but by unstated consent it always included two essential elements. Drinking and looking at chicks. Noah had no problem with either, so even if he was nowhere near as aggressive in either area as his new workmates, he still fit right in. Frankly, with his three best friends indefinitely out of his life, it felt good to have some guys to hang out with.

There was only one issue which could have been a source of tension and animosity.

As the preview in the parking lot after his job interview had portended — if he recalled it was a Slayer song being played at a mind-numbing volume that day — the other members of the Full Metal Jack Its worshipped at the altar of heavy metal rock music. Not even pop metal like Bon Jovi, Def Leppard or Guns N' Roses. That was wussy boy stuff. They liked the dark, dirty and demented. The stuff that would rip your brain out of your skull and tear your mind up into a thousand little pieces. Even Motley Crue, despite their appetite for wild orgies, sprees of random destruction, harrowing drug abuse, and near death drinking, were looked on as posers. Pussy rock for pimple-faced metal head wannabees.

Basically, the original four Full Metal Jack Its loved the stuff that the religious right hated. The stuff that would send them on an express train to Hell. And paralleling the vehement vilification of those who would condemn them, their love of death metal burned with a religious fervor that made evangelical Christians and the Islamic jihadist mujahidin look like lethargic hobbyists.

Enter into the picture Noah.

Noah unequivocally hated metal music but he respectfully remained mute on the subject. He always smiled noncommittally and tried to hide the physical and aesthetic torture listening to it caused him. Obviously he never mentioned his own fanaticism for the music and videos of Michael Jackson. That would have been like taking out a contract on himself.

One time during a cigarette break out behind Bldg 5, in a rare moment when he actually put together a verbal stream more than two consecutive words in length, the usually silent Steve Toblinski philosophized about metal and its place in their world.

With an interesting ontological leap — a Unified Field Theory for work and play — he carried on for several minutes, as if during the hundreds of hours of muteness which preceded his soliloquy, he had been constructing his new theory and now it was ready to be made public. Some highlights ...

"Think about the men working in the mines, the ore being loaded into box cars, the smelting factories, huge ships carrying the refined metal to ports, then it being brought here. Thousands of men across the world. Strong men. Moving the metal. Working the metal. Constructing buildings and bridges. We're part of a huge army. Soldiers of steel."

"Uh, Steve ... we're mainly doing tin here."

"Steel. I meant it as a symbol, asshole. And if you can shut the fuck up, it'll make sense. Because it's all just energy. Nothing is solid. In the Universe, there is more space than substance. Just like music. They say in music it's more important the notes that are not played than the notes that are played. You know. Like the silences. Like the silence of outer space."

Noah had a little problem with that one. It seemed to him that heavy metal never let up. There was no space. Everyone played and screamed as much, as fast, and as loud as they could. It was like having a mountain dropped on you, with about as much "space" and wiggle room as you would have at the Earth's core. But he kept quiet.

"Music is vibration. Metal is the best conductor of vibration. Heavy metal music and real metal — I mean the stuff we handle every day — is like the perfect mating of everything in the world. It's the perfect mating of mass and energy. Like Einstein."

Fat Fuck lit up like he was getting it.

"Ah! Are you saying Einstein was a headbanger?"

"No, you dumb fuck! Heavy metal music wasn't even around then. But maybe ... yeah. If he was around now, he probably would have been. $E = mc^2$ says it all."

Noah might go along with that on some level. The bands they really liked — Megadeath, Anthrax, Slayer, Venom, Motörhead, Sepultura — were about as subtle as a hydrogen bomb.

The five Full Metal Jack Its sat in silence for a while.

Tal, Steve and Ghost puffed away on their smokes. Fat Fuck ate M&Ms. Noah sipped on an orange Fanta.

Then Tal took one last drag, stubbed out his cigarette on the heal of his work boot, and summed it all up with his own burst of eloquence: "Dude! When it comes to metal, either hearin' it or movin' it, we're the most kickin' ass motherfuckers in the world!"

Exactly. And it was a beautiful thing.

Pride in workmanship.

Male bonding.

Music.

Fuckin' eh.

Yo motherfucker!

But time to go back to work.

Noah had his own perspective. Working there at Merkel? Sure it was just a factory job. But it was a job. Almost 18,000,000 Americans were out of work. Just not being one of them stood for something.

It meant an honest day's wage for an honest day's work.

Food on the table. Gas in the machine.

What were his options?

There weren't any. That was the cold, hard reality.

It still didn't change his primary focus. Just slowed things down.

In some recent conversation over flat watery tap beer that for a nanosecond rose above the usual banality of bar chat, someone asked him what his long range goals were.

"I need to get out of here."

"Good luck, dude."

"Gotcha."

It was obvious it wasn't going to happen.

At least not right now.

Noah took another sip of his tasteless beer. Metallica's *Welcome Home* started playing over the sound system …

> "Welcome to where time stands still
> No one leaves and no one will
> Moon is full, never seems to change
> Just labeled mentally deranged"

Maybe there was something to this heavy metal music after all.

> "Sleep my friend and you will see
> That dream is my reality
> They keep me locked up in this cage
> Can't they see it's why my brain says rage"

Gotcha.

My Fair Lady

The poster was Pulnick at its most pathetic.

"That girl's got a terminal case of assphasia. Her face looks so much like her ass, her bowels don't know which way to move."

Noah and Sam the Ghost were looking at a poster for the Monroe County Fair posted next to the Building 4 time clock. Usually Ghost was pretty reserved and non-judgmental but apparently this pushed even him too far and he felt obligated to say something rude.

"What is wrong with those people? Have they got hockey pucks for eyes?"

"Come on, Ghost. She's not that bad."

"She could turn Leonardo Dicaprio into a homo!"

"I think his credentials speak for themselves."

"So dude! Are you going?"

"Not a chance!"

"Right."

"You couldn't pay me any amount of money to go there. I have been every year of my dreary life. Twenty-three years running now. It's always the same. I ain't going this year."

"Who are you kidding, Tass. You can't resist. See you there, chump!"

Sam walked away smiling a cocksure smile.

Noah really had no intentions of going. He held out best he could. Then on the last day, he finally succumbed and drove over to the Fairgrounds, about 11 miles away in nearby Paris. He just hoped that whatever happened he didn't run into anyone from Merkel, especially Ghost.

The fair had been going on for five days already. Today was the final opportunity to visit the booths, catch some terrible live music on three small stages, jump on a few lame carnival rides, maybe see some planting and harvesting equipment demos, breathe in the stink of the farm animals, and if he stayed till the end, watch the closing ceremonies and the grand finale fireworks display. The whole way there he wondered why he was bothering to go. Was he just another pathetic creature of habit?

Noah had already missed most of the major mainstay events.

He missed the crowning of Miss Monroe County Fair 2011, the bovine-human hybrid who appeared on the poster the Ghost man was deriding. The coronation, which had taken place the previous Saturday, was performed by Pulnick's own most highly visible public official, the Honorable Judge Herzog M. Clay, presiding judge of Missouri's 10th Judicial Circuit.

He had also missed the slow pitch softball tournament; the dog show; the truck and tractor pull, youth rodeo, horse show, the judging of prize hams; the bucket calf show; a number of photo ops featuring rabbits, poultry and dairy goats; the baby show, bicycle rodeo and pedal pull contest; cow chip bingo, a teen dance which he couldn't have attended anyway; the apple pie and hot dog eating contests; a private fashion review — would Karl Lagerfeld be there? — a demolition derby, the Paris Gun Club invitational shoot; the toddlers taffy pull, the four-county 4-H awards; a parade featuring the dazzling baton twirling of Kelly's Baton and Poms all the way from St. Louis; two performances by Monroe County's own special darling of the country music scene Becky Blackaby; and the hand-wringing heart-pounding grand prize raffle drawing hosted by Paris Mayor Pro-tem, Jim Buckman.

What to do? Was life worth living now?

The good news was that all his favorite fair foods and beverages were still available — genuine Polish sausages, hot and sweet chili con carne, crispy deep fried onion rings, corndogs, ice cream filled crepes, cotton candy, kettle corn, Budweiser "the king of beers".

If he was really in a masochistic mood, he could attend the Farm Bureau ice cream social — average age 80 and counting — or the livestock and ham sale, both at the end of the evening.

He had gotten a late start and arrived mid-afternoon. He wasn't quite ready for the orgy of face stuffing he had visualized himself doing, so he decided to wander around a while until hunger pangs started their urgent throbbing on the inside lining of his tummy.

He walked through the carnival ride area — the "carny rats" made the Pulnickians look like members of the royal family — took a pass on the show barns and adjacent corrals, then wandered into the main staging area consisting of a long L-shaped lane, lined on both sides by booths of every shape and size.

Besides the food gallery booths — he would be getting to them later — there were all sorts of arts and crafts displayed, community organizations represented, activities and history associated with Monroe County touted and promoted, and finally a booth that lit up a giant light bulb over Noah's head like a holographic celestial body.

A plastic banner stretched over the modest booth.

Monroe County Sheriff Department

"Here to serve and protect."

Sheriff Ricky Dean Hoffman, chief law enforcement officer of
the county welcomes you to the 2011 Monroe County Fair.

Maybe there was a good reason for coming here after all.

As with most guys his age, it hadn't occurred to him before this very moment, to solicit the help of the police. Law enforcement officials were almost exclusively regarded as the enemy. They were looked on as just uniformed stiffs who one way or another were always engaged in cramping the styles of the younger generation, if not completely taking them out of circulation. Cops of any shape and size, of any ilk or variety were typically avoided at all costs.

But this situation called for it. It made total sense. Whatever evil person or persons had descended on Pulnick, first appearing at the rave party and then setting up what Noah was convinced was a drug manufacturing facility, needed *their* style seriously cramped, needed to be taken out of circulation, before a lot of innocent people got hurt.

Noah gathered his thoughts as he approached the booth, then finally was standing directly in front of the table which stretched across the front perimeter of the sheriff's department open air tent. There were a number of pamphlets on display, emergency instructions and phone numbers, safety tips, a county government org chart and directory, a history of the department. Two officers stood behind the table at parade rest, ready to answer any questions.

They looked like Laurel and Hardy. The younger of the two was tall and thin, goofy looking, and seemed naked without a banjo. His badge identified him as Junior Deputy Sheriff Pete Forsythe. The older one was maybe in his late 40s early 50s, big, sweaty, self-assured, visibly annoyed about something. Maybe just being here. He had the gnarly, vericosed nose of a heavy drinker, pasty complexion, thinning red hair, and if he had lips, they were on the inside of his mouth. His badge, which sat under some ribbons and other metallic commendations, said he was Senior Deputy Sheriff Bert Toller.

Toller smiled professionally at Noah, which did not in the least mask his impatience.

"What can we do for you today, *sir*?" The 'sir' was drawn out sarcastically.

"Well ... I don't know how to ... uh ..." Why was he so nervous? "... see it's like this. There's this meth lab. It's only a few miles outside of town. Outside of Pulnick. Where I live. It's Clapper. It's an abandoned farm house out in Clapper."

Deputy Sheriff Toller gave Noah the once over, then looked side to side with a noticeable smirk on his face. He was taking his time. He tipped his sheriff's hat back a notch on his head and rocked to and fro, heel-to-toe-to-heel. He was an arrogant son-of-a-bitch to say the least. And fat — enormously fat. He proceeded to hook his thumbs into his pants, itself a minor miracle defying the laws of physics, considering how tightly his belt was cinched under his grotesquely huge beach ball belly.

Finally, out of the side of his inhumanly thin lips he replied.

"I see. So what do we have here? A CSI junior detective? Hmm?"

He leaned forward and looked Noah straight squarely in the eyes. Looking through him. Like he was trying to read something on a placard behind Noah's head.

Noah tried to regroup. To communicate.

"You don't understand. This is real! My sister is holed up in there. She's in trouble."

"Trouble? Runs in the family maybe? Tell us, Mr. uh ..."

"Noah. Noah Tass."

"Explain to the junior deputy sheriff here and myself how it is that you, an ordinary citizen is aware of a situation ..." He pronounced it 'sich-ee-ay-shun'. "... which we as highly trained officers charged with the enforcement of the law — local, state and national I might add — please tell us exactly how it is you came upon this piece of covert intelligence."

"It ... it ... was an inside source. Someone in the ..."

"Business? Someone in the business. I see I see. I am getting the picture. So I am now wondering if this purported ..." Pronounced 'purr-po-did'. "... meth lab you herein reference, is a place where you do business as well?"

The two deputies got a nice chuckle out of that one.

"No! Of course not. Look. I'm just trying to let someone know. This isn't some prank. I'm not making this up."

Senior Deputy Toller, not exactly a consummate actor, suddenly changed gears and now appeared to be more sympathetic. Or was he just playing? Noah clung to the hope that they were through having fun and would now take him seriously.

"I think what we need to do here is look into this particular matter. I'll file a report on it. Please, if you would, let me see some identification. That will get the ball rolling."

The senior deputy pulled out a small note pad. Noah handed over his license, and Toller copied down the basic information from it, then requested and wrote down Noah's cell phone number, place of employment, and both his mother's and sister's name.

The deputy sheriff gave Noah his license back and stuffed the note pad in his back pocket.

"*Mister* Tass. I have to say this is a very serious matter." Pronounced 'fairy-see-russ-may-ter'.

The smirk was back. Toller glanced sideways at the junior deputy and winked.

Why was this asshole being so patronizing? Was smugness and sarcasm just his regular MO, the product of too many years as a fat ass in a comfy job he probably thought was beneath him or that he somehow was over-qualified for? Or had he immediately taken a particular dislike to Noah personally.

"Now if these people are as dangerous as you say, we don't want you going off half-cocked trying to do the onerous ..." Pronounced '*own*-russ'. "... work of highly trained specialists in the field of law enforcement like Deputy Forsythe here and myself."

Okay. It was both.

He was an arrogant fuck who had definitely taken a special dislike for Noah.

"Here's what's gonna happen here. You're just gonna sit tight. You hear me? And we're gonna get that sister of yours outta any trouble she's mixed up in."

Right.

What an asshole!

Noah wanted to kill the guy.

Pulnick's finest. Here to serve and protect.

Noah hoped the contempt he was feeling was not written all over his face.

This was not at all what he had expected.

What had he expected? These rubes were so pathetic.

"Thanks for your time, officers. If you need anything else from me—"

"We'll let you know, Mr. Tass. Have fun, now. Last night of the fair. There's an ice cream social in about an hour. Maybe you could pick up a nice piece of ... I mean, meet some real nice young lady there." Snnk! Snnk! Snnk! The junior deputy snorted when he laughed. Boogers playing pong inside his nose. "A good lookin' guy like yourself should have no problem in that department."

"Right. Ice cream. Nice babes. I'm all over it."

Then an amazing and incomprehensible thing happened.

Deputy Sheriff Bert Toller extended his hand homey-style to do a fist bump with Noah.

He had to be kidding! What a total fucking loser.

Yo! Right! We be bad brothers, dude.

Noah gave him the peace sign turned around and walked away.

Well. That was a total bust. What do taxpayers pay those idiots for? Kicking shit around the parking lot of the police station?

This was not good. A complete waste of time and energy.

He walked back down the row of food and display booths. If he had an appetite earlier for all of his favorite county fair junk food, it was definitely gone now. More than anything, he just needed to think. All of the noise, people, rides, and stinking animals here were giving him a headache.

Noah cut a path directly to the parking lot, where he had left his mom's Caprice.

Just as he stuck the key in the driver's side door to unlock it, a big strong hand clamped on his shoulder. He heard a familiar voice.

"Knew you couldn't stay away. Pulnick's got a big noose around your cojones, dude."

Noah couldn't win for losing. It was the one person he hoped he wouldn't see.

"Ghost! How did you do in the Mark Twain Memorial pud pull?"

"No contest. Filled all the buckets in the barn."

"Pulnick is mighty proud of you."

The Short Arm of the Law

Over the next ten days Noah snuck out to the Clapper farm house seven times. Five times it was right after his work shift, twice on the weekend. The weekend visits were mid-morning, figuring he would try to catch someone as the day got started.

But the results every time were the same.

He saw nothing. Saw nobody. No active signs of life on and around the property or from inside the house itself, not while he was there anyway.

Somebody was definitely coming and going because things were moved. Some furniture appeared on the porch one time. Next visit the same furniture was stacked by the tool shed. One time a car was parked in the drive. He felt the hood but it wasn't warm, so whoever drove it must have arrived at least a couple hours before. That particular time he hung around for over four hours but no one ever came out.

Noah even tried being more brazen, more aggressive.

He yelled and pounded on the door, but he got no response and heard no sounds coming from inside.

He sensed they were in there. He was sure of it. He was sure his sister was right on the other side of the door, playing some stupid game to fuck with his mind and frustrate him.

The last evening he stopped by, he did see someone about two miles from the farm house. It was killer brute in a huge Dodge truck headed the other way on Monroe Road 487, the route going through Clapper. Beside him in the cab was someone Noah had never seen before. Another huge, frightening looking guy who looked like a cross between a pirate and an ultimate cage fighter. From the glimpse Noah got as they sped by, it was obvious they both subscribed to the same fashion credo. Tattoos, piercings, posts, leather, chains, spikes and studs. Meant to intimidate. The human version of a product warning label.

On the flip side of the coin, it also became apparent that Noah's little talk with the sheriff patrol at the county fair had actually made an impression.

It had an effect.

But not the intended one.

They were on the case alright.

His case.

Five times in the same ten day period, he was pulled over driving. They searched his car without his consent. They made him empty all of his pockets and patted him down. Then they subjected him to a battery of sobriety tests. These included close penlight examinations of his pupils; then having him stand on one foot, spread his arms directly out to the sides like a bird in flight, close his eyes, and using one hand at a time, touch the tip of his nose with his index finger. Noah thought a person would have to be pretty plastered to not be able to locate his own nose. But it was their game, so he played along.

They didn't issue any citations — never actually explained to him why he was being stopped — then typically told him to be on his way, with a piece of paternal advice like: *"Now stay out of trouble and trouble will stay out of you."*

The last time they pulled him over was around 10 p.m. To rub salt in his wounds, it happened about a mile from his own apartment, as he was returning from the meth lab farm — yet another unsuccessful attempt to contact his sister.

After a warrantless and unwarranted search of his vehicle, the pat down and shake down which was becoming a hackneyed and annoying ritual, the settling on the one and only possible conclusion that just as Noah had repeatedly stated, he had not been drinking or abusing any controlled substances, the officer — a particular deputy who had stopped him three times before — asked Noah to turn on his parking lights, then walked around to the rear of the vehicle.

"Mr. Tass. Look. Your right rear tail light lens is broken."

Sure enough, it was. What did this mean? Thirty days in the clink?

"This is a dangerous situation. People coming up behind you aren't seeing the appropriate red color of your tail light. You need to get that fixed."

And in the meantime? Do I need a lawyer? Bail?

"Tell you what. We don't want anything to happen to you. Accidents happen, you know. Crazy stuff. I see it all the time."

The officer went back to his patrol car and returned with a roll of translucent plastic red tape. He tore off a couple pieces and covered the jagged hole in the lens of Noah's vehicle.

"There you go. That should help until you get that fixed. Have a good evening, Mr. Tass."

"Uh ... thanks."

"Just doing my job."

The officer then got in his car and drove away.

Noah just stood there and looked at the temporary repair of his broken tail lens.

Just doing his job.

To serve and protect.

Pulnick was a damn good place to live.

Maybe the cops harassed innocent people. Maybe they ignored meth labs belching toxic gases and inflicting violence and drugs on an unsuspecting community. Maybe Noah's sister was holed up with some horrible gang of drug dealers, withering away and dying.

But at least his tail lights were now both visibly red.

This was law enforcement at its best.

It was like the man said.

Just doing his job.

Chapter Five

July 26 ...

A Swinging Door

If you approached the swinging glass door to enter Fuller's Apothecary on Main Street in downtown Pulnick from the outside, you could not help but notice that right above the bar handle was a decal that said 'Push'. Then as you left the apothecary from the inside to return to the street, the decal facing you also said 'Push'.

In another town, too much push and no pull might have caused problems. It might have at least been perceived as a source of potential conflict. Confrontation. Stalemate. Showdown.

But this was Pulnick. And Pulnick after all was an aw-gosh-golly-after-you-neighbor kind of town. Nobody wanted trouble. A nod. A wink. A smile. That was the Pulnick way of doing things.

So for the hundreds of Pulnickians who had passed through that swinging door at Fuller's Apothecary coming and going, the Push-Push decal situation was never an issue.

Nor was it an issue for whoever entered the building at approximately 2:30 am on Sunday, July 31st. Because they drove a heavy-duty diesel-powered truck with thick pipe fortifications welded to the front bumper and frame, right through the entire front of the building.

After completely destroying the facade, the vehicle came to a stop somewhere in the middle of the shop, meaning most of the displays and shelving were in ruins. Then to complete the job, the perpetrators went through the entire rest of the apothecary, bludgeoning everything in sight with some massive implements — probably crowbars or sledge hammers. There would be no salvaging of anything. The entire store was demolished.

The really strange thing was that just about all of the stock, which included thousands of dollars worth of prescription and non-prescription drugs, cosmetics, candies, snacks, school supplies, stationery, miscellaneous household items, toys, nearly the entire inventory was still there scattered about or in piles on the floor. Even the cash in the cash register was untouched. There were only two items missing.

All of the over-the-counter anti-allergy remedies were gone.

Plus they took a large jar of peanut brittle.

Postcards

Noah hadn't heard a word from Jeff for over two months. Then the mail arrived.

Apparently he was in the thick of it. Still in boot camp. Stupid fucker. He was playing the sympathy card. Or was it the guilt card?

Sexually
Deprived

(For your freedom)

What the postcard lacked in profundity, it made up for in penmanship.

> Jiffer here!
>
> Man, they're busting my balls. Almost a month to go and instead of waking up with a stiffy, I wake up stiff and full of aches and pains. Actually, I still have a stiffy. But the idea is to turn me into a lean, mean, fighting machine. Which is working. Tell Jinx when I get out of here, I'll be able to kick his ass with one arm tied to a monster truck.
>
> The chicks here are grizzly bear ugly, dude. What was I thinking? They all look like bull dogs. Which makes sense. They're all bull dykes! Except for one. She's from Minnesota. Blonde and built like Jessica Alba! I'd crawl on my belly through a mine field to pet that kitty.
>
> That's it for now. Sign up. Uncle Sam wants YOU!!
>
> Jiffy

Very cute. Hadn't he heard of email? Or maybe the army didn't have computers.

Three weeks later, Noah received an update.

> I did it! I made it through boot camp. Now we're getting ready for deployment. These guys don't fuck around. It's from hell into super-hell! I think they need me in Buttfuckistan (aka Syria). Have you seen this in the news? Of course not. But we're doing major shit over there right now.
>
> Jiffy

The front of the post card was especially lame. It was a human skull wearing an Army Ranger beret.

What was that supposed to mean? Another poor slob went to his death? Or was Jeff anticipating what his own fate would be?

Why would he send this? Was it supposed to be amusing?

Noah was glad he had never, nor would he ever, consider joining the military. War, killing, military conquest, it all repulsed him, made him sick to his stomach. Jeff could have it, if that's what he wanted. But it certainly wasn't for Noah.

It definitely wasn't amusing.

Not much was these days.

Billboards

Noah received his first paycheck, bought a new motorcycle, and renewed his membership at the YMCA gym in Hannibal.

Life was back on track.

Riding his new Kawasaki Ninja 250R was the ultimate joy. It was much faster than his old bike, cooler looking, and being a heavier bike, tended to be a much better ride. It was a 2009 model, so it wasn't really new. But it might as well have been. It had less than 8000 miles, and the original owner had taken perfect care of it.

The day he picked it up was one of his days off work, so he figured he would head over to Hannibal, register the vehicle in his name, then go to the gym to start working out again. Hannibal overall was pretty cool. Maybe he'd spend the rest of the afternoon and evening there.

It was incredibly hot — over 90 degrees — and one of the best ways to stay cool was for him to generate some serious speed and keep the breeze rushing by at near hurricane velocity. Take heed to the need for speed!

It was only noon, so there was plenty of time left in the day. He decided to take the long way around, which happened in terms of motorcycling to not only be the most interesting, but typically the route most likely to be free of pesky state police patrol cars and radar guns. He pointed himself down through the Mark Twain Recreation Area, then headed directly east through Perry and northeast toward Center and New London.

When he got to the appropriate place in the road, he looked back over his shoulder and noticed that the billboard of the girl in a blue dress was gone. But it had been replaced by one that was even weirder.

B e w a r e !!

The Large Hadron Collider will destroy the World!!

"The black hole of infinite sadness will swallow you."

11 - 11 - 11

Excuse me?

Large Hadron Collider? Infinite sadness?

What was that all about?

Things got stranger as he entered New London. Within the small confines of the village limits there were three more billboards — *three!!* — which monopolized all of the available billboard space for the entire town, population 3,768. These had just a lavender wallpaper of 11s and the unique 11-11-11 logo.

It didn't stop there.

He saw two more of the *Beware!* billboards on his way north along Highway 61, then the one with just the 11s again a little further on.

The best, however, was saved for last. He spotted it as he gently eased off on the throttle and entered the outskirts of Hannibal from the south.

"11 is the King's ransom."

And what do you have left?

**Pass through the 11th Gate, into a Greater Love.
To ascend from duality into Oneness.**

*'And thou shalt eat the fruit of thine own body, the flesh
of thy sons and of thy daughters' - Deuteronomy 28:53*

11:11 is an encoded molecular trigger!

11 - 11 - 11

In the lower right hand corner was a picture of Jesus looking very solemn, offering His divine blessing with His right hand. His left hand pointed to His heart, which mysteriously glowed through His chest like a large ember.

Noah decided this billboard warranted some serious scrutiny. He pulled his bike to the side of the road, slipped off his helmet and stood directly in front of the huge sign.

The King's ransom?

11 what? Shekels? Pontius Pilate tribute pennies?

What do I have left? Not much after taxes.

The Biblical passage from Deuteronomy seemed to be recommending cannibalism.

Pass through the 11th Gate? What about the other ten gates? What about Bill Gates?

Duality? Oneness? One is the loneliest number.

Encoding? Molecular biology?

Even Jesus looked confused.

Noah considered himself a smart guy — because he was — and prided himself in generally being able to comprehend what he read, whether in a book, magazine, school text, technical journal, instruction manual, product label, whatever. But no matter how many times he went over it, this billboard made absolutely no sense to him.

Maybe it wasn't supposed to.

Maybe it wasn't directed at people like him.

Maybe it simply wasn't supposed to make sense to anyone.

But what then was the point? Why was it here? What were the hundreds of people passing by this billboard supposed to take away from it? What kind of thought-provoking discussions was it intended to kindle?

Noah thought back on the town hall meeting his mother had dragged him to at Salem First Baptist Church. Most of the people there had lapped up the ramblings of Dr. Theodore Clemus like thirsty dogs. He thought about the upcoming visit by spirit guru Björn Agynn in September. And about his whacked-out sister. The tattoo. Then dumb ass Phil! Who also apparently was somehow caught up in this 11-11-11 nonsense.

There sure was a lot of this crap floating around these days. What was going on? What was the occasion? As far as Noah was concerned, everything he had heard so far had consisted of a lot of nonsensical blather. A lot of other people obviously felt different.

He wondered if this was some local underground cult phenomenon which had randomly bubbled to the surface — like a cracked sewage main oozing its contents onto the crumbling cobblestones of his hometown — or if 11-11-11 was in fact gaining some traction on the national stage.

His curiosity finally got the better of him. He jumped on the internet and did some snooping. Of course, any nutcase with a computer could float stuff out there. But with 11-11-11, it was clearly way beyond that. Without a doubt, it was popping up everywhere, the exact same kind of weird stuff he was seeing around him locally. And the level of buzz was by every measure increasing exponentially each day — in volume, intensity, hyperbole, noise, sheer wackiness.

What about the legitimate media and press?

Noah didn't watch TV, thus had no cable service into his apartment to feed him the news. But he was able to watch various television feeds on his computer. And sure enough. There it was, in all of its baffling stupid splendor. CNN and MSNBC had their share of it. The network stations did their part, particularly with comedians doing bits and take-offs on it. Saturday Night Live was starting to incorporate a regular skit about it called "The Quakers Dozen", which featured an eleven-headed space alien whose ship had landed in a Quaker community in Pennsylvania. On Comedy Central, both Jon Stewart's The Daily Show and the Colbert Report had some hilarious segments on the topic.

The most annoying coverage came from the Fox News Channel, which in contrast to a lot of the exposure it was getting elsewhere, was taking it very seriously — or claiming to — brandishing themselves as *"first in the nation to bring you everything you need to know about the coming 11-11-11 crisis"*. Fox just couldn't pass up such a perfectly packaged pile of poop, shovel-ready nonsense guaranteed to scare the shit out of its viewers and further boost its bloated ratings. This created a domino effect. Since no one in the media world wanted to be left behind in the stampede to stupidity, the blind followed the blind (or maybe it was the unglued followed the shrewd). Noah saw a lot of copycat coverage slowly emerging in normally responsible and respectable news sources like the New York Times, Washington Post, Time, Newsweek, the Christian Science Monitor, Los Angeles Times, New Yorker, and so on.

There was no doubt about it. 11-11-11 was everywhere.

Noah had already drawn his own harsh conclusions

It was a cancer of the mind — or was it of the soul? — spreading like some mutant virus.

It was classic epidemiology. First in anomalous isolated appearances, it showed up here or there. Someone noticed. Maybe filled out a report. Then it started to pick up momentum. Take hold. More people noticed. Everyone started talking. Suddenly, it was everywhere! There was no hiding. People were afraid and wanted to know.

Ohmigod!! Is it the next plague? Help! We're doomed!

11-11-11.

What a joke!

It was always something. Nuclear holocaust. AIDS. Sunspots. The Anti-Christ.

The Apocalypse!

It's the end of the world! That had certainly been a mantra throughout history.

Granted, there would be a time when they finally got it right.

But it was sure a pretty dismal record so far.

Wrong 1,956,832,514 times.

Right one last time.

Nice work!

Sweet Tooth

"I kept asking her, 'Why don't you brush your teeth?' I even bought her a new toothbrush. She just looked at me like I was crazy."

Imagine that.

Noah was on the phone with his mom.

Gretchen had suddenly and mysteriously dropped by the house. She just breezed in and made a beeline for her room. What prompted the surprise visit soon became clear.

"When? When did she show up?"

"Two days ago. I was afraid to tell you."

"Is she still there? Should I come over? I should come over."

"Then she starts talking about her birthday. What am I going to buy her this year for her birthday? It's not for five months, six months. I don't know. What month is this?"

"It's July. Two more days it's August. I'm coming over right—"

"Noah. She's not right. I think you'll upset her."

"She's never been right. I couldn't make things worse."

"Anyway, for her birthday she wants money."

"Don't give it to her! Whatever you do—"

"She says it's for school. She wants to go to junior college."

"Mom, don't! I see what's going on. I don't think you understand."

"Well it's too late. I just gave her $200."

"I'm coming right over!"

By the time he got there, Gretchen had made another quick cameo downstairs in the living room, looked enigmatically at her mom, then retreated back to her room.

Noah found his mom sitting staring at the television. It wasn't on. Probably for the best. If it was tuned to the Home Shopping Channel, he would have been talking to a feather duster.

"Is she still here? Where is she? In her room?"

"I tried to talk to her, Noah. I'm her mom. I know what's best for her. I made all sorts of food, all her favorite dishes."

In her typical rambling, semi-coherent fashion, she then went on to describe how Gretchen was acting. Her pacing around the room, her biting her fingernails till they bled, her staring at some object she would fixate on, her warnings to her mom that the days were numbered, that on November 11th people were going to be herded like cattle onto a long river of fiery coals, that cockroaches and new bacterial life forms would inherit the Earth, and how sad she was because there would be so much suffering.

"She talks to strange creatures that live in the trees and make fun of us. She says they are the monkey demons. They talk to her because she is one of the chosen ones. They tell her they think it's funny that everything has been poisoned and we don't know it. We're all going to bloat up like dead cows and explode. Noah, I think she might be crazy!"

Noah took the stairs two at a time. He knocked on Gretchen's door.

"Gretchen. It's me. Noah. I'm not going to cause any problems. Promise. No arguments. No pissing contests. Let's just talk."

He could hear her moving around. He tried the door. Locked.

Faintly, he heard a motorcycle. Then closer. It was approaching the house.

He took a step back, tucked slightly, then put all of the power of his 172 pound frame behind it, as he rammed his shoulder into the door. The flimsy old door jamb gave easily.

The window was open. She was gone.

He ran down the stairs as fast as he could. Just in time to see her speeding off on the back of a Harley Davidson. Either brute man or one of his look-alike protégés was driving.

Noah stepped into the kitchen. His mom sat at the table. Either caught by surprise or paralyzed by her sense of helplessness, she apparently had not done anything but watch her daughter race out the door.

"I just don't understand. She's so thin. You'd think she'd want to eat something. I made her all her favorite stuff. BLT sandwiches. Linguine and clam sauce. Fried chicken wings. Pepperoni pizza."

She stood up and picked up something from the counter. It was a stack of some sort of confectionaries or candy bars.

"This was all she would eat. So I even bought extra for her. And ... now she's gone."

His mom put them on the table. He recognized the label. It was a very popular brand all through this part of the country. Colonel Tucker's Old Fashioned Home-Style Treat For The Whole Family. Americas Finest. Since 1877.

Peanut brittle.

His mom just shook her head.

"My little girl. She always had a sweet tooth."

Family Values

A few days later, Noah was back again sitting in the kitchen with his mother. They had just finished eating dinner.

He hated her cooking—if you could call what she did cooking — but it was an opportunity for them to visit, talk, put their heads together, and just try to figure out what might be going on these worrisome days with respect to Gretchen.

His mom's fashion statement tonight again told a strange tale. Apparently, she had jumped into some new orbit, an elliptical path which soared out even further than usual from any of the recognizable conventions of contemporary American dress. She was wearing a dark green track suit which had been accessorized with shiny sequins, jewels, and strips of fake rabbit fur. It was inexplicably cut out in back and showed the top of her leathery ass crack. She had a black vinyl New York Mets baseball cap sideways on her head, and additionally wore a thin woven leather headband which she might have gotten from a *Last of the Mohicans* memorabilia catalog. Instead of running shoes, she shuffled around tentatively on black plastic platforms, embossed with white Chinese characters.

Perhaps the gamma ray gun they were using as part of her post-operative radiation therapy was being aimed too high and it was dissolving her brain.

"Interesting meal, mom. I really liked the shepherd's pie."

"That was pumpkin bread. I didn't have any flour, so I used ground beef."

"How are you feeling? It's been two months. What do the doctors say?"

"They keep changing doctors. Now I have some Mexican. Dr. Rajesh Gupta."

"Mom. That's an Indian name. From India. Like Gandhi."

"Same difference. I can't understand a word he says. When he talks he sounds like his mouth is full of guacamole. Have you talked to Gretchen yet? I'm worried sick about her!"

"Mom, I can't tell you how many times I've tried. I am pretty sure I know where she is. But she's never there. Or I should say she never answers the door."

"Why do you hate her?"

"Mom. I don't hate her. I just have never liked her."

"That's not true, Noah. You were crazy about her when she was a baby. You used to play with her all of the time. You called her 'Itchin'. You used to protect her. You made sure the other kids didn't ever pick on your little sister …"

"I don't remember."

"… or hurt her. Till she was three, maybe four years old."

"Dad left. Everything changed. I didn't hate her. She just became a pain in the ass."

"So … tell your mother. Are you worried about her now? Are you really trying to—"

"Mom! Lighten up. She's my sister. She means a lot to you. Regardless of whether she and I get along, I don't want anything bad to happen to her."

"What's going on, Noah? Why is she acting like this?"

His mom started crying. Really crying. It was like someone had just opened the floodgates of the Hoover Dam.

Noah went over and tried to comfort her.

As soon as his hand touched her shoulder, she pulled back, whipped around, confronted him. She looked furious.

"What did you do to her, Noah? My baby! Something happened! Why won't you tell me what happened?"

"Mom … I … I had nothing to do with this. She's … I … I don't know. But it's bad. She's mixed up in something—"

"Do something about it, Noah! Goddamn it! Do something!!"

Her livid face melted back into a mask of despair. She turned her back to Noah and buried her face in her hands. Her weeping was something horrible and barely human. Like the shriek of an air raid siren combined with the hungry howl of a wolf. She cried so hard she was soon gasping for breath. Coughing. Hiccupping. Gagging. Her eyes rolled up in her head and she looked like she was going to faint. When she recovered her breathing, she then started sobbing and wailing again even louder. Noah knew from prior experience this could go on for hours. The roaring storm in her head would drown out everything else and she would be carried along in the torrential floodwaters of her own tears.

Through the wailing could be heard her whining plea.

"Do something about it. Do something."

She just kept on repeating.

"Do something."

The words, the agony, the desperation, rode the surface waves of her torment, and underneath, the riptide of her helplessness pulled her drowning into the dark abyss of despair. This was his mother at her worst. There was no dealing with her when she was in this state. He had seen this before, too many times. *Way* too many times.

Was she crazy?

Noah didn't like to think about it. This was his mother. For better or worse.

He wanted to believe at least technically she was sane. But it was tough, especially when she got like this.

How could his mom conceivably think he was to blame Gretchen's situation, whatever it is? Maybe he never went out of his way to be nice to his sister. Maybe if the truth be known, he had gone out of his way to avoid her, especially the last few years since he had left home to live on his own.

But what was he supposed to do?

Gretchen could be such a bitch! She used every opportunity to put him down, humiliate and denigrate him. It seemed to be her major mission in life.

Maybe it was her only mission in life. She sure didn't seem to have anything else going on.

Gretchen barely finished high school. Couldn't find a job. Constantly sponged off their mom. Went through boyfriends faster than most people go through sandwich bread.

She had the mouth of a truck driver, the social graces of a pit bull.

She was voted by her school as the most likely to fail.

She named Kelly Osborne as her role model.

She couldn't take 'yes' for an answer.

She walked like a prison guard.

And … it was no accident.

It was just Gretchen.

While Noah was no fashionista, he knew what was happening locally — what the twenty somethings in and around town were wearing, how they looked. From the internet and music videos, he was also quite aware of the edgy stuff going on in the rest of the country and around the world. He couldn't help but conclude that Gretchen literally went out of her way, went to exhausting extremes, to make herself unattractive.

Her hair looked like last year's hemp harvest left out through the worst of winters, then treated with rust-inhibiting spray paint. It was some indescribable color — a greenish purplish brown — which wouldn't look good on a tractor-drawn beet harvester, much less a human being. Her makeup on a good day would give pause to a vampire, if not induce immediate cardiac arrest. She had shaved her eyebrows, then inked them back on like two opposing Nike logos, a comic effect that would have been the envy of Groucho Marx. She bought all the right clothes but combined them with such obtuseness and anti-aesthetic zeal, the sum was always less than the total of the parts. Often the sum was less than zero. Admittedly, when she walked into a room, she caught the eye. But then the eye pleaded to be excused from having to look at her again.

Rebellion was one thing. But Gretchen appeared to be on some mission. Its unstated but clear objective was to shock or repel people into thinking she was ultimately and incomprehensibly cool. From what Noah could see, they were just shocked and repelled.

This had been going on for a long time. A really long time.

Once when Gretchen was in junior high school, Noah watched as a human-shaped entity, something of a hybrid between a life-size cabbage patch doll and an Amsterdam hooker, marched through the kitchen, then headed up the stairs. After accepting that this was not a hallucination but was in fact his sister, he turned to his mom.

"What is wrong with her?"

"I tried to tell her. Acrylic nails are the only way to go."

Right.

Like asking the kettle why the frying pan is black.

Gretchen made it through school pretty much a complete loner. It never seemed to bother her that she had no real friends, that there was a revolving door of girls and sometimes guys, who would come along, check her out for a while, and hold out some small promise of actual friendship, then soon disappear. Two weeks seemed to be the most anyone could take. Gretchen always dismissed these obvious rejections with smart-alecky sarcasm, flippant condemnations and brutal personal attacks. Finally with shrill arrogance she'd claim the other person was a waste of *her* time, not up to *her* high standards. He or she could just "fuck off and die." Her state of denial about how unpopular she was appeared to be total. "Who needs these losers anyway?" she would say as she strutted around cocksure and wholly comforted by the delusion that she had some vast back-up reserve pool of friends to draw from.

In terms of her behavior over the years, nothing ever changed. With no anchor in reality and the tacit approval of an equally unhinged mother, she kept on getting weirder and uglier, more and more alienated. The problem was, it wasn't a game she could play forever. Pulnick was a small town and Gretchen had by now gone through just about everyone.

It was easy to see how Gretchen and their mother had become so close. Mom had flipped out and become completely isolated. Gretchen similarly underwent social ostracism at school. They were driven into one another's arms. More and more so, as time went on.

Their shared obsession with Addams Family cosmetics and bizarre fashions, became the adhesive for their intense bonding. Perhaps because there was thirty years difference in their ages, they never shared clothes or exchanged specific makeup tips. But there was definitely some implicit and powerful dynamic uniting them. The competition in their race to the bottom seemed to provide energy and inspiration, driving them to new heights, or depths depending on your perspective, of absurdity in their fashion choices, the vandalizing of their individual personas, the perfection of off-putting others. They were Siamese twins of fashion suicide.

So what happened?

Why had Gretchen by choice so inexplicably written off her mom?

There seemed to be no plausible reason. Not even an implausible reason. It wasn't like there had been some big blow out between them. Or that she had been kidnapped. There were the two brief visits she had made. Gretchen had acted casual, like everything was fine between them. She looked thin, not very healthy. Seemed a little weird. Made some crude reference to Jesus. Sported an 11-11-11 tattoo. She asked her mom for her birthday present early.

But she didn't appear to be especially upset about anything.

Then back out the door she went.

Except for the two visits ... not a word. Not even a phone call. Nothing.

While it didn't impact him one way or the other, it was certainly the last thing Noah would have expected. Certainly the last and most painful thing his mom could have imagined. And it unfortunately came at a time of enormous emotional need and vulnerability for her. She was still recovering from the surgery, was now going for regular chemo and radiation treatments, and despite the reassurances from the doctors, had to be wondering if the whole business was over, or if she would be facing another round in a life-and-death struggle against cancer.

Noah couldn't share with his mom his own thoughts about what a screwed up and dangerous situation Gretchen might be in. It would upset her too much.

But his conclusion seemed unavoidable.

Everything he read about the effects of meth offered the most straightforward answer. Use of and addiction to the drug produced dramatic and unprecedented shifts. Totally impulsive, unpredictable, irrational behavior. Dramatic mood swings. Hostility. Paranoia. Withdrawal.

Noah spent the night there at his mom's house. Her caterwauling finally stopped when exhaustion overtook her. She finally slumped over at the kitchen table and fell asleep. He gently helped her sleepwalk her way to her bedroom, then crashed on the living room couch.

Next morning they ate breakfast in total silence. Her face was still puffed and blotchy from the torments of the prior evening. His face still bore the indentations of a night on the sofa.

She walked him to the door and finally said something. "I just want to be a family again."

"I understand, mom."

A family? Fat chance.

When had they ever been a family?

Chapter Six

August 19 ...

Alien Abduction!

It was the last straw!

Well ... the last straw till the next straw.

Now there were small handbills, posters and bulletin board notices popping up everywhere — at BP and Shell gas stations stretching from Monroe City to Paris, at Breaktime and all of the Casey's convenience stores, even in the employee cafeteria at Merkel — announcing a special "citizens emergency meeting" being called to inform the residents of Pulnick and surrounding communities of an "alien threat" that was gathering on the not too distant horizon.

Alien threat? From where? Guatemala? Pakistan? Neptune?

This really pissed Noah off. There were some very serious problems in Pulnick right now. Yet here was more evidence of Pulnick's complete disconnect. He wished he could take the whole town by the shoulders and shake some sense into them. Hello! Wake up! It's not about space invaders, folks! There are *real* issues to be dealt with.

A young man was recently killed at a rave party. The police report was just made public. It said that the county coroner concluded that the hapless fellow was high on drugs and had suffered an unfortunate and fatal fall. Right. And bounced twenty three times, which is the only way to explain all of the contusions on his face and body.

If murder were not serious enough for them, Noah could take officials to the site of what he suspected was a fully functioning meth lab, or at bare minimum the headquarters of a meth distribution ring, which had moved to Pulnick to spread death and chaos. If anyone would just take the time to notice! The Sheriff Department claimed they were there to protect and serve. Where the hell were they?

On a more personal note, his own sister had disappeared, probably along with the neighbor boy he had grown up with. This was sleepy boring Pulnick. People don't just up and disappear. Was it too much to ask to get some help finding them and getting them back?

Alien threat!

What a bunch of idiots!

Noah was 110% positive this poster had nothing to do with a real emergency. It was just another ridiculous distraction being foisted on a clueless and gullible citizenry.

According to the posters, the meeting would be hosted by the current and soon to be re-elected mayor — it was a given that Aldous Penthe would again win and sit at the head of the town council, since he had been mayor for over fourteen years and faced no opposition — and feature a very special guest speaker, a man who was no stranger to Pulnickians for 2½ decades now.

As with many remote communities scattered like tiny blackheads across the pale face of mid-America, Pulnick had its own special saga of visitors from outer space. And its own special liaison for these intergalactic encounters.

The father of one of Noah's high school classmates, a Mr. Elmer Huck, claimed that over several months during the summer and autumn of 1986, he was abducted by a race of alien beings, lifted by some mysterious energy beam right off terra firma into the metallic bowels of a huge saucer-shaped space ship. Inside the craft, he was placed under hypnotic anesthesia, which left him immobilized but conscious, then subjected to various tests, probes, samplings, biopsies, and other experimental procedures. He could and did describe all of this in lurid detail, but confessed he had no idea what exactly the aliens were after. He also gave a meticulous account of the physical appearance of his abductors, and though it strayed a bit from one telling to another, the creatures bore an uncanny resemblance to the little space midget in the movie *E.T.*

This was two years before his son, Noah's classmate, Findley Huck was born.

With that in mind, what would have been entirely believable about this story was that Findley was the product of a genetic experiment by the putative extraterrestrial scientists, gone awry. For if anyone was a mutant species, possibly of non-earthly origins, it was Findley.

Findley was odd in every respect.

He was randomly proportioned, an assemblage of anatomical parts from at least twenty divergent body types and maybe even other bipeds. His neck was thick as a telephone pole. His head was the size of a small coconut. He had one thick eyebrow which bisected his forehead midway to his hairline. His ears were pointy and stuck out horizontally like the wings of a fighter jet. His torso was narrow at the chest and wide at the hips. Deeper front to back than side to side. He had no ass. One arm was long, the other short. His elbows looked like golf balls. His thumbs were as long as his index fingers. His Adam's apple looked more like Adam's summer squash. In short, Findley could have modeled for Picasso.

Socially, he was a complete and total misfit. No one would go near him, hence he had no friends. He was easy to pick out in school. In every class, he was the kid sitting alone in the center of a circle of empty desks.

Not surprisingly, it didn't bother Findley in the least. He never seemed to notice.

During his puberty years, he masturbated constantly. Privacy was never an issue for him. None of the many witnesses to his pud pounding — which included just about everyone at school — ever recalled him having an orgasm. Which apparently prompted him to keep at it, resulting in three years of steady crotch grinding with the heel of his hand, and delicately executed caresses, using just the tips of his fingers, to the feels-so-good underside of his penis.

This took place in class, in the halls between classes, in the cafeteria, at school assemblies, and finally even at graduation ceremony. He spent so much time with his eyes rolled up in his head, bets were on that they would eventually get stuck and he would spend the rest of his life looking like they had been replaced with hard-boiled eggs.

Findley arrived at school precisely at 8:00 a.m. at the first bell and left precisely at 3:20 p.m. at the last bell. Never a sideways glance coming or going. Every moment outside of school he spent at home, tucked away from the world with his hopeless old maid sister of twenty-six and his Virgin Mary obsessed mother. The Huck family lived in a gloomy century-old barn-shaped gabled house, set back from the road and shaded by giant ancient maple trees. Their property was three miles south of town, right on the outskirts of the Mark Twain Recreation Area.

Findley's father, like his father before him — and his father's father — was a farmer. Common wisdom held that Mr. Huck spent way too much time alone, which is probably why he passed father-to-son absolutely nothing in the way of social graces, and entirely why there was never a witness for the twenty odd times he was allegedly taken up into the flying saucer back in 1986. It's a lonely life out there among the stalks of corn and rows of sugar beets.

Farming, of course, makes nearly superhuman demands on the serious farmer. Sometimes the days stretch out to twelve, fourteen hours.

Even so, Mr. Huck was never exactly forthcoming about what he was doing riding his tractor in the pitch black of those many Missouri midnights, during which he experienced his encounters with the alien visitors.

This was how he told it.

There he was, just minding his own business. The business of making things grow. When out of nowhere appeared a giant spaceship. It hovered above him for a while, sizing him up perhaps, making sure that he and the tractor he rode posed no threat to the advanced 7 million ton super-alloy craft, which had survived collisions with every conceivable kind of space debris, encounters with four black holes, a high-intensity gamma ray supernova, and hyper-space travel along the high-energy event thresholds of the space-time continuum. You can't blame them for being careful. No way of knowing what those Missouri farmers might have up their sleeves.

Finally after about an hour of hovering and humming — an eerie electronic hum that he claimed sounded like an old toaster which had gotten stuck and couldn't eject its bread — Elmer was floated off the seat of his tractor right up into the hull of the space ship.

He was quickly surrounded by chattering little aliens. They were all short, giggled a lot, and in terms of their generally upbeat dispositions, seemed to have a lot in common with the Munchkins in *The Wizard of Oz*.

They placed him on a very comfortable medical examination table, and had him stare at a spheroidal glass knickknack, small enough to easily fit into the palm of the hand. It resembled the little liquid-filled winter scenes which when are shaken make it look like it's snowing. This one had a beautiful butterfly-winged planet, not unlike the Earth, suspended in the middle. One especially cute alien creature shook it for him and held it up for him to see. The globe became filled with swirling twinkling points of light, which ever-so-slowly settled to the bottom, forming what appeared to be a glowing snow drift. By the time all the swirling stars fell and became completely motionless, Elmer was deeply hypnotized and could no longer feel a thing. He felt more weightless than numb, and since he weighed over 280 lbs it felt pretty good.

Now the probing began.

Orifices are the preferred way to go, according to most accounts of alien abduction like Elmer's. His was no exception. Into the ears, nostrils, mouth, throat the tiny creatures went with their various instruments. Even into his urethra.

But for whatever reason — and who could begin to second guess these strange little beings — the anal probe seemed to invite most of the fascination. They probed and probed. Elmer felt no particular pain. If anything, it was pleasant, so he offered little resistance.

When they were done with the entire battery of procedures, they passed a light over his eyes from a hand-held de-hypnotizer that looked like a simple flashlight, and normal feeling returned to his body. They then sat him down, and as if they could read his mind, served him his favorite meal — spare ribs, string beans with bacon and onions, whipped potatoes, and head cheese aka gelatinized cow brains, with mayonnaise and ketchup on the side. They included his favorite beer with the meal and topped it all off with hot cherry pie smothered in whip cream.

He couldn't complain. This was certainly better treatment than he got at home from his cranky wife, who was too busy asking for blessings from the Virgin Mary to ever make him any kind of outrageously delicious meal like this. She usually served him eggs in the morning that had the consistency of linoleum, and in the evening, meat loaf that tasted like pressboard.

Elmer finally claimed that for some strange reason then, instead of using the proton tractor beam to return him to the ground, when they were done with him they lowered him on a swing. It was definitely not smooth going, and he had to hang on for dear life, as they extended more and more rope. The swing would sway back and forth, shake and bounce as it abruptly stopped and started in its long journey earthward. It was the truly harrowing part of the abduction, since the ship had to at least be a thousand feet off the ground.

But he always made it back safely. He maintained that he had never felt so clean in his life. All of his orifices had been ungunged and exorcised. His butthole and upper intestine were scoured and scrubbed so thoroughly they became a high-colonic super-Chunnel, which assured pleasant and effortless defecation for days.

He was emphatic that this was exactly how it happened the first time, and this was exactly how it happened for each and every subsequent alien visit. The only very slight variation was that after the caution of the first encounter, all parties now seemed entirely comfortable with the arrangement, meaning the initial one hour of hovering and humming was omitted and he was sucked right up into the ship immediately after they arrived.

By some mechanism Elmer never identified or pretended to comprehend, by the third encounter with the aliens he began to be able to understand what his new little friends from outer space were saying. Similarly, they understood him. He claimed to have had some lively conversations with them about all sorts of things. When reporters started coming around for interviews, he often described these exchanges, offering precise quotes of what the aliens had said. Unfortunately, since most of it tended to sound nonsensical, very little of value could be derived from the rambling interviews he gave over the years.

There had been quite a number of these interviews. When he first announced that he had experienced a close encounter of the alien kind, there were both local newspapers and the usual national tabloids — National Enquirer, Tattler, Daily Mirror, Chicago Sun-Times, Midnight Globe, Star, National Examiner — who flocked to his isolated farm to get the scoop. Whatever his agenda, if he had one, he wasn't very media savvy in the early stages. Reporters initially found him to be an uncooperative witness — unenthusiastic, reticent, inarticulate — an unwilling participant in the story and the firestorm of media attention he had himself unleashed. One article described him personally as a big, boorish, dull, fat slob, who had suffered brain damage sitting on his tractor in the sun for too many years.

After a few months of disastrous interviews, he loosened up a little and found his groove. This produced a number of notable, if bizarre and inscrutable quotes, usually following some attention grabbing header like, *MISSOURI MAN ABDUCTED BY SPACE ALIENS SAYS* —

"They don't want our women. They don't mate like us."

"Their breath smells like gasoline."

"They love rock 'n roll and are big fans of Bill Haley & The Comets."

"I met St. Augustine. He looks the same as ever."

"I tried to teach them the Star Spangled Banner. They are terrible singers."

"They sometimes live to be over 800 years old."

"For them 2 plus 2 can equal 4. Or 7. Or 3. Just about anything."

"My space alien nickname is Flij Maut Klak."

Elmer had been quiet for quite some time now. This was primarily because the alien visits had stopped. Predictably, he went back to doing what he did best, which of course was farming, and the media moved on to newer bigger better things.

Moreover, toward the end of Elmer's salad days of fame — and even now when some obscure magazine would dig him out of the historical woodwork to bring some new set of readers up to speed on his experiences — he was repeating himself. Saying things over and over that weren't really all that interesting the first time around. The strange quotes which were central to whatever curiosity people might have about his freakish adventures in intergalactic anthropology — that is, the crazy shit which sold newspapers to idiots who would believe almost anything they read — had trickled off and ceased entirely. Now he mainly talked about how the alien visitors felt about farm subsidies. They were passionately in favor of them.

Which made this new surge of interest in him curious to say the least. Noah couldn't help but think: Something smelled rotten in Monroe County. It was the smell of exploitation.

Who had gotten to him? Who was resurrecting this ancient hackneyed news story and its sub-stellar luminary and for what purpose? Who exactly was using Elmer Huck?

There was only one way to find out.

Noah would make a point of being there.

What did those idiotic posters say?

Sunday 8 p.m. September 11.

September 11th?

That figures.

Salem First Baptist Church.

That place again!

Oh great.

Fear

For now they at least assumed Gretchen was still alive. But that didn't solve anything. And increasingly his mom was driving Noah crazy. On the phone or in person, she either cried pathetically or screamed frantically. There was little in between. Pauses to breathe was about it.

It wasn't always easy for him to convince himself it was *his* duty to try to find her and do something — anything! — to get her to come home and stay home.

Certainly he wanted to relieve his mom's anxieties. But he feared that even getting hold of Gretchen would be opening a Pandora's box, that then the real problems would surface and totally send the old lady off the deep end. His mom was completely clueless. She thought Gretchen was just mildly confused right now and her physical condition was some simple health issue, maybe not enough potassium in her diet. She offered not the least hint of suspicion that Gretchen might be involved with anything as untoward as addictive drugs, and she certainly knew nothing of the crowd Gretchen apparently was hanging out with these days.

But there was another side of Noah — admittedly an insensitive side — that prompted him to just say 'Fuck it!' If Gretchen was stupid enough to get herself into whatever mess she was in, she should have to live with the consequences. There was frankly so much bad blood between them, built up over the years, that for him to generate the enthusiasm his search and rescue mission probably warranted, was next to impossible.

Still he kept at it. His deeper conscience and the shrill pleadings of his mother egged him on. He continued reluctantly going through the motions of being a good son and a protective brother.

The truth be told, it always ended up being more than a mere token effort. Noah was not a half-measures kind of a guy. And certainly taking on what he suspected was a gang of meth peddlers did not respond well to casual and half-hearted measures.

He kept asking anyone and everyone if they had seen her. Not her close friends. She didn't have any. But people in her general age group who might ever so briefly have caught a glimpse of her. She must go somewhere sometime to do something.

He kept coming up empty-handed.

It completely baffled Noah how Gretchen had become so invisible. This was a small town. A *really* small town. He was constantly running into just about everyone he knew, ones he barely knew, people he wanted to see, people he didn't want to see. It was inevitable.

Not even Gretchen's most casual acquaintances, ones who might have taken notice of her just as a data point for the stream of gossip which was constantly enlisted to fill the yawning void in their lives, not even these frenetic blathering busybodies had anything to offer him in terms of her movements. Had she completely bailed? Was she holed up now in a commune in Sedona, AZ or a cult cloister in Amsterdam?

Finally, one of the pus-faced night clerks at Casey's in Shelbina — was it a job requirement that these guys have aggressively erupting acne to operate a cash register? — seemed fairly certain he had spotted her.

"If it's the one I'm thinking of, she comes in with some very scary dudes."

Shelbina. That made sense. Directly north on County Road V, then west on Hwy 36. Twenty miles round trip to get groceries and beer. Not as close as Pulnick, but if they wanted to avoid drawing the attention of the Monroe County Sheriff's Department, this was the way to do it. Shelbina was in another county, incestuously named Shelby County.

"Is she kind of a scaggy bitch? With a really bad attitude?"

"That would ring true."

"Two guys she comes in with I've never seen around before. Two big hairy dudes. I mean like long hair and beards. Tattoos and shit. Their trucks have Texas plates. We're supposed to notice those kinds of things, in case we get robbed. Sometimes there's a couple others along. I'm sure they're local, though."

This might prove very convenient. Merkel Industries was located about three miles east of Shelbina, which was why it was so convenient for him to buzz by the abandoned farm in Clapper. Though the ride was incredibly boring, in terms of a direct and quick route for getting to work, this was it. And the farm was basically right on the way.

Now he would make a point of zipping over to Shelbina occasionally and staking out either Casey's or the main road in and out of town. It would probably turn out to be a huge waste of time but he was getting desperate. He naturally wondered if Gretchen ever made the trip by herself. It was hard to imagine that she did. Not in a big truck or on a Harley.

But there was a slim chance.

Then what? Kidnap her? Invite her for a cup of coffee?

He hadn't thought that one out. He needed to do that. Come up with a plan of some sort.

Before he made any more excursions to Shelbina, Noah continued to stake out to the farm.

It was always the same. Signs of someone being there at one time or another. But never any signs of life when he was there.

At least until his most recent visit.

This particular occasion was one of Noah's days off work. So he had to make a special trip. Since he wasn't confined by his work schedule, the advantage was he had complete freedom to choose when he would show up.

He arrived around 10 a.m. He didn't know why, but for this particular visit he was more apprehensive than for the many prior occasions he had sneaked onto the property, though he certainly always felt a gnawing pit of fear in his stomach as soon as the farm came into view. He had taken to parking his motorcycle way off the side of the drive, back behind some trees, maybe five hundred feet from the house itself.

He knew from all previous experience that the house would be a waste of his time and energy. So this time he circled wide, walked around behind the barn, across the wildly overgrown back area behind the house, then down a path parallel to a small grove of trees growing behind an old post-and-beam fence.

Looking through the trees, he saw something. A plume of smoke rising from a shed he had never noticed before. He scissored over the fence, then made his way through a not very densely overgrown copse, to get a better look.

Sure enough, there was what looked like a tractor shelter or equipment shed which had subsequently been closed in and weatherproofed. There was a tiny entrance porch, a proper door, and two small windows. The four panes of glass in each window, and those in the door itself, were incredibly filthy. He couldn't see clearly through any of them. But in the window furthest from the door, he could just barely make out a couple moving shapes, working away at a bench. Directly above them poking through the roof was the galvanized rain-hooded chimney from which the plume of smoke Noah had spotted was rising.

Noah approached very cautiously, attempting to keep whatever shrubs and tree trunks were in his path, between him and whoever was in the shed, to avoid being noticed. As he got closer, he couldn't help but smell the acrid chemical fumes which filled the surrounding air. It was the very same smell he had detected on his first visit to the farm, only much more intense, burning his eyes now and catching in his throat.

He decided to try to see who was inside.

Noah could make out that one of the figures had his or her back to him. The other one stood sideways to the window and was very focused on something directly in front of him.

Staying low he made a dash for it.

He watched them the whole way. They remained preoccupied and he was positive they had not seen him. He stopped next to the window and pressed himself flat against the outside wall. He needed to catch his breath and muster some courage.

Very slowly and carefully he edged his closest eye to the window and looked in.

It was Gretchen. It was Gretchen and one of the gorilla men.

Gorilla man suddenly stood up and turned.

He walked right by the window. Noah couldn't have been more than a foot away.

Then he saw Gretchen pass.

Shit! The door was opening.

Noah slipped around the corner of the shed. There was no place to hide. He had to stop moving because they were out of the building now and he was afraid they would hear him.

He heard Gretchen's grating voice.

"So Satch. Is that it for now?"

Satch? Short for Sasquatch?

"We're cool. We can finish this afternoon. I'm hacked. Fuckin' chemicals, man."

Gretchen pulled out a cigarette. Something new. One of the only good things Noah could say about the girl was that she didn't smoke. So much for that.

She pulled out a lighter. Just before she lit it, gorilla man grabbed it out of her hand.

"Wait till we get away from here. That shit's like nitroglycerin."

In that exact moment, Gretchen was passing the corner of the building. She was literally inches from Noah. Had she not turned her head in reaction to the abrupt snatching of the lighter from her, she would have caught the sight of her brother in the periphery of her vision.

Noah held his breath as he watched the two of them walk away. They never looked back.

What was she doing here? It didn't look like she was *with* King Kong man. No magic. No romance in the air, from what he could tell.

It had to be the dope. She was here for the ride. That's all he could figure.

They disappeared down a narrow but well-worn path through the trees, which Noah hadn't noticed. Just to be safe, he ducked out of sight on the opposite side of the shed and waited.

He waited and waited. No way was he ready to confront ape man.

This was not turning out anything like he had expected. He saw his sister but …

Which made him realize he didn't really have any expectations. Because he had no plan. He had been plunging headlong into this business thinking that he just wanted to talk to her, reason with her brother-to-sister, but without hesitating long enough to arrive at the obvious conclusion. The only conclusion.

It wasn't going to happen.

She didn't want to talk to him. She made that clear.

And gorilla man and whoever else was in that house certainly weren't going to let him.

He thought about what had happened to the kid at the rave. Yes. That would be him. Noah would have his head bashed in by these brutes. Because they didn't like him bothering Gretchen. Because they didn't like his looks. Because they felt like it.

Suddenly Noah's entire body shook with fear. With more fear than he had ever felt before. With greater intensity than he could have ever imagined possible.

He waited.

He waited and waited.

At all costs he must get back to his bike without being seen.

An hour went by. He remembered ape man say they would be returning this afternoon.

Time to go.

Noah avoided the path they had taken, since they would be coming back that way. He stealthily crept back through the copse of trees, keeping an eye out for anyone exiting the farm house. Once he made it to the clearing, which opened to the front yard area at the front of the house, there was really no place to hide. He would just have to take his chances.

With fear at his back, he made a dash for it down the drive, only looking behind him as he ducked into the trees where he had hidden his motorcycle. No one was following him.

He fired up his Kawasaki and off he went.

About a mile down the road, just after going through Clapper, his engine began to sputter and cough. Then it stopped completely.

It sounded like maybe a carburetion problem, like either the air or the gas had been choked. Noah got off and started to stoop down to look at the intake filter, in case it had gotten clogged.

That's when he noticed it.

The lock cap on his gas tank had been jimmied. It was severely bent and had obviously been pried off. In his haste to leave the farm, he hadn't even glanced at it.

It took him four hours to hitch a ride home, then to arrange for his bike to be picked up and hauled all the way to the motorcycle shop in Hannibal. Old Farrell in the service department, who was an expert in everything that was combustion-driven and rode on two wheels, gave him the bad news. Someone had intentionally sabotaged his new bike. The engine would have to be rebuilt top to bottom.

They had known all along he was there. They were just playing with him.

This was a warning. Sugar in the gas tank.

Noah got the message.

Next time it wouldn't be so sweet.

Man-Up!

Missouri was particular about its exploitation. Selective. Discrete.

Slavery had been outlawed by Governor Thomas C. Fletcher in 1865 by executive act but estimates had the current illegal immigrant population at over 200,000. Many of these illegals worked at sub-standard wages under abhorrent conditions.

To prevent the use of women as embryo factories, stem cell research was largely banned. But it was not very difficult to find a good cockfight in rural Missouri and root for your favorite rooster to tear his opponent into bloody strips.

A person could play bingo, buy Missouri state-run lottery tickets, play high-stakes games like black jack and roulette in riverboat casinos, but not gamble on the internet or have a for-money poker game in their own basement or backyard.

To keep a man from marrying his best male friend or his horse, the only marriage permitted in Missouri was between a man and a woman.

While strip mines were still legal in Missouri, much to the chagrin of the Full Metal Jack Its, strip clubs were not. At least the ones where they got to see the full female monty.

Which is not to say that they couldn't go to an all nude strip club.

It just made it inconvenient.

Strip clubs were not only legal but thriving in adjacent Illinois. In fact, the Puritanical laws of Missouri had created a narrow band of extremely successful strip joints right on the other side of the Missouri-Illinois border, scores of them right across the Mississippi River in Saugett, Brooklyn, Washington Park, and East St. Louis. It was free market capitalism at its best, demonstrating the efficiency of the marketplace and the efficacy of the laws of supply and demand. The wild-eyed horn dogs of eastern Missouri demanded hot, young bodies to drive their hyper-agitated libidos even higher into the stratosphere, and a host of clubs on the Illinois side was happy to accommodate them.

Strip clubs are a fascinating window into the twisted, delusional side of the male.

It is common knowledge that strip clubs are not whorehouses, nor are they places to pick up a girl for a quick non-paying piece of ass. They are certainly not the place to find a girlfriend. They are not even a good place to meet girls, delicious as they may look on and off stage. Most strippers are lesbians.

Whether they are just indifferently there to make a living in what they consider a non-threatening environment — nothing sexual will ever come of it, no matter how much they take off or how much they writhe and slither with feigned horniness and lip-licking desire — or whether it is the product of a man-bating, man-hating agenda, meaning they relish and thrive on tormenting men with their ooh-so-sexy-hot but completely unavailable bodies, is a whole other discussion.

Strip clubs. Look but don't touch.

If a guy wants a girl, a strip club is definitely the wrong place to go.

Regardless, men keep on stampeding to them in droves, each guy carrying to one degree or another, elaborate but completely erroneous fantasies about what could happen.

You never know. Tonight might be the night!

It came up over lunch one afternoon. Noah and his rough-around-the-edges compatriots in a rare, almost patronizing moment of laziness, decided to blow off the local tavern and eat lunch in the employee cafeteria.

The food there was surprisingly tasty, if a little greasy. The five Full Metal Jack Its were sitting together, not having much to say, just quietly chomping away from plates piled high with man-size portions of standard issue American sub-nourishment — meat, potatoes, fries, burgers, and a few token vegetables for color.

Suddenly, Tal perked up like he had just been goosed by Daisy Mae.

"I got it! Yes! Blow me! Dudes … tonight is *Man Up!* night."

"He's got it, alright. He's got a brain-eating virus."

"Are you having a Tony Robbins moment?

"No no no! Listen, guys. We owe it to ourselves. We've been kicking ass here."

Noah of course, not being privy to the entire array of testosterone-driven rituals, was in the dark. What the hell was he talking about?

"We're going to man up? Man up about what?"

"You don't get it. *Man Up!* is our favorite club, dude. Over in Brooklyn. You gotta come. It's way fucking awesome!"

"You'll have a good time, my man. A *real* good time."

Noah had nothing against having a good time, though he sometimes had to wonder about what these guys considered a good time. Then again, nothing ventured, nothing gained. So he went.

Billed as a "real man's night out", Noah, silent Steve Toblinski, Samuel 'Ghost' Leek, and Freddie 'Fat Fuck' Stangler aka F, piled into Talbert 'Blow Me' Caswell's Chrysler Aspen, and headed toward the Illinois State line.

It was a two-and-a-half hour drive to the *Man Up!* and they refused to tell him what kind of club it was. It became pretty obvious when they pulled into the parking lot. A giant sign with the neon outline of a two-story high naked girl standing astride it, announced their wares: *All Nude - The Hottest Sexiest Girls In The World!!*

The bouncer at the door was as wide as the door. He checked them for weapons and eyed them warily, but he probably eyed everyone warily. They each paid the $10 cover and stepped inside.

Noah tried to take it all in. It was a lot to try to grasp. He would be embarrassed to admit — he certainly didn't tell these jokers — that he had never been in a strip club.

Frankly, it was exciting. *Really* exciting! The biological bottom line was, he got a rock hard boner as soon as the Full Metal Jack Its swaggered in, and he immediately got an eyeful of the girls prancing about in little more than they had worn coming into the world.

They headed toward a large circular table maybe ten feet in front of the main stage.

The club was not at all the way he had imagined it. He had assumed that it would be more of a theater setting than a disco, that such places were dark and grimy, poorly lit pits of iniquity, where desperate old men and weirdoes made some shadowy bargain with the Devil for a quick glimpse of hairy forbidden fruits, and maybe some bulbous cellulite-blighted mammary glands.

Was he ever wrong!

The stage was a slightly raised platform with highly a polished wood floor, with par lamps and pin spots illuminating the area with shifting colors and beautiful swirling patterns of light. There was a gleaming pole in the center that the dancers used to great effect, twirling around, climbing, and assuming extremely flattering positions guaranteed to provide the best visibility for the prized parts of their anatomy.

The entire club glistened with mirrors and chrome, had brilliant rock-concert lighting all around, a pumping pulsing sound system better than any he had ever heard before, and two high-tech bars presided over by scantily-dressed, breathtakingly beautiful female bartenders, whose smiles alone could send a man reeling in whirlwinds of sexual fantasy.

And the strippers!

Again he had no idea where his preconceptions had come from, since he had seen strip bar scenes in any number of movies. Maybe he thought that these were just more examples of the separate reality that pervaded everything Hollywood, that even if these places actually existed there in Los Angeles, they didn't any place else, except for maybe Las Vegas, but certainly not in this part of the country. After all, this was the 'Bible Belt' middle of America. With the men breeding with the animals, what were the chances of offspringing some real feminine beauty.

The girls filed out one after another, each one seemingly more enticing than the last. When they weren't onstage, some went back into the dressing room, but others circulated about outfitted in string bikinis, which were more string than bikini.

His eyes couldn't keep up with it all. He would probably have neck cramps tomorrow and have to wear a cervical collar. Of course, the real action — the dancing, the erotic posing, the seductive removal of what little costume they had on — was up on stage.

At first he held back, preferring to just sit tight at the table where they were initially seated. Tal and F didn't even pull out their chairs to sit down, but headed right for the 'firing line', as they called it. This was the area right at the perimeter of dance stage itself. There were seats one next to the other, and a narrow counter which wrapped all the way around the stage, for the guys to set their drinks on. This also provided a convenient surface to put their elbows for leaning in to get a better look. The girls would sometimes park one foot or stand on this surface so that they could get right in a guy's face with the parts of their bodies that held the most fascination. He watched as both Tal and F pulled some singles out, slapped them on the counter, and started to savor the girl whose performance was already in progress. She spotted them and gave them each a warm welcome by squeezing her breasts and fondling her nipples tantalizing close to each of their faces.

For a while Noah, Steve and Ghost just watched. Curious. Fascinated. A few minutes later, a very busy waitress came over, placed napkins on their table, and took their drink orders.

It took about a half hour of coaxing and a lot of cajoling, taunting, then finally the ultimately de-inhibiting effects of the alcohol, but Noah eventually got up made his way over to the main stage, followed by silent Steve and Ghost.

The most myopic psychologist could learn more about a particular man's psychological profile by observing him for ten minutes in a strip club, than the most highly esteemed team of PhDs could garner from hundreds of hours of testing and therapeutic interviews under the controlled conditions of a lab or the meditative solace of a psychiatric couch.

Tal was the classic attention-starved class clown, extrovert, playboy, life of the party, who would stop at nothing to draw the attention of the girls and try to prompt a smile of approval. Much of what he did was showing off and showing up the other guys, especially the ones who seemed to take it all too seriously. He would hold his hands up and wiggle his fingers like he couldn't wait to grab those titties, never touching the girls, of course, since that would have gotten him immediately thrown out. He would pucker his lips, wag his tongue, and make sloppy licking motions. But he would always grin ear to ear to let it be known it was all in good fun. Twice in the evening, he stood up on his ringside chair and did a perfect mirror imitation of the erotic posturing of the girl dancing in front of him. He writhed and wiggled, bent over and spread his cheeks, ran his tongue around his lips, tweaked his nipples, all done with his clothes on, of course. The bouncers trying to keep a straight face finally came over and made him sit back down. He was hysterical and had everybody laughing.

The dancers all think he's funny. He *is* funny. An asshole. But funny. A funny asshole.

Through all this, Tal's mind is going a mile a minute, and he imagines he'll get one of them laughing — he's got his eye on a large-breasted Swedish blond — all the way to a nice horsy ride on his hilariously hard member. Blondie alone made over $40 from Tal on tips.

The joke was on him.

Then there was Steve.

Steve played the same game he always played with women, the Master of Hard To Get. They always came to him. He sat on the firing line with his arms folded on his chest, leaning back in his chair, above giving even an inch of territory. His body language said 'Come to me, if you like what you see.' It worked. They did come to him. They played his game. But on their terms. They knew the strong, silent type. These arrogant dickweeds were a dime-a-dozen. The girls hung it out there just the way he *made them* do it. Their tits and the lips of their shaved vaginas within a breath of his face. Make him look. Make him smell it. Almost taste it. Let him hold out as long as he wanted to. They had all night.

Of course, there would be the occasional reminder, "Hey, you handsome hunk. I don't do this for free." He would predictably roll his eyes and shell out another buck or two. Or three. Or as the evening wore on, and the whiskey straight-up he was drinking started to wreak havoc with his judgment, he'd shell out a fiver. Or a ten. Just to show these cunts who was in charge. He'd do whatever he felt like doing. He was no slave to a pink pussy sprinkled with a little rainbow glitter, no matter how much they waved it in his face.

The interesting thing was that at the end of the evening, it was Steve who had spent the most money of any of them. Not counting drinks, he had shelled out over $140 getting these bitches to do everything in their power to break him. They didn't break him. No way. He still had the smirk on his face, never said a word to a single one of the girls, and still had $2 in his pocket. Actually, $1.75 but you know, rounding up.

Freddie "Fat Fuck" made no attempt to conceal what a good time he was having. Or his total elation at being so close to so much beauty and sexual potential. Though in some remote and inaccessible chamber of his psyche he probably harbored the incomprehensibly tiny hope of a sympathy fuck from one of these lovelies, he was probably the least delusional of any of the men at the club about the possible outcome of the evening. It was plain and simple. He merely loved what he was seeing, enjoyed every second of it. He was like the window cashier at a McDonalds who would go to the BMW lot to look at a car he knew he could never afford and would never own.

The girls didn't really mind the fat guys. The blobs, as they called them, were the least intimidating, the least likely to get obnoxious and cause problems. The lesser of the evils. There was even the slightest shred of sincerity to the good will they directed toward them.

The dancers still liked to make fun of them in the dressing room.

> *When that fat blimp stands on a bathroom scale I'll*
> *bet it reads, 'Only one at a time, please.'*

> *Holy shit! They probably have to iron his*
> *pants in the driveway.*

I'll bet when that blob wears a raincoat,
people yell 'Taxi!'

Guys always say, to fuck a fat chick you just roll
her in flour and look for the wet spot, right?
With a fat guy, I know where to look.
I just don't know where
the where is!

That fat guys had small penises was a big favorite.

He hasn't got a dick. He's got a scale model.

That blob's got a shrink-to-fit weenie that went
through the wash way too many times.

Fortunately, this was all unbeknownst to Freddie. He just sat there good-naturedly, more than happy to just be in the proximity of a world he knew nothing about and had certainly never experienced. Not even close. For the truth was that F had not only never had sex, he had never ever touched a girl, or even kissed a girl. Not once in his entire life, excepting of course his mom and a few old wrinkled aunts and grandmothers. But that was something else entirely. This was about guys and girls and sex. And outside of the thousands of frequent frantic dates with his own hand he had been having since puberty, Freddie had no concept of sex. None whatsoever. And tragically — though he hid it well behind his happy-go-lucky fat guy persona — he had serious doubts that this would ever change. It looked like a lifetime marriage of convenience between him and Rosy Palm.

Ghost wasn't much better off.

Tonight as was typical, he was wearing a shoulder strap muscle pullover that displayed more of his torso than it covered. His muscles were pumped up like those of a prize fighter just before a championship bout. Interestingly, the thin plastic baggie aspect of his skin, conferred by his extreme albinism, heightened the effect. His pumped veins and the sinewy texture of his muscles literally jumped out of his dermal sheath. He looked like the Incredible Hulk on steroids, who if the tabloids were correct was already on steroids.

Ghost had an interesting effect on the dancers. They thought they had seen it all, but he was so strange looking, he piqued their curiosity. Not only did they talk about him in the dressing room but each tended to give him just a little extra time when his turn came up on the firing line. It wasn't in the least that his features were out of the ordinary. Had he not been an albino, he would have probably been considered fairly handsome. But his coloring was off. Way off. And just the way that the face paint of a mime, by eliminating the normal shades and variation in tone and coloration, can transform an otherwise pleasant face into something comic or even otherworldly, his albinism transformed him into something which seemed outside the human realm. 'Ghost' was the perfect nickname for him, not just because he was so white, but because he really did look like a visitor from the other side, from some world of phantoms and occultist oddities.

Despite this, or perhaps because of it, most of the girls, though they never openly showed it, were intrigued. Little did Ghost know that if these lovely sex goddesses were asked to pick a "favorite" customer from the vast pool of men in tonight's packed house, it was him.

There was another factor in his appeal. While most men brazenly exhibited an overbearing arrogance, an ugly machismo-driven swagger, and right of privilege and claim on the girls, Ghost was quite the opposite. Without seeming weak or pathetic — nearly impossible anyway considering how his imposing muscle bound bulk would intimidate anyone who even casually noticed him — he gave the impression that he really didn't know what he had done to deserve to be so lucky. So incredibly lucky to be here tonight. But here he was. Sitting and staring, mere inches away from such female physical perfection. Unlike other men, when he studied a dancer's breasts or pelvis, or leaned back to savor the innocent beauty of her face hidden under layers of harsh stage makeup, there was something soft and almost feminine in his eyes.

Thus Ghost breathed a refreshing, if brief and very temporary air of civility and kindness, into a room predominantly seething with explosive sexual tension and macho savagery.

Tal yelled out for another round. He was good at keeping the flow of alcohol flowing. The owners of the bar loved the Tals of the world.

The drinks, a sweet concoction Noah had never heard of before called Buttery Nipples, arrived at the same time the next dancer hit the stage.

As Noah sat there, doing his share of looking and leering, something odd occurred to him. Here he was with his buddies, the guys he spent nine hours a day with at work—the same guys he hung out with socially at least once a week. Tonight something was missing. Entirely absent was the usual camaraderie between them. Every time their attention locked on the girls, they were strangers to one another.

In fact, despite the loud music and raucous party atmosphere, there was no sense at all across the entire varied pool of customers there, of a club full of guys out having a good time. He would have thought that if there were any situation where there would be male bonding going on, it would be in a room full of naked girls. Guys hooting hollering. Us against them. All the usual chest pounding and back whapping that you see at football or hockey games.

But everyone here was on his own. Every guy in his own little world.

It was a classic example of being alone in a crowd. But with a testosterone twist.

It wasn't competitiveness. Because each man was convinced there was no competition. Noah concluded that each and every guy there, himself included by the end of the evening, was possessed by an unassailable sense of entitlement, an absolute and exclusive right of ownership.

As they stared at a dancer's nipples, gawked at her supple little butt, gaped at her breasts, and salivated over the thin pink line between her legs — truly a fountain of infinite fascination — each one said to himself: *"That! She wants me to have that. That right there? That's mine!"*

It was astounding. Literally, no one acknowledged the existence of anyone else in the room! When a guy's turn came up for a dancer to ply her charms on him, the others weren't merely irrelevant. They didn't even exist!

Sure. The girl would move along, give each guy on the firing line a little taste of her erotic charm. But each guy sitting there knew the real story. She had to do that just to keep her boss happy. It was just part of the job. She really couldn't wait to get back to *him*. He had something special going on with her. These other guys might as well hang it up.

Then there were the silent auctions. They were really great!

Some guy instead of putting down the standard acceptable tip of $1, would put down $2. The guys around him without telegraphing their contempt would notice. *What a fucking cheap shot! That ugly motherfucker thinks he can buy her. But she's mine. I'll show her how much I dig her and appreciate her.* $3 goes down. Some other arrogant idiot knowing for 100% certain that *he's* the one, plops down $5. A $10 bill appears. Maybe even a $20.

It was this ridiculous, fantastical, delusional, masochistic, almost laughably simplistic cranial malfunctioning, replicated man for man in every occupied seat in the club, night after monotonous night, which the girls counted on. It was what they built their meager fortunes on. Night after night they sold themselves to the highest bidder, kept all of the bids, and never had to deliver the goods.

Now that's a solid business! It was hardly surprising that some of these girls, lacking any marketable skills other than their good looks, kittenish spunkiness, and hot sexy bodies — many lacking even a high school diploma or the capacity to get one — walked out of there every night with $300, $400, even $500.

What an education this was turning out to be! Noah's very first evening in a strip club. Bets were on that they didn't teach any of this at college.

His turn came up. The dancer who was onstage slithered over in front of him. She was down to nothing. So was his drink. He toasted her anyway, popped an ice cube in his mouth, then raised his glass for the waitress to bring him another. Buttery Nipples. Damn good drink when you're looking at a girl's shaved crotch.

Noah usually drank in moderation. If at the end of the evening he couldn't precisely nail the official benchmark for Designated Driver, he was always the most *designatable* driver.

But tonight even drinking in moderation only went so far. He had been there for almost three hours, moving little more than his eyeballs, bringing his dominant hand up just enough to dribble between his lips an overpriced drink, and of course reaching with his other hand into his trousers to get another tip for whatever fine young thing was entertaining him at the moment. Not exactly burning a lot of calories. His alcohol blood level was definitely building up.

Thus it went. The girls came and went. The money just went.

There were only so many girls on duty. They rotated on a pre-programmed schedule. At first Noah took special note of a girl when she came back around. As if their familiarity conferred something special to the unfolding dance. As if they had a relationship, or at least some history, they could continue to build on.

Now he didn't even bother looking at their faces. He just stared. Hypnotized, mesmerized, transfixed, captivated. Captivated and captured by the allure of those anatomical parts which have since the dawn of time assured the absolute enslavement of the male *Homo sapiens* and guaranteed the perpetuation of the human race.

Tits. Ass. Pussy. Tits. Ass. Pussy.

Round and round they went.

Tits. Ass. Pussy. Tits. Ass. Pussy.

A lazy Susan of erotic delights.

Tits. Ass. Pussy. Tits. Ass. Pussy.

If Noah thought he was turned on when he first arrived, now his dick was so hard it could have been used as a jack handle or a crowbar.

Then something happened which brought it all crashing down.

The *Man Up!* had three stages. The Full Metal Jack Its had been sitting at the main stage, but off in the corners of the club were two others, a little smaller but set up the same, with the firing line counter around three sides. They had fewer chairs and provided a slightly more intimate dance experience. Like the main stage, by now all of the seats were filled.

The girls danced three-song sets. At the beginning of each set, a live DJ — he must be somewhere in the club though Noah never spotted him — would announce the dancers.

> *On stage three, to make your mouth water we*
> *have Ariel. On stage two you can fly to Heaven*
> *with Angel. And on the main stage, Crystal will*
> *sparkle and shine cause she just did a line. Keep*
> *those hands where we can see them, gentlemen.*

Noah had stopped listening quite some time ago but for some reason the latest introduction caught his ear.

> *... and making her international stage debut in the*
> *performing arts, tonight on stage three we have*
> *from heartland of America itself, from the flat*
> *farms of Monroe County, Missouri, where women*
> *are women and sheep are sheep and the men can't*
> *tell them apart, the lovely and enchanting Miss*
> *Eleven Eleven Eleven.*

He heard it but didn't really pay it much mind. Even the reference to 11-11-11 dispersed in the alcoholic vapor of his insensibility. It was just some local broad trying to break into this sordid business and make a few bucks. He knew what the girls looked like back home. Anyone of them trying to compete with what he had seen here tonight would be a bad joke.

The music started again. He recognized the tall, thin redhead who was now strutting her stuff back and forth in front of his inebriated face. He should. This was the seventh time she had danced this stage since he had arrived and assumed his place among the other plastered and drooling customers.

Redhead extracted two more dollars out of him and got ready for the last song of her set. She was down to a tiny g-string about the size of a Band-Aid, which would come off next and give the final anxiously anticipated thrill to Noah and the other eleven panting dogs on the firing line.

For no particular reason, just a random movement of his wobbling head, Noah glanced over at stage three, where the newbie was making her debut appearance.

That's when he saw who it was.

Oh my fucking god!

Gretchen!

He couldn't believe his eyes. It wasn't possible. But there was no mistaking it.

The truly surreal thing was how she looked.

She was of course much thinner. That had been developing for some time.

But he had no idea! Nothing had prepared him for this.

He was now seeing in shockingly real 3-D that underneath her baby fat and obtuse clothing had been hiding a very nice body. Perky firm breasts. Shapely butt. A torso which had for so long been a tube was now an hourglass.

It didn't stop there, however. Gone were the snarls of ratty hair, the horrifying paint job that constituted her complete inept attempts at applying makeup. She had three tattoos now and tiny chunks of polished metal in her earlobes, eyebrows, lower lip, and — holy shit! — her nipples.

His own little sister!

This was really fucked up.

Noah felt a kick to the back of his head. Redhead stripper wanted some attention. Actually she wanted to make sure he coughed up some money at the end of her dance. Nothing personal. Each seat on the firing line represented a monetary reward for services performed. She did not want this son-of-a-bitch looking across the room at some other dancer and forget to pay up.

Noah had to force himself to turn back around. He smiled weakly at Miss Redhead, whose name now completely eluded him, slapped a five dollar bill on the counter to comfort her, then used the rest of her dance to regroup, try to clear his head enough to think. Good luck on that.

Gretchen. What should he do?

The music ended. He jumped to his feet. Gretchen was making a hasty retreat backstage. The entrance to the dressing room — or was that undressing room? — was only ten feet away from the stage. She was through the curtain flap of the doorway before Noah even got close.

A bouncer stood next to the door. He eyed Noah suspiciously as he saw him approach.

"Listen. That last dancer. Could I talk to her?"

"If she wants to talk to you, she'll come out."

"No. Really! I need to talk to—"

"Right. You guys all need to talk to her. If I asked every motherfucker in this joint, they'd all say they need to talk to her. Back off."

The bouncer positioned himself directly in front of Noah. He was huge and his bulk pretty much filled the entire entrance to the dressing area for the girls. There was a slight gap between the black velour curtain and the door jamb and Noah stood on his tiptoes and leaned to one side to get a look.

"Gretchen! Gretchen! It's—"

There seemed to be no transition. One second Noah was standing there. The next he was flat on his face on the floor in an arm lock. The pain was excruciating.

Then he was on his feet. Not through any effort of his own. The bouncer lifted Noah like he was a small sack of groceries and was now carrying him toward the exit. Three more burly bouncers appeared out of nowhere and were right behind them.

Tal, Steve and Ghost saw what was happening and jumped up. Fat Fuck was just coming back from the lavatory and joined them. Tal tried to apply some diplomatic charm.

"Hi guys! What's going on? This is my friend. Hey! Come on. He's harmless."

One of the Ten Commandments of bar bouncers declared that troublemakers traveled in packs. Tal, F, Steve and Ghost had just established the precise membership of the pack that Noah belonged to. Two more bouncers appeared. Were these guys dropping out of the ceiling? No one had noticed that a small army of buffalo-shaped guys in black pants and white shirts were there in the club when they walked in. The boys were a bit distracted at the time by a lot of skin.

The Full Metal Jack Its were all now being escorted to the parking lot.

> *Keep those eyes in their sockets, gentlemen. On stage three, we've got a sexy young thing who'll put a bulge in your trousers and make your girlfriend or wife look like a mangy old dog. Yes, it's the delicious and talented ...*

Full Metal Militia

Noah crawled out of bed.

The memory of his first evening in a strip club and its abrupt ending at the figurative end of a large boot — clouded as it was by high residual levels of alcohol in his system six hours later, and clenched in the mean headlock of a throbbing headache — was still vivid.

He could ignore his humiliation.

His hangover was the least of his concerns.

But there was one thing he couldn't handle.

His sister dancing at the *Man Up!*

Noah was totally freaked out. Things were really getting out of control.

Time for action. Drastic action.

It was the last Friday of the month. Payday.

After work, the Full Metal Jack Its all went out for a beer.

The other guys were in rare form and Noah took a sizable ribbing for getting them all kicked out of the club last night. Even the normally silent Steve and the ruffle-no-feathers Fat Fuck got in some good shots. But it was all in good fun and spirits were high.

The jokes eventually had run their course, however, and then the conversation just drifted. Noah seized the moment.

"Guys. I have something serious to talk about. Something I might need your help on."

He laid out the whole deal for them, everything that had happened: The first time he saw the new rough characters in town. His finding the meth lab. The indifference of the cops. His many attempts and utter failure to locate and try to help his sister. Finally his complete shock at then seeing her dancing at the strip joint.

Everything he could think of.

As would be expected, Tal was all over it.

"Your sister was the short haired chick with the great tits?"

"No no. You didn't see her, I don't think. She was off on one of the side stages. But—"

"Well, we might have seen her if you hadn't gotten our asses thrown out of there."

Fat Fuck perked up.

"She had tattoos! And a shaved pussy!"

"They all had tattoos and shaved pussies. Jesus Christ! Are you guys going to come up with something useful here or what?"

Tal moved around the table next to Noah and put his arm around him. Not only was he a true leader but a guy with a sensitive side.

"Listen, dude! We're here for you. You can count on us."

The others raised their glasses and gave Noah reassuring nods. Tal continued.

"Frankly, I think you need a plan. This isn't something we can just jump into blindly. But if these pushers or whoever they are can be ruthless assholes, so can we."

He turned to the others.

"Are you guys with me?"

With about as much enthusiasm as kids walking to school on a Monday morning in a cold blizzard, they embraced his call to action with the ambivalence and degree of trepidation it probably warranted. What after all were they committing themselves to?

Tal sensing their anxiety, quickly walked over the bar and ordered a special round of inspirational drinks.

The five cocktails arrived — a sweet concoction made of butterscotch schnapps and Bailey's Irish Cream — and Tal proposed a toast to the great State of Missouri, to the United States of America and its allies, to God, to Lars Ulrich (drummer for Metallica), to pussy, to tits, to ass, and to the Full Metal Jack Its, "the baddest dudes east and west of the Mississippi. Yo!"

Noah took a sip and instantly recognized what it was.

"Buttery Nipples! This is what I was drinking at *Man Up!*"

Tal gave Noah and the others a smile of cocky assurance.

"See, gentlemen. We're already off to a good start."

The plan was simple and guaranteed to fail. Noah had mentioned that he overheard the big brute coming out of the shed say that the stuff they were using to make the meth was like nitroglycerin, that any fire in the proximity of the shed posed the danger of an explosion.

"So we drive out there, blow up the shed, wait in the bushes and when your sister comes out, we grab her!"

Admiration and confidence in the plan built and finally peaked with the arrival of the fifth round of Buttery Nipples at their table. Tal had just finished detailing his brilliant strategy.

"Excellent!

"Awesome, dude!"

"We'll be on television!"

"Alright. Let's go!"

"Was your sister the blond? The one with that puckery little mouthwatering butt hole?"

Noah, even feeling the glow of the sweet warm syrup coating his tongue, sitting in his stomach like a relaxing evening naked in front of a fireplace with Penélope Cruz, was still a bit uncomfortable.

"Guys. Listen. This isn't going to be a walk in the park."

"Whatever. Let's just do it. Tonight! As soon as the sun goes down."

"It's been dark for three hours."

"I knew that."

They took three vehicles.

It didn't quite go as planned.

On the way into Clapper, they were pulled over by the Sheriff's patrol. None of the drivers passed the sobriety tests. Fortunately, only Steve had something important to do the next day. Spending the night in jail can really cramp a person's style. Steve wasn't behind the wheel and was sent home with a gruff warning and unsolicited advice about the company he was keeping. Noah wasn't driving either but was hauled in on general principles. Something about seeing him on this stretch of road a little too often.

They could have used the time behind bars to refine their plan for rescuing

Noah's sister but instead fell asleep on the metal benches attached to the walls of the community cell.

The next morning, as they gathered their things, thanked their protect-and-serve babysitters for their hospitality, and stepped out into the bright summer morning air, Tal was right back at it, picking up the thread of his concern for Gretchen.

"Was your sister the tall long-haired brunette with the really perky nipples?"

The Slippery Slope

The next two weeks would go down in the collective memory of the people of Pulnick, as the strangest two weeks in its history.

A freak late summer thunderstorm sent fierce bolts of lightning through the high-tension wires that provided electricity for most of Monroe County, cutting service for over 72 hours. Several fires in surrounding fields ignited among the drying weeds, then spread and destroyed over 600 acres of grain sorghum plantings.

Alerted by a school nurse, three children just returning from the summer break were diagnosed by the county health department as having a rare, highly contagious gum disease, sent home from school, and quarantined until further notice.

The oldest sitting member of the Pulnick town council committed suicide. Rumor had it that his wife found out about an affair he had had thirty five years before and he couldn't bear the shame.

A tornado touched down just east of Paris, uprooted a huge forty year old sugar maple tree, then deposited it on the roof of a florist shop right in the center of town, killing the owner and injuring one of his employees.

A tanker truck coming out of Ohio jackknifed and overturned, sending hundreds of gallons of sulfuric acid sloshing across and dripping over the sides of a highway bridge on Route 24. The paint on one of the bridge abutments blistered and peeled. For several days, people visited the site of the accident staring at the cement wall, awed and amazed by what everyone agreed was the face of Jesus Christ looking back at them.

Finally, a few days after Labor Day the body of a young male was dumped in a ravine, doused in gasoline and set ablaze. The body was burned beyond recognition or any possibility of determining exact age or identity. The Saint Louis County Medical Examiner's Office sifted through the bones and ashes and made a educated guess that the victim was between 20 and 28. Since no one in Pulnick or the surrounding communities was reported missing, it was assumed that the individual was from out of the area, probably out of the state, and the incident was a case of random dumping of an unknown murder victim.

Two months later, under circumstances nearly as horrible for him personally, Noah would find out that the incinerated young male was his childhood friend, Phillip 'Zipper' Roswell.

Chapter Seven

September 11 ...

Patriotism 102

It was the tenth anniversary of the destruction of the World Trade Center Twin Towers in New York City and the jetliner attack on the Pentagon.

This would be a big day for the country. Lots of out-of-tune marching bands, red-white-and-blue, hot dogs and cotton candy, flag-waving, endless replays on the boob tube of the jets flying into the Twin Towers and their subsequent collapse, eye-grabbing newspaper headlines like *It's Been 10 Years* and *Our Heroes Will Live On In Memory*, patriotic billboards for everything from toothpaste to tampons to tough stain removers, ceremonial wreathes, stars-and-stripes bikini dancers, a special episode of Jeopardy featuring 9/11 tragedy questions, the release of a book called "Stories of the Twin Towers: A Retrospective" which was a collection of anecdotes by survivors of the victims, and a plethora of related memorabilia trinkets, from key chains to refrigerator magnets to collector's edition ceramic plates.

The television would be full of talking heads, politicians and obnoxious celebrities from all corners of America making completely predictable, pompous, sanctimonious and self-aggrandizing statements about the greatest tragedy to visit the greatest country in the world. How amazing we are. How lucky we are to live here in the land of the free. Blah blah blah.

A good reason to turn off the TV.

It was Sunday. Noah hadn't looked at his mail from the day before. There was a new postcard from Jiff.

**BE A MAN
AMONG MEN**

RHODESIAN ARMY

The written message was another comment on the human condition. What it lacked in erudition, it made up for in heartfelt and virulent racism.

> Dude!
>
> The Army truly sucks!! It's really hard to believe that we ever won a fucking war. These guys are so disorganized. So now they're telling me I might be

patrolling the Mexican border. Like, I want to stand on this side of a fucking chain link fence and watch for a bunch of taco belching border bandits coming in to suck on the American handout tit nipple. Am I supposed to shoot them or give them a chili relleno and directions to the nearest welfare office so they can live off the dole?

Maybe I should've joined the Rhodesian army. I could at least deep 86 some nigglies! Bang bang! Gotcha motherfucker!

Jiffy

Like all of the bigots who insisted on securing the borders, Jiff had such an uninformed perspective on American history. Last time Noah checked, neither Jiffy or any members of his family were Native Americans. How did he think he got here?

The migrants from the south were America's new favorite whipping post for everything that was wrong with the country. Noah thought that a good honest look in the mirror would be a sobering wake-up call for most of his TV-lobotomized fellow citizens. They would be looking at the descendants of the previous batches of immigrants which now populated the country from sea to shining sea. Everyone ultimately was from somewhere else.

There were plenty of Mexicans and other Hispanics in Monroe County. Especially around end of summer when there was harvesting to be done. Noah could honestly say he had never had a problem with any of them, not even once. Not a single incident. Not a cross word.

Then again, he had never spoken to any of them.

God bless America.

For Whom the Bell Tolls

When Cindy Fleischer was nine years old, she stood before her 4th grade homeroom class and announced to the world in no uncertain terms what she was going to be when she grew up. No one in the room, including the teacher, had any idea what she was talking about until she explained.

"You know. At boxing matches. Between rounds. Like after the first round ends, they ring this bell. And a girl comes out carrying a big cardboard sign with a '2' telling everyone that now it's time for the second round."

For thirteen years, she relentlessly pursued that dream, never wavering in her resolve, never questioning whether she would fulfill her passion. Finally, tonight she would make her debut as a ring girl.

As Cindy prepared for the big event, Noah was also getting ready. It was the night of the town hall meeting at Salem First Baptist Church, featuring Pulnick's own Elmer Huck in a public discussion of the imminent alien invasion.

When Noah arrived, with only minutes to spare, he was surprised to see how many people were there. The parking lot was full and cars lined both sides of the lane entering the parish grounds.

He was even more surprised that things were already underway. It wasn't quite 8 p.m. The mayor of Pulnick, Aldous Penthe, hardly a riveting orator by any measure, was mid-speech as people continued to shuffle in and look for seats. They were already filled. Noah joined those he was arriving with in lining the walls of the tiny church, as the mayor droned on about the importance of coming together and being there to support one another in times of crisis and need.

After a final reminder that election day was only three months away and he hoped he could count on their votes — he could — Mayor Penthe brought out the next speaker.

Dr. Theodore Clemus stepped up behind the lectern.

Him again? Well … that figured. Same church. Same dumb crowd.

As good fortune would have it, Clemus was mercifully brief. At least for now.

"As John Donne, the famous 17th Century British poet said, 'Therefore, send not to know for whom the bell tolls. It tolls for thee.' And indeed it does."

Over the P. A. system there was the loud thump and the scratchy sound of a needle being dropped onto a 33 rpm vinyl record. People still had record players? Then again, this was Pulnick. They still lit fires by rubbing sticks together.

The room was suddenly filled with the loud deep ringing of a bell.

A girl emerged from behind a portable screen off the side. A very special girl. Pulnick's own Cindy Fleischer. Barefoot and wearing only a string bikini, she walked across the front of the stage swaying her huge gelatinous hips. High over her head she carried a large cardboard sign with a number on it.

11

A collective gasp went up from the audience. Not that they were anticipating a rip roaring eleventh round. They simply weren't used to seeing in the house of the Lord so much … so much … skin! Flesh! Pulchritude. Overt sensuality. Erotic potential!

Some women shielded their eyes. Some shielded the eyes of their husbands.

Cindy, oblivious to the inherent outrage and general level of indignation she was stirring, just kept strutting her stuff back and forth. Finally, she retreated back behind the screen.

Having seen more than his share of bikini babes — ones who were a helluva lot more sexy and not nearly so pudgy — Cindy Fleischer's immodest display was hardly something to make Noah bat an eye. But what he saw next did.

Elmer Huck stepped out of the wings.

Talk about an extreme makeover!

Elmer was dressed to the teeth — as to the teeth as anyone was dressed in Pulnick anyway — outfitted in a grey three-piece pinstripe suit, a white shirt, which considering his bulk had to have been made by a tentmaker, and a lovely if conservative navy blue silk tie. Noah glanced at his feet under the lectern and noticed that incongruously he was wearing dirty rubber work boots. But at least from the shins up, the man was dressed like he was speaking before a joint session of the U.S. Congress.

As Elmer stepped up on the podium to join Clemus, the putative professor raised his hands to quell the applause which wasn't there.

"Thank you. Thank you. Ladies and gentlemen, I am proud to introduce to you a man who I am sure needs no introduction to you, the fine people of this community. A man whose distinguished reputation as a scientist and visionary speaks for itself."

Scientist? Visionary?

How about fat insane hallucinating farmer with a compulsively masturbating son?

"The distinguished Mr. Huck here, has in the past shared with you some of the insights he has gained by talking with visitors from other parts of God's marvelous creation, this Universe full of mystery and wonders. But tonight he comes to us with some sad tidings and dire warnings. Mr. Huck?"

Elmer cleared his throat and pulled out from the inside pocket of his suit jacket some notes written on wrinkled yellow note paper, glanced at them briefly, then addressed the audience. He was visibly quite nervous, and hazily stared at some point on the rear wall opposite him, high over the heads of the wide-eyed attendees.

"We need to get ready. This was told to me many years ago. But I waited till now because no one would have believed me back then. Later this year ..." He looked at his notes again. "... on 11-11-11 ..." He looked back up at the audience. "... the shit's gonna hit the fan. Thank you."

Dr. Clemus leapt forward and histrionically led at least two other people in applauding Pulnick's own scientific genius as he stepped back off the stage and disappeared in the wings.

For the next hour or so, unfortunately Clemus himself was not as wonderfully brief.

A lot of what he had to say sounded like the same incoherent blather that Noah had heard the first time when he was here with his mother.

But tonight there was some fresh spin. And one new and very significant twist.

"Just look at what we have experienced the past 14 days."

Aha! A whole deck full of fear cards!

"Tornadoes. Acid spills. Suicides. Epidemics. Ditch cremations. Fires. I ask you, my God-fearing friends, do we need any other signs of the coming reckoning? But there is hope. God does not abandon his children."

Clemus then, in the solemn tones of a used car salesman, described a special structure which could shield them all from the onslaught of negative spiritual energies — the "slings and arrows of misfortune manned by the legions of the Devil himself." Inspired by the pyramids, with supporting references from the Bible plus secret blueprints obtained from the archives of none other than Nostradamus, he was making available to persons of sufficient faith, a powerful cosmic and cosmological shield. It was a specially configured tent made almost entirely of tin.

Noah glanced around. People were swallowing it. They were mercifully being saved by one of God's brave soldiers in the fight against the doomsday designs of the Devil.

How touching. How noble.

Dr. Clemus, motivated only out of altruism and concern for the good God-fearing people of this beautiful Bible-belt land of the Lord Our Savior Jesus Christ, Monroe County, Missouri — one of the few remaining bastions of the true faith, in a world which was increasingly becoming a playground for the paganism of Islam and other horrific Godless heresies — was here to provide them what they needed to survive the coming holocaust. A shield. A guarantee. An insurance policy underwritten by the Holy-of-Holies Himself, so that they could go forth into a new post-apocalyptic world, one cleansed of the scourge of evil and sin, to establish and maintain for all eternity a pure Kingdom of Divine Worship. In the name of Jesus Christ. Amen.

Clemus announced he would be available now to talk to people individually.

Mayor Penthe came back center stage dragging a reluctant Elmer Huck. Cindy 'Ring Girl' Fleisher, still in her bikini, followed them unprompted and stood there smiling and waving. Mayor Penthe enthusiastically thanked everyone for coming. The meeting was now adjourned.

Clemus stepped away from the lectern and made his way over to sit behind a table set up off to the side of the podium.

People scrambled from their seats and made a disorderly, not very Christian charge to the front of the church to be first in line to take Dr. Clemus up on his generous and righteous offer.

The official part of the evening's program ended just in the nick of time — right before Noah's gag threshold reached the level which would induce uncontrollable vomiting.

There was so much chaos it was difficult to know exactly what to do.

Mayor Penthe was smiling ear-to-ear. Why, was anyone's guess. A political smile maybe.

Elmer Huck looked dumbfounded. Or just plain dumb.

Noah was tempted to leave. But where would he go? Curiosity and inertia got the best of him, so he hung around, drifting perceptibly toward the stage.

It was bizarre enough that to most everyone's discomfort, the flesh-baring Cindy had strutted around the church earlier in the evening in just a bikini. But still reveling in the glory of her career debut as a ring girl this evening, and completely oblivious to the stares and sniping going on around her, she stood alone, half-naked, blinking and smiling, still playing the beach bimbo card. Noah ambivalently strolled up to her.

"Well, Cindy. Congratulations! It's straight to the top from here."

Cindy just giggled and continued to wink and flirt with anyone who took notice of her.

Right behind her stood Elmer Huck. He was being interviewed by some reporter and Noah couldn't help but eavesdrop.

"Hi, Mr. Huck. I'm from the Riverfront Times. We're the other paper in St. Louis. Anyway, I was wondering how you got tuned into this whole 11-11 phenomenon."

"Well … uh … see one morning I came in from working the fields. I'm a beet farmer, see. So I look up. My clock says 11:11. Then I switch on the TV. What do I hear? The goddamn government's gonna cut my paycheck."

"Cut your paycheck? I'm not following you."

"Government running out of money, they says. Gonna cut all farm subsidies. Across the board. Right across the board! Then they announce it."

"Announce what, sir?"

"The amount. They say they gonna cut farm subsidies by 11%! It all ties together. 11%! 11:11. 11-11-11. What was I supposed to think?"

Over on the other side of the room, Clemus sat at a table. As fast as he could manage, he was handling out what looked like contracts to people reaching over, pushing and pawing one another out of the way, to get at them. These were the "guarantees" he had mentioned. Insurance policies against the inevitability of certain doom. Orders for single-dwelling and family-size tin pyramids which would soon be dotting the surrounding countryside. It was a feeding frenzy. People were filling in the blanks and writing out the checks.

Whoever was behind this — whether Clemus was operating alone or was part of some larger organization — was pulling out all the stops, or what they perceived to be the stops. They had Huck, Cindy, the Salem First Baptist Church, the Mayor. All there to crank up the fear factor, win the loyalty and trust of the local yokels, and empty some wallets.

Noah got the picture.

There was money to be made.

No idiot left behind.

Ka-ching!

Allergy Season

A strange thing happened shortly after Fuller Apothecary was demolished by an as yet unidentified vehicle, driven by as yet unnamed assailants, at ram speed over a month ago. From outward appearances, the drugstore was closed. The front windows of the building at 312 Main Street were boarded up. Anticipating a sizable settlement from his insurance policy, Mr. Fuller had moved to Biloxi, Mississippi to begin an early retirement. All outstanding bills were paid out of his savings and all of the business bank accounts closed.

But from another perspective, that of several of his wholesale suppliers scattered around the country, Fuller had actually expanded his business. Significantly expanded. There now were at least on paper, six branches of Fuller Apothecary, consisting of the original store and a circle of satellite franchises in nearby Shelbina, Paris, Mexico, Monroe City and Perry. They all shared the distinction of having no physical addresses, only post office boxes.

They also shared the distinction of being in an area of the country which appeared to have epidemic levels of common respiratory allergies, usually treated with over-the-counter drugs containing pseudoephedrine hydrochloride. This was the active drug in a number of extremely popular remedies for relief of the annoying, sometimes debilitating symptoms of hay fever: Sudafed, Contac, Claritin-D, Unifed, Zyrtec-D.

More significantly, pseudoephedrine hydrochloride was the key ingredient for making methamphetamine.

With the rapidly spreading scourge of meth addiction becoming the number one drug problem in America, pseudoephedrine compounds were supposed to be a carefully monitored and controlled substance. But the slash and burn policies of a Congress, obsessed with reducing the mushrooming government budget deficit, had so thoroughly gutted the resources of the relevant agencies — specifically the U.S. Drug Enforcement Administration (DEA) and the Bureau of Alcohol, Tobacco, Firearms, and Explosives (ATF) — no one could keep up with it. Despite their valiant and highly publicized efforts, the necessary manpower just wasn't there and a lot was slipping through the cracks.

Thus, no one took special note of the fact that the amount of various over-the-counter anti-allergy remedies being drop-shipped into the several branch stores of Fuller's Apothecary would be more than adequate to serve the combined populations of Kansas City and St. Louis.

Monroe County must be having a real bad allergy season this year.

Blitz and Krieg

If it wasn't being totally orchestrated, then coincidence had become the bastard child of calculation and manipulation.

The day after the town hall meeting at Salem First Baptist Church, a media blitz — or at least what passed for one in Monroe and surrounding counties — filled the local papers, billboards, air waves, shop windows, telephone poles and fence posts, bulletin boards, and even the skies via the periodic use of skywriting biplanes, inundating the region with announcements of the coming of Björn Agynn.

Even Walmart found it impossible to get billboard space for their back-to-school and fall harvest sales, as the event's advertisements became ubiquitous across four counties.

Rapture of the Ascension

"The beginning of the end is not the end of a beginning. Praise God! Let us begin again. To be born again."

Wednesday Sept 28th 10 am - 10 pm

(Next to Rockcliffe Mansion Estate in Hannibal, MO)

"Dearest Lord, our prayers have been answered!"

11 - 11 - 11

For the first time that Noah was aware of, there was a picture of the man prominently featured in the ad.

Björn Agynn.

Wayfarer. Prophet. Visionary. Seeker. Guru.

The man who had seen the frightening face of the Apocalypse and who destiny had chosen to shepherd the weak and the wary of the world through the terrifying days ahead! He was coming to Hannibal, Missouri on Wednesday, September 28th, for a full day of contemplation, spiritualization and triumph over inevitability. It was a celebration of the power of spiritual cognition and eloquent prayer in the face of certain annihilation.

And it only cost $199 per person to attend. A real bargain.

The *Rapture of the Ascension* would be an all day affair held at a 190-acre vacant field adjacent to the Rockcliffe Mansion estate, a historic spread where many prestigious receptions and festivals had been held over the years. The increasingly familiar 11-11-11 logo of course appeared on all of the advertisements, but now they were also adorned prominently with the intense, some thought handsome face of the man who would lead the meditations, prayers and group hugs. The event was going to be Missouri's Woodstock for the end of the world.

Within a few days, it was on the lips of everyone who had lips.

"He is a good friend of Benny Hinn!"

"He knows Rod Parsley!"

"And Jerry Springer!"

"I think he looks like George Clooney!"

"I loved 'O Brother, Where Art Thou?'!"

"I heard he travels in a flying saucer."

*"Foreign governments have tried to kill him. But they can't.
He has powerful angels as bodyguards."*

Mayor Penthe, magnanimous public servant that he was, with the best interest of the citizens of Pulnick in mind, made his office available for ticket sales. In spite of the relatively steep price, they were flying out the door as fast as he could print them. Pulnick would be well-represented that day of glory and brotherhood of spirit in Hannibal.

During the same two-and-a-half weeks that the people of northeastern Missouri were being seduced and brainwashed by all of the promotion for Björn Agynn's *Rapture*, the area was also being visited by a blitz of a different sort. This had no connection whatever with Björn Agynn or 11-11-11 or any of the metaphysical stuff. It was by pure coincidence, that the historically blissful and safe Ozzie-and-Harriet communities of Pulnick, Paris, Monroe City, Shelbina, Center and even Hannibal itself, were now also experiencing something normally only seen in the Bronx or south side of Chicago.

A crime wave had suddenly descended on this pastoral patch of Missouri countryside.

The panicked municipal and law enforcement officials branded them "random altercative and disruptive incidents". Unfortunately, this euphemistic invention could not hide the sinister reality of the situation. It had been slowly and secretly brewing in the equipment shed of an abandoned farm. Now the poison was starting to boil over and bring suspicion and terror to the local residents. If left unchallenged and unchecked it would slowly eat what was left of the delicate frail fabric of this boring, backward, but generally peaceful patch of farmland and small-town cities, dotting mid-America at its plaintive worst.

Between making personal pitches for the *Rapture of the Ascension*, and putting his personal imprimatur on the event by announcing to everyone that he himself had bought over twenty tickets and was taking his family and a number of close friends, Pulnick's Mayor Aldous Penthe with Sheriff Ricky Dean Hoffman at his side, made a public statement under the pealing wood portico of City Hall.

> *"Our God-fearing, peaceful and freedom-loving community has been the random and arbitrary victim of some unusual and disturbing acts of violence recently. Let's just say we are experiencing a few wrinkles in the road. But let me publicly declare that all of this is being brought to an immediate halt. As your mayor, I can unequivocally state*

that we have the situation completely
under control. God bless America."

The known, elected and familiar politicians and officials could declare what they wanted. Some unknown, unelected and unfamiliar miscreants had declared otherwise.

They had declared war on Pulnick and Monroe County.

Mean Streets

The destruction of Fuller's Apothecary back in July had been dismissed as an anomaly. Now it was viewed as a warning shot.

A herald of bad tidings.

A preview of coming attractions.

There were no fatalities on record for the recent spate of criminal occurrences. But there was quite a rash of petty and not so petty disturbances. A bad rash. And the doctor wasn't around to suggest a cure. In fact, the local law enforcement officials, normally addressing nothing more serious than someone backing their car into someone else's fender, or having to give a stern lecture to some kid who had just shoplifted a candy bar, were scratching their collective heads, unable to compute what was happening in their normally straight-arrow little fiefdoms.

At first, because the crimes were scattered over such distances, no individual sheriff's office grasped the larger picture. But the old boys did regularly talk back and forth, exchanging by FAX and email everything from ethnic jokes to pornography. And when they got around to tall-telling about some of the unusual and rather serious stuff going on, eventually it became clear to everyone responsible for keeping the peace in the counties of Monroe, Shelby, Marion and Ralls, that they were in the midst of a shit storm.

In just two weeks, there were three car-jackings, one in Monroe City and two in Hannibal. Five other unoccupied motor vehicles were stolen from residences. One in Paris, one in Shelbina, and three in Hannibal. Several purse snatchings had occurred in broad daylight on two consecutive Sundays in Monroe City and Hannibal, the victims being geriatric ladies strolling home after morning services at their chosen house of worship. At least thirteen houses had been burglarized across the four counties. These were the nicer homes sitting on the newly developed outskirts of several communities. The owners came home to find missing all of their stereo equipment, jewelry and whatever cash might be lying around, plus the nasal decongestants they might have had in the medicine cabinet.

The most frightening incidents, and ones which should have supplied some description of the perpetrators, were nine reported robberies and rumors of several others. But the victims were too embarrassed or had been too drunk to want to engage any active official involvement.

All of these took place at knife or gunpoint. The guns were described as sawed-off shotguns either 10 or 12 gauge. One victim off the record said he felt like he was looking down the barrels of a meat-and-blood explosion of carnage waiting to happen. One point of agreement: Two of the perps were depicted as being WrestleMania-huge, half-human half-animal.

The most spectacular hold up took place on a Saturday night in Palmyra, at a local bar that specialized in Buffalo wings and Coors on tap. Three assailants, all wearing ski masks, two carrying shotguns and one a machete, walked into the crowded bar around midnight, and within 45 seconds had everyone prone on the grimy beer-soaked floor. They proceeded to relieve the terrified customers and employees of their wallets and all their cash, then empty the cash register, before only minutes later, bolting out the door. On the way out, one of the huge gun-toting hulks yelled, "Thanks for the business, assholes!"

The sheriffs finally had something to work with. Look for big rude ape-shaped men wearing ski masks and carrying weapons of personal destruction.

Now they could serve and protect.

Knowledge is power.

Chapter Eight

The Ugly American

Why was there mail? With the internet and cell phone technology, paper was prehistoric. Anything that needed to be communicated could be communicated without cutting down trees.

Noah now only bothered to retrieve his mail once a week. Every day at least twice, he walked by his personal mail box next to the front door, but didn't have the curiosity or inclination to reach over and grab the contents on his way up the stairs. It was a waste of time. Whenever it got to the point where the box could hold no more, Noah would grab the handful of fliers and miscellaneous junk mail which had accumulated, then spend the next twenty minutes throwing all of it piece by piece into the trash.

This time he didn't throw it *all* away.

There were two recent postcards from Jiff. The first one showed some swimsuit model in a bikini. But she was accessorized with belts and pouches full of infantry stuff — grenades, magazines full of bullets, a canteen, and so on. A knife was strapped to her arm and a pistol to her leg.

Completely unrelated to the picture was an update.

Noah couldn't accuse Jiff of subtlety or good taste, that was for sure.

Noah, my man! I'm in Pakistan!

These Muslim girls can really fuck! None of the Muslim guys ever touch them. It's against their religion. So they're like a powder keg waiting to go off. The only problem is that I've like bonked three of them and I have no idea what they look like. It's Halloween 24/7/365 here, with these costumes the women have to wear. After the recent action, now every time I see a burka I get a boner! Ha ha ha ha!!

The local guys here are a bunch of homos. They don't even look at the chicks and some of the young ones are beautiful! The old ones tend to spread and look like big cows walking down the street in tents. But the young babes are hot! I think most of them are virgins. How else could it be? Until I got here, there was no one to shred their lovely little hymens.

… continuing on a second post card which on the front featured the picture of a machine gun and a slogan which should tickle the hearts of terrorists across the globe …

> **I'll see your JIHAD**
> **and raise you a**
> **Crusade!**

There for all the world to read and share was Jiff's message of love and cultural sensitivity.

> Like I said, Muslim guys must be homos. They walk around holding hands and God only knows --- oh excuse me, ALLAH only knows --- what else goes on. I think they might even be fucking the goats.
>
> When are you going to man up and do your patriotic duty? Come on, do your part, Pvt. 1st Class Noah Tass! Spread some American love around the world. I can't do this all by myself (though I'm trying!). My dick is going to get calluses.
>
> Jiffy

Mother Knows Best

Noah would never in a million years consider spending $199 to attend Björn Agynn's all day *Rapture of the Ascension*. But a few days before the big event, a ticket arrived in the mail. The enclosed receipt noted that a Louisa Tass had sprung for the price of admission and had requested that the ticket be mailed to Noah.

He hit speed dial and started in on her as soon as she picked up on her end.

"Mom! You don't have this kind of money to be throwing around. Besides—"

"Noah, this is important. And you are my son."

"Both of those statements are questionable."

"What is that supposed to mean?"

"Just joking. But seriously, I don't want to go to this. This is just a bunch of—"

"The world only ends once, Noah. It's a good idea to be prepared."

"I am prepared. I stocked up on Top Ramen and toilet paper."

"I get it. Trying to be funny. You were always so cute. I'll probably see you there."

Click.

End of discussion.

Rapture of the Ascension

Björn Agynn's much anticipated and fanatically heralded all day *Rapture of the Ascension* was thoroughly unspectacular in all respect but one. That was the amount of money it raked in. With people coming from as far away as Kansas City and Peoria, Des Moines and St. Louis, Indianapolis and Omaha, to jam into the seven gigantic tents set up at one end of the 190 acres of open field next to the historic Rockcliffe Mansion Estate, it was estimated that over 30,000 had come and gone over the course of the day — at $199 a pop.

The tents themselves could have been spectacular, and arguably were when viewed from high above, since they sported several highly recognizable emblems pointed directly at the sky. These included a Christian crucifix, a star of David, the Islamic crescent moon, a giant Yin and Yang, a peace symbol, the Buddhist Wheel of Life, and predictably, a huge '11-11-11'. But only a few passing airplanes would have seen these. The people on the ground were subjected to drab and grimy canvas surfaces, all the worst for wear from the hectic tour schedule that took Björn's *Rapture* to 4 continents and over 25 countries.

The two center tents were joined to form a big auditorium, with folding-chair seating for two thousand. This is where Björn addressed as many people as could fit inside, a sizable number of them crouched in the aisles, lined along the sides, generally compressed and vacuum-packed like human sardines. There was a stage that ran across the entire front of the room, featuring an odd and mismatched assortment of entertainers. There was a Thai dance troupe, five didgeridoo players, three Tibetan Buddhist monks dressed in full ceremonial garb holding huge curved horns and bronze gongs, a barbershop quartet outfitted in candy cane jackets, and to finalize the surreal incongruity of it all, a 20-member satin-robed gospel choir conspicuously lacking any people of color or anyone who could sing.

The onstage entertainment had the potential to be interesting, perhaps even enjoyable, except the entertainers entirely lacked enthusiasm, performing with such unalloyed indifference, it seemed plausible that someone had sprinkled animal tranquilizer on their Wheaties that morning.

The other five tents were filled with every conceivable marginally relevant and borderline insane sort of sales and display booths. Björn Agynn's traveling road show had picked up quite a range of New Age, end time, cult and cloister hawkers from everywhere it had thus far visited, each selling their own version of the disconnect from reality that had snowballed into the 11-11-11 phenomenon. Of course, fundamentalist Christians were there in their sanctimonious severity, as well as a wide variety of other Bible thumpers. These included 7th Day Adventists, Christian Scientists, Mormons, New Apostolics, and Jehovah Witnesses. Uncomfortably mixed in with the Christians were the numerous upstart metaphysical communities: the crystal people, Yoga masters, astral travelers, channelers, healers and spiritualists of every size and shape, and what might be called alternative religions like Scientology and the International Association For Krishna Consciousness. Hundreds and hundreds of booths and stalls combined to create a one-stop-shopping flea market for every imaginable journey of the soul.

There were also some exhibitors which did not quite fit any particular category. All one could say about them was they were uniquely and amusingly enigmatic.

One had a huge banner which asked: *What Is Your Cosmological IQ?*

Frankly Noah couldn't remember this ever coming up before. He was sure he had never been tested for it in high school.

Another sign declared: *The Meek Shall Invest In Gold Futures*

It would be interesting to see how that investment strategy played out after the destruction of the world.

Another queried: *What Is The 5th Dimension?*

If Noah's memory of his mother's record collection served him right, they were a pop act from the 60s and 70s, which had a hit song called 'Up, Up and Away'. That couldn't be right. What were they getting at? It didn't appear that anyone was going find out, since absolutely no one walked up to the booth for the entire day. The bearded man slouched in it was sound asleep.

In sharp contrast to the *5th Dimension* booth, there was another one which was mobbed with people. It was a huge stall with many tables and row after row of computer monitors. Here they were claiming to have an internet connection to the other side, as in the world of the deceased. Their one-of-a-kind uplink-downlink made it possible for a person to contact and converse with someone close to them who had passed away. It was kind of a Facebook for the dearly departed. Dozens of people were typing away in supernatural chat rooms, with hundreds in line waiting for their turn. The whole area was charged with raw emotion, ranging from hand-wringing anticipation to shouts of joy and disbelief to tears of relief and comfort.

There was one variety of display booths that was duplicated many times over, across the spacious dirt floor of the gigantic tents. These displayed and offered for sale the writings of the man of the hour himself, Björn Agynn. Apparently he was quite a prolific writer, as there were over thirty titles available, both hardbound and paperback editions of his wizardly tomes.

Objectively speaking, some of the titles were intriguing. Others were just weird.

"Are You Experienced?"

Wasn't that a Jimi Hendrix song?

"What I Learned From Amelia Earhart"

Make sure there's enough gas in the tank?

"What Goes Up Stays Up"

Fly balls? Hot air balloons? Erections?

"The Science Behind The Séance"

How about the folks behind the hoax?

"God Can't Keep A Secret"

Why should He? And who's going to call Him on it? *'But God, you promised not to tell ...'*

"I Am My Own Siamese Twin"

Like a 3-dimensional Möbius strip? Which one lived when they were separated?

"We Are All Gilbert Grape"

More mash potatoes and gravy, mom?

Some of Björn's time was spent signing copies of his books, but most of it was devoted to conducting special intimate workshops — no more than 20 people at a time — where for an additional fee, select attendees could benefit more directly from the sage wisdom of the man. There were even a handful very special by-invitation-only one-on-one encounters with Björn. The impact these sessions had on three of the participants — all of whom happened to be rather attractive, nubile young women in their early 20s — was evidenced by positive results on their home pregnancy tests two months later.

Björn Agynn did give two addresses over the course of the epic event. One was the long welcoming speech at noon. The other his metaphysical magnum opus, which droned on for an interminable hour to officially close the *Rapture of the Ascension* and finally send everyone dragging their weary bodies and dazed minds to their automobiles, some of which were parked as much as two miles down the road from the site.

11-11-11 naturally was mentioned countless times.

But it was more revealing what was not mentioned. There was nothing about what was going to happen on that date. Only that it would be incredible, mind blowing, cosmic. Nor was any reference made to a rapture or an ascension. Those attending who had been seduced by the title of the event and were expecting to be given some pipeline to Paradise and the keys to the Kingdom, were certainly disappointed. At least the ones were who happened to notice the mystic guru's oversight. Most didn't. Most were either in a hypnotic stupor from listening to Björn's humorless monotone speech, or punch drunk from trying to make some sense of it.

He could have spared the audience hearing all of his long-winded convoluted blather, a serpentine line of reasoning and vapid supporting anecdotes that would have required an army of the most attentive linguistic analysts and sharp-witted scholars to reconstruct into something meaningful.

It wasn't that difficult. Noah got it. It was at best a yawn.

In a nutshell the message was: You can't save the world but you can save yourself.

Armed with this bland bit of encouragement — a smiley bumper sticker for the fatalistic underdogs of the world — and unburdened of $199 plus whatever they were foolish enough to spend at the event itself, people went back to their homes, or maybe their tin pyramids, to await the Apocalypse.

Or something.

Bad Cop Bad Cop

It had been two months since Noah had seen any sign of Gretchen. She hadn't been at the 11-11-11 town hall meeting featuring Elmer Huck. There was no sign of her at Björn Agynn's *Rapture of the Ascension*, though realistically chances of finding her in that huge throng were nil and none.

He couldn't even be sure that she was still in town. The daytime cashier at the Casey's in Shelbina, one of the convenience stores that had been recently robbed, said the owner thought there was a girl with the two ski-masked robbers, standing next to one of the Harleys out by the street, who then jumped on the back as they sped away.

Not much to go on.

When Noah walked into the local Sheriff's Office, something he had never voluntarily ever done before, it was almost as if they had been expecting him. Sr. Deputy Sheriff Bert Toller — this was one of the officers Noah had talked to at the County Fair back in July — was sitting behind his desk, hands clasped behind his head, leaning way back in his chair to offer an unbecoming view of the entire bulbous bounty of his stomach straining the buttons of his shirt to their limits. He was again sporting the standard issue smirk that Noah had been assaulted with when he tried to talk to him that first time. A cold cup of coffee with a thin film of scum floating on top, sat untouched next to the phone. A cigar lay in an ashtray issuing a thick plume of smoke which filled the room with a sickening stench. Deputy Sheriff Maxwell Tandy — at least as fat as Sr. Deputy Toller, and carrying a reputation among everyone under 25 for brutality to the boys and opportunistic fondling of the girls — was sitting on the corner of the desk. He turned slightly to look when Noah walked in. Both of them just stared at him.

No warmth. No greeting. No love.

Tandy picked up the cigar and took a long carcinogenic drag, as Toller finally parted his linguini-thin lips and grunted just one word.

"Yes?"

Noah thought he could pierce their frigid antipathy with a little light joshing.

"I can see you are pretty busy. Maybe I can come back around midnight."

"At midnight we'll probably be rounding up you and your heroin addicted friends in some field and calling to a halt your latest orgy. I just can't figure out with all of the shooting up, smoking crack and whatever else you're doing, why any of you are still alive."

"I guess we're just young and tough."

Noah accepted the hopelessness of telling them that his own personal drugs of choice were beer and Buttery Nipples, or trying to explain to them the enormous difference between the party drugs like Ecstasy and pot typically used by his peers at their so-called raves, and the highly addictive, often lethal drugs like heroin and meth.

"Look Sheriff ... I mean Sheriffs. Everybody knows there's been a lot of bad stuff happening around town—"

"Yeah. A shitstorm of bad stuff. What do you care? Are you part of the problem?"

Noah was taken aback. There was always bad blood between the younger members of the community and the "establishment". Boys liked to party. Girls just wanted to have fun. Domesticated citizens settled into the monotonous rhythm of family life wanted lights out at 9. There was bound to be friction.

But it was obvious that there was some severe undercurrent of hostility here, some simmering disdain that went way beyond that.

"I just wanted to—"

"All of you Tass's are a barn full of trouble. I was around when your father left. I saw first-hand what was going on. Before then and since then, it's been one thing after another. What do you have to say about that, Deputy Sheriff? You probably know better than me."

Deputy Sheriff Tandy looked like he was going to enjoy this.

"Well, to start off, the only people in this town who don't know how crazy your mother is, are the ones crazier than her. And I can't off the top of my head think of anyone that fits that description. I hear your sister is caught up in some loony business. Well, ain't that a surprise!"

"But that's why I'm here. She's missing. She's been missing for over—"

Toller lumbered from the comfort of his chair and stood up.

"Right right right. You think she's out at some farm in Clapper. You think I didn't hear you the first time. I remember what you told me. My memory is like a steel trap."

"They're running a meth lab. I've seen it with my own eyes."

"I'm sure you have."

"Did you check it out?"

"Well, as a matter of fact we did. Not that you have much credibility around here. But on the off chance that you might have stumbled onto something, we did pay a visit to the farm."

"Then you saw—"

"Someone's been holing up out there. Not that unusual these days. There's four million homeless scumbags wandering around this country like it's some big national park and they are on permanent holiday. But no one was there. And there was no suspicious activity."

"What about the shed in back? Didn't you notice a funny smell?"

"Yeah, there was a funny smell. Deputy Tandy here farted in the car on the way back."

They both found this rollickingly funny. It was interesting to see grown men laugh and remain so essentially angry at the same time. Even the hateful like a good joke.

Noah hoped they couldn't read his mind. All he could think was what stupid, worthless, obnoxious creeps these guys were, what a complete waste of taxpayer money sat here filling the room with their lazy corpulent incompetence. He forced himself to laugh along.

"But the crime wave that's been—"

"The 'crime wave' as you call it is just a blip. The state's Attorney General Office says that these statistical anomalies ..." Pronounced 'dese stat-stickel nom-lees'. "... occur from time to time. You see, on the whole crime is down. No thanks to you and your animal friends."

Noah couldn't believe what he was hearing.

And he shouldn't have.

What he didn't know was that, despite the appearances of stupid calm and indefensible lethargy, this Sheriff Department and every single other one in the four affected counties were in a full-tilt panic. They had a big problem on their hands and no one knew what to do about it.

What they didn't tell Noah — in fact had lied to him about — was that when they casually investigated the farm in Clapper just three days ago, they were fired on and driven off the property. Humiliated and outgunned, they returned to Pulnick and were now in the process of planning a siege, led by a highly trained State of Missouri SWAT team, with the assistance of federal agents from both the DEA and ATF.

Noah glanced at the shiny metal name plates mounted above the pockets of their shirts.

"Well, Deputy Sheriff Toller and Deputy Sheriff Tandy. Thanks for your time."

"Anytime. Serve and protect. That's why we're here. Stay outta trouble."

"And trouble will stay outta me."

"You got it."

Shell Game

There are no secrets in a community the size of Pulnick. It took Noah all of 24 hours to find out about the siege on the meth lab farm house. Not only that it was happening, but the date and time it was going to take place.

Early morning October 6. Right after sunrise.

This was something he didn't want to miss. It would be cause for serious celebration if the authorities could flush these venomous bastards out for good. On the other hand, he tried not to get his hopes up too high. As the disastrous siege on the Branch Dividian complex in Waco, Texas back in 1993 had demonstrated — and Noah could still remember watching it on TV when he was a young boy — these things didn't always go as planned.

And then too, what about Gretchen? Noah couldn't help but have serious concerns about what might happen to her, if she was still holed up there. Would there be a big shoot-out? If so, was she stupid enough to try to fight the authorities alongside whatever crazies were bunkered in there?

There was no point in trying to talk to the sheriff department about her. It was already obvious that no one would listen and he doubted if they gave a damn about her welfare. Their view was if she was in there, she either would surrender or get what she had coming to her for the company she kept.

He'd just have to hope for the best.

The morning of the siege, Noah left his apartment a little after 4:30 am. If he was worried as he drove his motorcycle through the cool pre-dawn air about being shoved aside or prevented access to the farm, his apprehensions disappeared as soon as he got there. Apparently, the press had been tipped off and there literally was a media circus already well underway. Broadcast vans and other vehicles bringing cameramen, photographers, reporters and support staff lined the road in front of the property. A yellow-ribboned police line well onto the property itself had been established which offered a good view of the farm house, barn and front yard area. The media had set up their tripods and other video recording gear along that strip of yellow tape and crews were fine tuning camera angles and lens settings for the coming police action. Apparently this wasn't going to be a sneak attack.

While the enforcement officials tended to be quiet to the point of grimness, there was a lot of joking and conviviality among the media types. Confidence was high. Not necessarily that the best efforts of the nearly seventy law enforcement officials would be successful. But that they were going to get some good video footage for the daytime and evening news. Or better yet, that some drama could unfold which would capture the attention of the national and international broadcasting channels.

It was safe to assume that once the request went out from the Monroe County Sheriff's Office, that the Clapper property had been put under close surveillance. That the highly sophisticated electronic monitoring equipment of the DEA and ATF had been employed, that every available form of advanced technology was being engaged to assure the safety of officers storming the buildings, in short, that nothing was held back in terms of bringing the mission to a successful conclusion.

Which made it all the more astounding what they found, after the property had been completely surrounded by over forty shotgun-bearing local Sheriff patrolmen drawn from four counties; after one federal surveillance and two air assault helicopters hovered ominously over the farm house; after the command was finally given and the farm house and equipment shed doors had been kicked down by armored, helmeted, and heavily armed police storm troopers; after the entire property had been thoroughly secured and locked down.

They found some greasy pizza boxes, several cases of empty Pabst Blue Ribbon bottles, candy wrappers, a couple of unused condoms, a back issue of Maxim magazine, and a dead goldfish floating in an unflushed toilet.

The entire meth lab and its inhabitants had moved.

To where was anybody's guess.

Chapter Nine

October 17 ...

Walk Like an Egyptian

Tin pyramids everywhere. Stooped over Pulnickians were seen ducking in and out of them. To Noah it looked like they were going inside to collect the fresh eggs. Or make cave paintings. Or see if the hickory ham was done smoking.

Some of the pyramid dwellers had seen fit to get a jump on 11-11-11 and had already set up housekeeping. Late at night, the flickering glow of television screens could be seen through the entryways. Dogs sleeping outside looked quizzically at the flimsy tin structures as if to ask, 'Why am I out here and they're in there?' Bird droppings collected on the painted tin roofs. The sky was falling. Shit happens.

It was easy to see why all of this was occurring here. Nature abhors a vacuum. But when nature doesn't fill it, humans will surely come along and do the job. Sometimes it's a wise man. Sometimes it's a bullshit artist. Sometimes it's a bullshit artist disguised as a wise man.

Or several such malefactors.

If there's money in it.

Against the numbing simplicity and flat line monotony of their sub-ordinary lives, the *Rapture of the Ascension* for the residents of Monroe County had been a big deal. A really big deal. Quickly forgotten was how lackluster Björn Agynn himself was personally, how incoherent his message was, what a incomprehensible hodgepodge every aspect of the entire event had been, and what a blatant and unabashed cash grab it had turned out to be. Forgotten was the boredom of listening to Björn speak, the weariness and induced torpor of wandering around for 12 hours in hot threadbare dirty tents, looking at a seemingly endless array of nonsensical kaka. Pride in just being able to say *"I was there"*, and enthusiasm for everything 11-11-11 had taken on a life of its own. It just kept growing and growing in the telling and retelling of stories about what many characterized as the biggest day of their lives, the day under the big top of a world-famous spiritual leader all the way from Sweden, all in preparation for the biggest thing that would happen in the entire Universe since God had sat down on the seventh day and declared 'Mission Accomplished' — the impending Apocalypse, the final encore, big boom and doom, the Grim Reaper's roundup, last call, Rapture, Second Coming, the zippity-do-dah, crimson curtain cul-de-sac, deep space crematorium, check-out time, the autobahn to nowhere, or whatever the hell was on its way.

As vague and ill-defined as people's expectations were, as to what exactly was to occur on 11-11-11, anticipation and borderline hysteria was easily being whipped into the frothy foam of fear by ongoing national media attention to the topic. Reinforcing this locally, fuel was in no small part being added to the fire of foreboding through the magnanimous entrepreneurial efforts of Dr. Theodore Clemus in a silent partnership with Mayor Aldous Penthe.

It wasn't in these fine gentlemen to abandon the frightened flock, leave them in the lurch, jettison them like worthless wastrels into the slapdash slipstream of ex hypothesis extinction. Hardly could they call themselves men of God and followers of Jesus Christ, were they to just turn away and let the good people of Pulnick and other area communities suffer the annihilating effects of whatever was heading their way.

Based on the excellent research of Dr. Clemus, and the ungrudging capitalization by Mayor Penthe and a coalition of a few of the well-to-do who had supported his meteoric career in politics, a build-on-demand fabrication shop was set up to provide the necessary cosmological-ontological-theological astrological shelter from the storm. A finely orchestrated advertising blitz kept the public informed of its options.

Billboards were popping up everywhere. Pictured were two models of the tin alloy pyramids, one blue and the other white.

To add some spiritual clout to the huge ads, they also included a big picture of Björn Agynn, quoting him as saying *"The end is just a new time to begin."*

Noah himself passed on buying a tin pyramid. It would have only marginally been an improvement on his apartment, and certainly not have been as roomy.

However, the mania for setting up housekeeping in a metal shelter smaller than a garden tool shed, did impact him personally. Merkel Industries was now swamped with orders for raw sheet metal of the tin alloy variety. Consequently, the already-screaming engines of production were revved up even higher, and Noah found himself working seven days a week, ten hours a day, with no end in sight. Other than, of course, the end of the world itself.

Effectively, Merkel was pushing tin out the door like there *was no tomorrow!!*

As a result, Noah was too slammed to do much of anything, much less take the few precious moments of free time he still had, to listen to his mother's caterwauling about Gretchen. He assiduously avoided home.

As did Gretchen still.

His mom called him and left several messages about how much she missed her baby, that thanks to Noah she was probably dead, that if he loved his sister he should find her, and if he hated his sister then shame on him, Gretchen was a good girl, and she was a good mom and how could Noah turn out to be so uncaring and heartless. Noah felt like he had been kicked in the balls. He didn't return her calls.

He hadn't given up on his sister but had to be honest with himself about it, if not equally candid with his mom. As far as he could see, his hands were tied and any effort he put forth at this point was the impossible confronting the inevitable. What was going to happen simply was going to happen. What that was certainly was anyone's guess. In the meantime, he would take advantage of the windfall in wages he was experiencing, put the money aside for the distant day when he would try to jump the Riker's Island moat around Pulnick, and finally escape to whatever was out there — which no matter how you cut it had to be an improvement on what was in here.

As if to reinforce his complete antipathy toward Pulnick and his fatalism about the immediate future, the "random altercative and disruptive incidents" continued unabated. If anything, they appeared to be increasing, both in frequency and severity. The cops were such useless dorks. They couldn't find a criminal in a high-security prison.

Noah truly wished he could put some stock in what the idiotic 11-11-11ers were saying. One thing was obvious. Mankind certainly had a lousy track record. Its days *should be* numbered! War. Famine. Genocide. Racism. We-ism. Me-ism. Greed. Ignorance. Intolerance. Idolatry.

How *could* we claim that we deserved to keep going? As if anyone could look at human history, hook their thumbs in their suspenders, rock back on their heels, hold their head high and declare: *'Yup! We've done a mighty fine job here. Mighty fine!'*

Moreover, God as described in the Old Testament is a pretty cranky son-of-a-bitch. If He does exist and has half a brain, it seems unlikely He's going to put up with our nonsense forever. It *is* His call. And He *is* given at times to throwing some very serious temper tantrums.

He's probably overdue for one right now.

Sometime around 990 BC, the ancient Egyptian Pharaoh Amenemope in his Instructions on Wisdom said:

Man is clay and straw,
And God is his potter;
He overthrows and he builds daily,
He impoverishes a thousand if He wishes.

Sometime in the mid-80s, the pop band the Bangles went into the Sunset Sound Factory in Los Angeles and recorded their hit song "Walk Like An Egyptian". The tune opened with timeless profundity:

> "All the old paintings on the tombs
> They do the sand dance don't you know
> If they move too quick (oh whey oh)
> They're falling down like a domino"

Sometime around 8:30 pm on September 11th of 2011 at Salem First Baptist Church in Madison, Missouri, Elmer Huck told the audience:

> *"Later this year ... on 11-11-11 ...*
> *the shit's gonna hit the fan."*

What else is there to say?
Oh whey oh.

Mission Implausible

"You run the farm. We'll run the lab."
"What lab?"
Elmer Huck, who looked puzzled 99% of the time anyway, really looked puzzled now. Confused but not especially threatened. Not much could surprise him anymore. He had just walked into his house to find six complete strangers making themselves at home. They were drinking his beer and had already made serious progress on two jumbo-size bags of potato chips and his favorite snack, chocolate pretzel sticks.

It was a few days before the combined armies of the DEA, ATF, Missouri SWAT, and local constabularies would mount their assault on the farm in Clapper and come up empty-handed. Elmer found himself sitting before a motley contingent who claimed to be emissaries from the very race of extraterrestrials, upon which he had built his questionable and marginally international reputation.

A young man about his son's age who Elmer vaguely recognized, was doing the talking.

"You are friends with the Pleiadians, right?"
"I've met with them many times."
"When was the last time?"

"It's been a while. A long time ago."

"But you know how they think. You know their plan."

"Well … uh … yes."

It had to be a qualified 'yes' because all of Elmer's alleged conversations with the Pleiadians had taken place in dreams. Very special dreams. Occasionally even he was haunted by doubts.

Elmer joined the air force when he was nineteen. It had been his only option. He was shipped overseas, and it was while he was stationed for over a year at Clark Air Force Base on Luzon Island in the Philippines as a mechanic, that he discovered the joys of opium. Manilla, on the mainland but a mere forty miles away, offered every form of depravity and hedonism which American servicemen were willing and anxious to buy, but it was the opium dens secreted deep in the dark alleyways of Chinatown which held an irresistible lure for the young impressionable Elmer. There he discovered how the dense pain of reality could be replaced with the light euphoria of alternate worlds, dreamscapes he could define and walk through, no longer as a weak and helpless loser, but as the commander of his own fate. There he made a friend that would be his constant company over the rest of his life.

As a boy, Elmer had been as brilliant as he was unappreciated. His parents had no mechanism by which they could understand or measure their son's enormous curiosity, dazzling imagination, his achievements in school, his precocity and intelligence. Neither had made it past the eighth grade. They were hopelessly ignorant and proud of it. If they had somehow noticed how gifted their young Elmer was, they might have resented it, but since they didn't, they credited their dogs with more practical worth and genuine talent than they did their son. People would ask young Elmer what he wanted to be when he grew up. When he replied either an astronomer or an astrophysicist, his parents just laughed through their mostly missing teeth, believing he had just made up some words to be funny.

His teachers recognized what a gifted child he was, and of course offered him every possible encouragement. But by the time he reached high school, the vacuum at home had suffocated him. As his parents drowned themselves deeper in the whiskey they consumed with addictive abandon, Elmer was forced to do more and more on their meager, unproductive farm. Enslaved to seven days and long hours of tedious manual labor which kept the family and the pantry shelves from ever being empty of Jack Daniels, but accomplished little else, the boy was usually permitted a few hours of much-needed sleep, but no time for that "silly book-learnin' stuff." He fell further and further behind in his class work and eventually graduated high school with just above a C average. The poverty of his life was absolute. There was no money for college. There was no love and appreciation for anything about him other than what his strong arms and back could provide. There were no hopes and aspirations that reached any further than a hand stretching to pour another dirty glass full of the brown liquid opiate of today's dead zone stupor. A cirrhosis of the spirit spread through the entire household, and soon the bright flame of Elmer's idealistic dreams and youthful passions became the doused cold embers of despair and resignation.

With no hope of continuing his education, he joined the Air Force. After three years of active duty he came back to Pulnick, to find that the family farm had fallen into total disrepair and dysfunction. He threw himself back into working the land, while attempting to care for his parents — also in total disrepair and basically dysfunctional — two withered and decaying people who never seemed to tire of proudly toasting with copious amounts of hard liquor, his recent service to his country. It was not long after, that he buried them both. They died only a few weeks apart, within a mere fifteen months of his return.

Elmer spent the next few years rehabilitating the farm, got married, and started his own family. Through all of this, completely unknown by anyone he came in close or casual contact with, including his immediate family, he carefully orchestrated the regular delivery by clever machinations and a number of highly secretive arrangements, an ongoing supply of the black tar he was now completely addicted to.

It was not stupidity, or a neurological deficiency, or a congenital impairment, or any other physical or mental handicap which conspired to create Elmer's big dumb clod oafishness. It was merely that for a good part of his waking life, the man was stoned.

Nor was it an intentional act of fraud, a set of carefully calculated lies, a grandiose bit of mischief by design, that Elmer told the world of his wild side encounters with space aliens. Because as real as the dreams of life are for all of us, he saw and met and hobnobbed with his friends the Pleiadians, in the reality of the opium world within which he lived.

As opium dreams go, these encounters originally started out as mere vignettes, little puffs of entertainment that relieved the boredom but quickly blew away. These later evolved into complete stories, full of excitement and friendships, eventually assuming a powerful reality of their own. It was a reality that was far more compelling and certainly much more preferable, than the reality of his bland mediocre life, one which was a constant and demeaning reminder of how far short he had fallen of his boyhood aspirations to become a scientist.

If there was a time when he might have weaned himself from the opium, it was just before he got married. That window passed. Soon after, he was possessed by a loneliness that was the darkness of despair itself. He sought out and married a woman, who he only found tolerably attractive, never loved, probably never even liked, then eventually sired two children, who even in his doped-up state could see were at best mutants, at worst some sort of curse from a malevolent God up to pranks Elmer could not fathom, much less forgive. His fate was sealed. The routine trips two or three times a day to a special place in the back of the barn, the midnight puffing astride his tractor, and the dreams which became the floating fabric of his alter-life, followed as regular a rhythm as breathing itself.

Elmer's existential recipe was now, and had been for as long as his opiated memory would serve, the perpetual making of the dish of survival. Nothing mattered beyond keeping himself and his family alive. He lived in the now to survive the now of tomorrow and the now of tomorrow's tomorrow. He tilled the soil, the soil gave back what little it gave. He filled out the government forms and the government gave back what little subsidies it gave. He talked to his friends from the stars and they gave him the stories of worlds beyond our imaginations for him to share with the impressionable public, make a few bucks, and experience a tangential taste of what it might have felt like to be a respected man of scientific learning.

What the curious contingent sitting in his home that day in October proposed — these strangers who claimed also to know and speak on behalf of the Pleiadians — didn't fall outside the scintillating circle of illusion that circumscribed Elmer's ever-evolving dreamscape. They wanted to set up a laboratory to do some special experiments, and for convenience live in one of the small buildings at the back of his property. They would compensate him, and better yet, if their "experiments" turned out to be fruitful, allow him to share in the adulation and spotlight. Since his career as a media darling could use a boost, and his bank account always welcomed a few more greenbacks, he agreed.

Two of the members of the contingent Elmer had never seen before. They were brooding and bestial. They didn't utter a word, but merely sat back and drank his beer, looking mildly amused, and not so mildly sinister and dangerous. Two local boys, who Elmer faintly recognized, did the talking. There was also a girl. She looked terrified and terrifying. Terrified of her own mortality. Terrifying in the explosive potential for self-immolation that blazed in her darting, dilated eyes. She had a tattoo that caught Elmer's eye.

"11-11-11? What do you know about it?"

"That this is this and that is that."

"Oh? And so what is *that*?"

"The end ... nothing."

"Nothing? You mean death."

"Fuck you! No! Fuck fuck fuck! FUCK!"

She was still crying when the others led her out the door to settle in their new quarters.

Mischief Night

Mischief night — also called Devil's Night in places like Detroit and Chicago — was still alive and well in Pulnick, despite its near extinction in most of the country.

This was the night before Halloween when a community was subjected to a battery of innocent and not-so-innocent pranks by the local youth, mostly adolescents. These ranged from soaping and waxing of automobile windows, toilet-papering trees and the fronts of houses, graffitiing walls and billboards, letting air out of tires, stacking or hiding lawn furniture, putting foaming bubble bath or detergent in fountains, slingshotting passing cars with marbles, trying to get all of the dogs in the county or at least within earshot simultaneously wolf howling, and even placing burning paper bags of cow poop at the front door of select town curmudgeons, then ringing their doorbells and running like hell.

Noah's phone rang again. This was the eighth time in the past 30 minutes. His patience had run out. He grabbed it and yelled.

"Fuck you, you demented asshole!!"

"Help me ..."

It was Gretchen.

"Noah ... you've got to help me ...."

She sounded drugged. Her words were sluggish and slurred.

"Gretchen! Where are you?"

"Elmer Huck's—"

Suddenly he heard a muffled scream and the phone on the other end drop to the floor.

Did she say Elmer Huck's? What was she doing out there?

Noah bolted out the door and was buttoning up his shirt as he leaped onto his motorcycle. It was cold and he hadn't grabbed a coat. He would just have to shiver. Within less than a minute of the call, he was on his way to Huck's sprawling farm.

When he pulled up, he saw the old man himself. Elmer was sitting on his tractor at the end of the drive which led onto his property. He was not in a good mood.

"Go away."

"Mr. Huck. I'm Noah Tass. Is my sister here?"

"Go away. Don't bother me."

"But sir. Please. I just got this call—"

Elmer pulled a rifle from a holster that was hidden from Noah's view. He brought it up to his shoulder and pointed it at Noah's chest.

"Maybe I need to show you what 'go away' means. If you don't leave, you will go away. Forever."

There was no doubt in Noah's mind how mentally compromised the man was. He just had never seen or suspected Elmer had a violent side. The man was such a big garden slug, an amorphous bag of unruly mucous. Was he bluffing? Noah decided to not take any chances.

"Have a nice day. Good luck. It's mischief night."

"That's the point. Nobody's getting away with anything this year."

Elmer's prediction was premature and ultimately very wrong.

As much mischief as was inflicted in and around Pulnick and the surrounding farm estates, it tended to be fairly evenly and randomly distributed. There was one exception to this rule. That exception was the inordinate amount of harassment Elmer and his family had to endure every October 30th.

They were an easy target. Elmer was considered a nutcase, with his stories of flying saucers and extraterrestrials. Harassment and ridicule followed his son Findley around like a shadow. His personal appearance alone brought out the worst in everyone who saw him. Findley's unsightly sister Charlotte — three years older — was type cast for *The Exorcist*. After the possession! She predictably had an obsession with witches, and the guileful look in her eyes could instantly make a Navy Seal pause and head back into the water. The mother of the clan, Regina Eloise Huck, whose antithetical obsession was with the Holy Virgin Mary, had literally hundreds of statues, figurines, pictures and the like, everywhere in the house. She dressed in turn of the century — the 18th Century — peasant garb, her hair looked like she had tumbled in a clothes drier on the heavy garments setting, and she constantly emitted a rumbling sound from her nicotine caked lungs that sounded like a didgeridoo in a fruit cellar. The Huck family made the Addams family look like the Kennedy's of Hyannisport.

The tradition of gathering like a small guerilla army on the edges of the Huck property and conducting mischievous sorties over several hours starting at sundown, had been going for nearly two decades.

This had apparently prompted the guard duty Elmer was doing this year, when Noah drove up mid-afternoon. Unfortunately, too many hits on the opium pipe, discrete as they were, rendered Elmer out of action by the time the sun had gone down, and he staggered a serpentine but generally westward course to see where the big light in the sky had disappeared to.

The tractor was still parked at the head of the driveway and became the first target for the mischief night pranks. It was spray painted the colors of the rainbow and then some.

The several mischief-makers then worked their way onto the sprawling property and spread out to find more inviting targets for their battery of tricks and annoying pranks.

Shortly after his two mutant children were born — this would be in the last half of the 80s — Elmer had partially cleared a copse of medium-growth trees in a back corner of his land, then used the cuttings and bought lumber to creatively erect three small buildings. One was a mini-barn which had no particular value other than its barn-ness. Another was a multi-tier tree house. Lastly there was a cottage.

The idea was to have a place for him to get away from his family. The aggravation and sheer perplexity which they caused in him, no amount of opium abuse could possibly mitigate.

It ultimately worked in both directions. At first, he was the one who slipped out of the house when no one was paying attention, which was most of the time, taking his pipe and the black tar of his dreams with him. Usually he drove the tractor and if he puffed enough along the way, often — especially during the hot summer months — he never made it into any of the new structures themselves but remained seated on his tractor, a happy happy dreaming man under the vast starry skies and all of the possible adventures they contained. Most of his encounters with the Pleiadians unfolded this way.

After Findley reached puberty, he suddenly took a hankering to spend time "out back", as the family called it. He was a new and enthusiastic fan of waxing the carrot and was always looking for new private places for the delicious pleasantries autoerotism. About the same time, his sister Charlotte was beginning to convene her first coven meetings, typically choosing the tree house for the witch sorority gatherings. With the kids out of the way, Elmer only had to wait for his wife to begin her hours of mantras with the plastic rosary she carried everywhere, and he pretty much had the house to himself.

The Huck property was well-charted territory for the pranksters that came around every year the night before Halloween. As usual, this evening's group of marauders started with the main house, egging the front of the barn-shaped dwelling and Regina herself — also barn-shaped — as she angrily screamed very un-Holy-Virgin-Mary-like obscenities at them from the porch. Her screeching and deep-lung rumblings were the only deterrents available, with Elmer out looking for the edge of the Earth, and her kids upstairs hiding under their beds.

The troublemakers next fanned out military style, to graffiti the barn with spray paint, set a huge nearby pile of hay on fire, sending the chickens and ducks scrambling for their lives, dripping candle wax all over the family car, emptying the tool shed of all its implements, and spray painting the cow to look like a psychedelic zebra. While this was going on, three of them headed for the back area where there was some conspiratorial talk about burning down the buildings. This was a very feisty group this year.

The structures at the rear of the property were where the meth lab and its executors had set up housekeeping. The lab was in the mini-barn, six of them lived in the cottage, and various numbers coming and going partied in the tree house.

Of course, as they approached, the mischief-making marauders had no way of knowing any of this. They did notice lights on in the cottage and some shadows in the tree house from a flickering candle or lantern.

The barn was closed up tight and there were no windows. But light filtered under and out through the cracks in the loose-fitting main door. An acrid-smelling smoke belched out of an improvised chimney cut through the roof. Empty cardboard boxes were piled on both sides of the main entryway, and large ten-gallon cans of some chemical liquids were neatly stacked just off to the side.

The pranksters whispered to each other, improvising a plan as they edged to the entrance. One held a cigarette lighter and a box of powerful M-70 firecrackers, sure to scare the shit out of Findley and Charlotte, who they assumed were hiding somewhere in or around. Who else could it be?

Unfortunately, in the darkness one of them bumped a stack of empty boxes and it came tumbling down. A sneak attack was no longer an option, so several firecrackers were handed around and hastily lit. They decided to create a reprise of the 4th of July for the two mutant Huck siblings.

Suddenly, the barn door opened and two huge gorilla hulks wielding shotguns burst out. Floodlights switched on, illuminating the area in front of the barn. And there they were. Three young deer caught in the headlights, lit fireworks in hand, conspiratorial grins and giggles replaced with the wide-eyed terror of staring into the barrels of two shotguns aimed squarely at them.

They tossed the firecrackers.

One of the hulks fired. Then in quick succession the seven firecrackers went off.

Two of the pranksters turned to run.

One of them tripped and knocked over a 10-gallon can of ether, one of the highly flammable solvents used in the manufacturing of crystal meth. The lid was loose just sitting on top of the can. The ether instantly caught on fire and a ball of hot flame drove the two gorilla hulks back and at the same time ignited the dry wood of the barn. The gorillas started to yell.

"Holy shit! Get out of there! Hurry! We got a fire."

Out came two young men and Gretchen. They started running.

The intense heat caused two more cans to ignite and explode, sending Napalm-like sheets of flames in every direction.

The two pranksters were fleeing as fast as their feet could carry them but then stopped when they realized their third was not with them. They looked back to see what was left of him laying in a pool of blood on the ground, a sloppy meat grinder pile of entrails pouring from the enormous hole in his stomach.

That was when the whole thing went up. The entire lab blew and in an instant consumed the barn in an explosion that could be seen and heard for miles around. The heat from the fiery blast set surrounding trees on fire, completely incinerated the tree house, and even charred the facing of one side of the cottage fifty yards away.

It was not your typical mischief night.

This one would claim the life of two people, and leave three others very seriously injured.

It would also put an end, at least for the time being, to the scourge of having a high octane meth lab right in the heart of the otherwise pastoral community of Pulnick. Something the sheriff's department and elite teams of drug law enforcement officers from both the state and federal governments, had not been able to accomplish.

A little mischief goes a long ways.

Family Reunion

Only twelve more days before the world ended.

But never mind about that.

It was Halloween!

Pulnick, unlike its urban counterparts where the risks of having kids roam the streets decked out in costumes were too great, celebrated a version of the holiday more like it had been in "the good old days." Downtown at least, youngsters as young as three and as old as fifteen, wandered the neighborhoods and scrambled from door to door, shouting, "Trick or treat!" hoping to fill their bags with everything from candy and gum to popcorn and fruit.

It was not quite the same cause for celebration and general giddiness for Noah.

True. The Tass family was back together again. Reunited. But it was in the Burnett Burn Center at the University of Kansas Hospital in Westwood, Kansas, a suburb of Kansas City.

Noah and his mom took a motel room nearby and would spend every day at the hospital, and every moment the medical staff would allow at Gretchen's side. This was limited since she was in very critical condition. But they got into the ICU section at least twice daily, for up to an hour.

Gretchen had been burned over 30% of her body. Her hair was completely gone. Most of her injuries were on her backside. Her back, shoulders, scalp, neck. Some burns on her chest as well. Her 11-11-11 tattoo was still there, but under the blistering of freshly barbecued skin.

Barring further complications, she was expected to live.

Unfortunately, there were further complications. With the urgency to treat her open running blisters, put dressings on her cooked flesh, and keep massive infection from setting in, there was no immediate comprehensive evaluation of the overall state of her health, which had been severely compromised by her near-starvation diet and extreme abuse of methamphetamine over several months. The fragility of her system became apparent, however, when her second day there, she suddenly slipped into a coma. Not long after, of course, a battery of tests revealed just how much damage her liver, kidneys and heart had suffered, not to mention her nervous system, which was functioning about as well as a toaster oven just struck by lightning.

She came out of the coma next day and by the evening was for a few short minutes somewhat coherent — as somewhat coherent as she ever was.

"How do I look?"

Noah almost said *'Like the barbecue sampler plate at Buffalo Wild Wings.'* He caught himself in time.

"Like a beauty queen."

"Is my lipstick smeared?"

"Define smeared."

She started crying.

"They killed Phil. Those fuckers killed Phil!"

"Killed … what … are you sure?"

She started to become hysterical. A sudden brief reprise of her typical venomous self.

"Am I sure? Am I fucking sure?! Noah, you are such an asshole! Asshole! Asshole!"

Two nurses came rushing into the room and signaled to Noah and his mom that they should leave. Noah walked his mom out to the waiting room, as one of the nurses administered a sedative to Gretchen.

His mother was wearing what looked to Noah to be a black satin formal evening gown. She had so much costume jewelry on — all of it pearls of one variety or another, mounted and strung together in tangled loops and other confounding configurations — Noah feared she would develop a hernia. She had said nothing all day, to either him or Gretchen.

Suddenly as if she had just emerged from a coma herself, she turned to Noah. Her eyes were full of anger and accusation.

"This is all your fault. You should love your sister. But you've always hated her."

Anger Management

Noah had been angry most of his life.

He was angry about his father leaving and abandoning them.

He was angry that his mom was demented, his sister a bitch, and that they were both fashion fruitcakes.

He was angry about the pure dumb luck of being born and raised in such a godforsaken place as Pulnick.

He was angry at his teachers and schools for imprisoning him and wasting twelve years of his life, while perpetrating the fraud that he was getting an education.

He was angry about big trucks and bad truck drivers.

He was angry that Michael Jackson died.

He was angry about Christianity and how perverted the message of Jesus had become.

He was angry about young people and old people and people in between, cowering and afraid, being manipulated and bullied and bled dry.

He was angry about Walmart and anything to do with shopping.

He was angry about being lied to and insulted by corporate America.

He was angry that the rich got richer and the poor got poorer.

He was angry about the military and the constant clamor for war.

He was angry about television and movies and music that numbed and dumbed everyone down into becoming docile robots.

He was angry about computers and YouTube and about his own obsessive-compulsive addiction to them.

He was angry about smart phones and Facebook and Twitter, because by falsely creating the illusion of belonging to a community, they reinforced loneliness and perpetuated isolation.

He was angry about the sameness, the maddening homogeneity of it all.

He was angry that the best minds of his generation — not that he had met any personally, certainly not in Pulnick — were having their talent and time frittered away on thankless dehumanizing jobs and empty desensitizing frivolities sold to them as entertainment.

He was angry at himself.

He was angry that he was so smart but acted so stupid, angry that he knew better, but just continually reinvented his own mediocrity.

He was angry at his own stubborn complacency.

He was angry for being able to see what was wrong but doing nothing to

166

right it.

He was angry at his own vulnerability and naiveté and powerlessness.

He was angry at his limitations, especially the ones he imposed on himself.

He was angry he had never seen a solar eclipse or saved a dog from being euthanized at the dog pound or known his grandparents or thrown a coin in a fountain and made a wish or ridden a horse or met Susie the MTV VJ or read the Constitution or even been to another country.

He was angry about hate crimes and highway litter and food additives and Wall Street and global warming and road kill and nutritionless white bread.

He was angry about over-the-counter drugs and infomercials and Hollywood gossip and flat tasteless beer and political pundits and rich politicians.

He could go on and on and on.

But sitting there in the waiting room, looking at his mother, seeing her and hearing her in that moment accuse him of hating his sister …

Something happened.

He had just suffered an insult of cosmic proportions. Hurtful, demeaning, humiliating recrimination from the woman who had birthed him. A baseless indictment so dissociated from reality it would have been laughable had it not been so corrosive. It was a moment of infinite sadness, galling absurdity, total helplessness, harsh injustice, abysmal rejection, an offensive disconnect from reality, a bludgeon to his integrity, a knife to his heart. It was a moment when his anger should have reached heights, intensity, proportions he had never felt before.

But …

Instead of feeling anger, instead of reaching some nuclear critical mass, instead of being justifiably infused and consumed with animal rage and fury, he felt his whole being empty of every possible human emotion. The cup that should have runneth over, emptied and became a sparkling clean pristine receptacle, as clear as the purest crystal, devoid of even an infinitesimal speck of contamination.

And for the first time in his life, he felt the gentle, calm, mothering comfort of peace.

Peace.

Total and absolute peace.

Plus a sure understanding of how it arrived.

Hopelessness can only exist where there is the possibility of hope.

Not even a vacuum can exist in the realm of pure nothingness.

Noah had in that very moment by some mutation of the geometry of Zen, a convolution of the algebra of Stoicism, been suddenly and unconditionally released from all of the cloying manacles, the tortuous delusions of believing for another moment, that any of this could and would improve. His mother. Sister. Pulnick. Life there. All of it. None of it.

What is … is.

Suddenly and dramatically after vilifying him, his mother had switched from hysteria to melancholy. She was hunched over staring into her lap, rocking to and fro, shoulders contracting with the initial tremulous shrugs of weeping. He knew she was on the brink of plunging into the abyss of self-pity and pointless loathing.

Noah leaned to her and whispered.

"Thank you, Mom."

She assumed he was being an upstart. She had seen this smart alecky side of Noah before.

"You should be ashamed. You'll be sorry. Yes. Someday. Someday … Noah … someday…"

He put his arms around her and fought back his tears.

No matter what … this was his mom.

She was his oyster.

He was her pearl.

Chapter Ten

November 10 ...

Patriot Act

Merkel was being very understanding with Noah. He had already missed nine days of work. But because of the severe nature of his circumstances, involving a member of his immediate family, they told him he could take as much time as he needed and there would be no repercussions. His job would be waiting for him.

Gretchen on average was about the same as when she had arrived at the ICU unit of the university hospital. She had her good days and her bad. But overall she was not improving, something which was of great concern to two of the three specialists on her case.

There was, of course, a burns specialist who determined that though 30% of her body had suffered severe exposure to the flames, the penetration was not great, and certainly not life-threatening. She would heal with some barely-noticeable scarring. Even so, at present her burns were a gruesome affair, especially for someone not intimately familiar with such things. Her dressings constantly needed changing, a stomach-churning procedure that Noah had witnessed only once — enough to last him a lifetime.

Unlike the burns specialist, the internist and neurologist were extremely concerned.

When her "numbers" indicated systemic problems, the resident expert on internal organs came into the picture. His prognosis was not very optimistic. Gretchen was a mess. The extent of damage to her heart, liver, spleen and kidneys became more evident each passing day. This was not related to the fire. When it was determined through blood toxicity tests that it was the direct result of her abuse of crystal meth, a neurology specialist also was assigned to her.

Twice in the first week in the burns ward, Gretchen had suffered dramatic episodes where she nearly stopped breathing, had mild convulsions, and slipped briefly into a coma.

At the end of eleven days, she was still considered to be in very critical condition. Most of the time she was unconscious, but occasionally she opened her eyes and languidly looked around the room. At least she wasn't yelling any more. She was far too weak for that. When she did speak, it was never to Noah. She would try to talk but it was mostly nonsensical mumbling, directed to her mom, maybe a nurse, and sometimes to someone who floated above her bed only she could see.

From all appearances, Gretchen was in there for the long haul.

It was decided that Noah should make a run back to Pulnick to pick up some clean clothes and various other things his mom wanted. Memorabilia.

Magazines. A 500-piece puzzle. Cosmetics. A manicure kit. His mother had this notion that if she did Gretchen's nails, it would speed her recovery. Image is everything. Noah wasn't clear on what research findings she might be basing this on, but under the circumstances he wasn't going to argue.

He left at the crack of dawn. The drive took him a little over three hours. He swung by his flat, looked at his mail — nothing there except a couple of bills — went to the family house to collect the odd assortment of items his mom had requested, then turned right back around to return to the hospital.

Noah was blasting through Pulnick about 20 MPH over the speed limit when he saw him. He pulled the car to a screeching halt and jumped out.

"Jiff! What are you doing here?"

"The fucking Army can't make up its mind. No. Scratch that … the fucking Army doesn't have a mind."

Jiff was standing by the curb, decked out in his full dress army uniform.

"You're looking sharp. Welcome home, my man!"

"It's a fucking dream come true."

"Can you get through a sentence without using the word 'fuck'?"

"Fuck no!"

The Department of Homeland Security was charged with protecting Americans and American soil against terrorist attacks from without and within, guarding against insurrection, preventing any organized mayhem, and generally maintaining a dumb calm throughout the land. However, the Posse Comitatus Act of 1878 strictly prohibited the use of the military — as in Army, Navy, Air Force, Marines — from acting in a law enforcement capacity on non-federal property under any circumstances. So technically the massive might of the U. S. military machine could not legally be used to keep the peace at home, regardless of the emergency.

Under President Bush and the current administration, it was a poorly kept secret that this act was honored more in the breach than in its observance. Even so, keeping up appearances had become more and more a priority lately. Numerous scandals had rocked both the executive and the legislative branches, many of them involving abuse of diplomatic power and the misuse of military personnel and materiel. So when paranoia about what might happen on 11-11-11 gripped the powers that be, they decided they needed to really think outside the box.

That something needed to be done — just in case — was not questioned. To be caught unprepared would be both embarrassing and irresponsible. As November 11th approached, the whole public discussion about what was going to happen got louder and louder, crazier and crazier, and had taken on a life of its own. It was a feeding frenzy in the media and eventually anyone who seriously questioned it — who even hinted that 11-11-11 was just a silly hoax — got no air time. The prevailing story line became not whether something was going to happen, but what was going to happen, what cataclysm or cataclysms we were in for.

Behind the scenes Washington insiders of every ilk — being high-minded, analytic and purportedly rational statesmen, with academic degrees from the best schools and memberships in the best country clubs — privately pretty much laughed it all off. Their public statements were vague and patronizing, impenetrable or cute, or merely 'no comment'.

But the truth was, there was some grave, very real concern about 11-11-11.

The concern was not about the potential for the end of civilization as we know it, or any of the other wild doomsday qua metaphysical claims being bandied about like a loose shuttlecock. It was about the potential for large segments of the population to plain and simply go bonkers. It was about the potential for riots, looting, shooting, for the pent-up emotions of a lot of agitated people being unleashed in chaotic and destructive ways. No one, for example, had anticipated that a little video tape of a typical boilerplate police beating by white officers of a troublesome black man, an itinerant named Rodney King, would result in the nationwide rioting in 1992. It was now even harder to predict how a population fed a constant diet of crime scene and reality shows, shock television, and processed foods laced with additives and hormones, might react.

The plan devised by the Department of Homeland Security was as simple as it was unorthodox. Military personnel would be "planted" in local communities. Huge numbers would be given leave and sent home to keep an eye on things. They would be given very specific but unofficial instructions — there would be no paper trail for watchdogs or whistleblowers to point to — on how to responsibly intervene, or if things got out of control, how to request military back-up.

That was how Jiff got sent home. He was instructed to stay in uniform, to show the local citizenry a "military presence" for whatever value that might have in mollifying the rabble. And he was to carry a special secure comm device to call for help if he saw any threatening activity developing.

What signs of an anarchistic uprising should he be looking for in Pulnick? People throwing unshucked corn at one another? Wild-eyed antagonists splashing each other from their canoes on Mark Twain Lake? Old ladies stabbing their orchids with crocheting needles? Bales of hay arrayed in front of city hall in the shape of a peace symbol? Drunken farmers square dancing on the sidewalks with unsheared sheep? Whatever the case, if a revolution picked up any kind of tailwind, at the other end of Jiff's secure cell phone were teams of highly trained urban fighting infantrymen, bivouacked next to Hellfire Missile-armed Apache helicopters, fueled and ready to go. Even though these same soldiers had frequently failed in the sands and mountains of Afghanistan, they stood ready to take on the residents of insurrectionist Monroe County, to keep the nation intact and on track.

Jiff and the three other soldiers sent home to Pulnick for this special assignment — two Army and one Marine — were the talk of the town. They were all formally and informally given warm and enthusiastic welcomes.

One young lady was particularly excited to see Jiff.

Margie Guster.

Seven months along now and showing it.

It had been a difficult time for Margie. She didn't want to be a single mom. The man who was responsible for this embryo taking up more and more real estate in her belly should be there for her, to hold and comfort her, ultimately be willing to walk the aisle and take up his proper role as father and husband.

The hitch was that she didn't know who it was.

She had made the rounds. Pointed the finger at every male who could potentially have impregnated her. The joke around town was that the hospital would have to DNA test every male within a hundred miles of Pulnick to figure out who the father was, since Margie was apparently anatomically ill-disposed to keep her legs from spreading in a wide welcoming, come-one come-all, statistically random invitation.

She even started trying to trick guys who couldn't have been the father, attempting with a midnight quickie to implicate them ex post facto, hoping they couldn't count backwards to nine. That was how Rich Flanagan had briefly slipped in and out of the picture. He slipped in — finally losing his cherry after eleven tormenting post-pubescent years — and ran like hell as soon as he saw what a nightmare he was in for if he stuck around, which was about five seconds after he splooged his love juice into her oft-used love canal.

Margie had worked all of the angles. She tried to pin it on every guy she could think of. Every single one of them managed to slip through her semen-drenched fingers.

Now Jeff 'Jiffy' Duncan aka Jiff, was back in town.

Poor Jiff. Unsuspecting. Unprepared.

He had pretty much forgotten about it. With the demands of boot camp, the general chaos and excitement of his brief deployment overseas, now his new special anti-terrorist assignment back in Pulnick, he never stopped to look back on the reason he had signed up for the Army in the first place. Which, of course, was to run like hell from what he assumed were Margie's baseless claims of paternity.

But Margie hadn't forgotten.

Small towns. There's just no escaping.

What are the chances of Jiff running into Margie at that very same moment that Noah was standing there greeting his old buddy?

In a town the size of Pulnick, about 999 to 1.

Noah saw her first. He tried to warn him.

Too late.

"Hi, Jeff. Remember me?"

End of the World Sale!

What part of "end of the world" were people not understanding?

If indeed the world was ending, trail mix, Kevlar underwear, purified water, skin creams and cartons of Top Ramen were not really going to help.

But Walmart was keeping busy.

Very busy.

Their most recent promotion had been going on for nearly a month now, touting Walmart as the only place you needed to go for all of your emergency needs. It was one-stop shopping for the disaster to end all disasters.

The best buying tips for the Apocalypse!

WALMART—YOUR "END-OF-THE-WORLD"

PLACE TO SHOP

That this was the Mother of All Catastrophes, the one which would terminate all life on Earth, vanish the Solar System, and possibly make the entire Universe go away, was not a factor. Logic step aside! There was money to be made!

One thing about capitalism. It was agile. It could sure move fast when it needed to.

And Walmart was the nuclear furnace at the center of the hot fireball of consumerism.

There was a thirty foot high LED countdown meter, visible from the next county if not Earth orbit, mounted over the facade of the gigantic building, directly above the main entrance. Its function was to stress the urgency of immediately buying the all of the things people allegedly needed. Today it read:

ONLY 1 MORE SHOPPING DAY TILL 11-11-11!!

A huge seller at the Big Box Store at the End of the Galaxy, was the hyperspace thermos bottle, called the Magnum Opus. Whenever it was moved or picked up, it played a disco version of Oliver Messiaen's "Quartet for the End of Time". Which, of course, nobody ever heard of. So it could have been playing "Little Latin Lupe Lu" by Mitch Rider and the Detroit Wheels and it would have worked just as well. Advertisements touted the thermos bottle's most amazing feature: *Dual purpose. Keeps your drinks either hot or cold!* Wow! Imagine that. Hot or cold! And you don't even have to tell it which to do.

There was a giant flashy booth in the center of the women's section of the store, featuring a new special array of cosmetics: Apocalyptics™ by Revlon. Several hyperactive sales girls, scantily dressed as sexy angels, demonstrated the proper application of everything from their Astral Lip Gloss to their Shadows of Nirvana face sculpting cream.

A whole range of over-the-counter medicinal products dedicated to addressing issues and alleviating any discomfort associated with rapture and trans-dimensional travel, packed the shelves. These included space travel motion sickness pills, SPF200 radiation block, creams for allergic reactions to space dust, anti-dehydration drinks — what? no drinking fountains on the Stairway to Heaven? — a quick weight-loss formula called *Slenderness Is Next To Godliness* (in order to look svelte when meeting your maker!), a product called *Geiger Balm* for gamma ray rash, non-prescription Duragesic transdermal patches to relieve any pain resulting from the elongating effects of near light-speed travel, even special soft 'astral traveling' non-chafing inflatable diapers called Bum Wraps, for hemorrhoid sufferers.

The Home Gardening department naturally devoted a lot of floor space to tin alloy pyramids, with special emphasis on the fact that they had been manufactured right here locally, and were endorsed not only by Björn Agynn, but by the Honorable Aldous Penthe, Mayor of Pulnick. Since time was running short, they were available for one day only at 40% off.

There was a Lost In Space Survival Kit, which included a talking GPS direction finder, a laser pointer pencil, a Pinochle deck, a baseball cap with a peace sign, cotton swabs, crackers with no expiration date, a tube of Velveeta cheese spread, Handi Wipes, a stick of 24-hour deodorant, and a multi-lingual phrase book which had in over 170 languages: *'I am from planet Earth and would like to be your friend. Take me to your leader.'*

And so it went: The same questionable or entirely superfluous products they typically sold — with the exception of the tin alloy pyramids — repackaged with a new spin. People clambering up and down aisles, climbing over one another, elbows flying, tempers short, grumbling and mumbling expletives, cash and credit cards flying out of wallets. Everyone finally lumbered back to their cars to try to stuff all of the stuff in and still leave room for the kids.

Since he worked the shipping and receiving area for the store, Jinx was up to his eyebrows. He felt like a one-armed wallpaper hanger. A one-legged ass-kicker. A one-titted pig with twenty hungry sucklings.

Being so busy had the advantage of making the time go by quickly. It became a big blur. Nothing particularly noteworthy stood out which might distinguish one from any of the other hundreds of forgettable days he spent there. The days just anonymously whizzed by.

There was one thing however, Jinx looked forward to. About a month ago, he noticed a very cute new girl working at the Dog-On-A-Stick eatery close to the main entrance of the building. She was a little overweight but had a lovely face and a great smile, and for whatever random reasons fueled such a response, she provoked a warm urgent swelling behind the zipper of his shrink-to-fit Levi 501s. He recently had been making a point of wandering by on his lunch hour. It was all fairly innocent. He didn't plan on pursuing anything with her. But it was nice looking at an attractive, sexy, apparently single girl five years his junior, and letting his male imagination do what male imaginations did.

Since he was showing up every day, she couldn't help but notice him, and probably just to alleviate her own boredom started being cordial to him. Not necessarily flirtatious, but certainly friendly and funny. They were fast becoming buddies. Joking. Goofing around. Sharing a few pleasantries.

It was all good. Something to break up the day.

The last few times Jinx had stopped by, he ordered his usual, but then they just kept on talking and he kept up the jokes and she kept on laughing and finally, he would sit down when other customers demanded her time. Same thing happened today. She got busy with other customers. He sat down and now was wolfing down his meal — it was the same every day, two dogs, fries and a Coke — hoping that she would get done before he had to go back to work, and they might have a few more minutes of silliness to get him through the rest of his busy day.

Jinx waited, but the line for phallus shaped fast food kept getting longer. Fun and games were over for today. He stood up. She waved and smiled, then went back to taking an order from an extremely obese woman with three obese kids. He waved, emptied his tray in the trash, then put it on a growing stack of identical trays by the turnstile exit, as he quickly strode out. If he hustled, he would be back on the loading dock with a minute to spare. They were expecting eight big shipments, so this afternoon would be particularly insane.

Relief *was* in sight. Tomorrow was the last day of the push on 11-11-11 merchandise. Then either the world would end or it wouldn't. Either way, the frenetic bustle of the past few weeks would be over. This mad rush shopping for the Apocalypse would finally come to an end.

There was a note on his desk when he arrived.

A note from his boss.

Report immediately
to my office.

What was this all about?

He would find out soon enough. He reported as requested.

His boss didn't wait for him to even finish crossing the room when he started to bellow.

"You were observed by security stealing food from the Dog-On-A-Stick. We are not running a soup line here, Mr. Jenkins. Your employment is terminated, effective immediately."

"But sir—"

"No 'buts' about it. Please collect your personals. You will be escorted out of the building. Have a nice day."

A hand reached out from behind him and took him by the arm. Jinx had not seen the uniformed security man in the rear of his boss's office when he walked in. They left together. Ten minutes later he was putting the key in the ignition of his Toyota Innova.

Jinx was fired for eating two hot dogs at the fast food court in Walmart and forgetting to pay for them. Technically, he didn't forget. He sweet-talked the pudgy little honey running the hot dog booth and she fluttered her eyelashes and giggled instead of collecting the $2.30 due for the nitrite-laced concoctions of ground up beef lips, eyeballs, testicles, ears, and other sinew. His excellent service at Walmart for several years did not factor in the decision to let him go, and he was replaced by yet another high school drop-out who would work unquestioningly for minimum wage and no benefits.

With a wife and four kids, the current Walmart sales campaign rang very true. Walmart *was* the end of the world place to shop. If he couldn't find another job really fast, it would certainly be the end of his world.

Then again, maybe after tomorrow he would have nothing to worry about.

Wonder what's on TV tonight.

Pickles

There were big flashy ads running non-stop on all of the cable channels and network TV stations, featuring swirling graphics, brilliant colors, explosions of light, mushroom clouds, spinning helixes, synchronized dancing angels, and images of every deity in recorded history. This was to be the biggest Pay-Per-View spectacular ever!

BA Ministries in association with
Don King Productions presents . . .

"The End of the World"
LIVE!!
FROM RACINE, WISCONSIN
HOSTED BY BJÖRN AGYNN
Subscribe NOW!!
Only... $199.95

It was going to be bigger than WrestleMania XVIII, bigger than Lady Gaga's *'Celebration of Lifestyle Options' Benefit Concert for the Lepers of Katmandu*, bigger than Iron Mike Tyson's 1 minute 29 second comeback fight with Peter McNeeley back in 1995, bigger than Pee Wee Herman's *But I'm Right-Handed* four-continent road show reprise of his once popular children's television program, bigger than Stephen Hawking's special guest cameo performance on Dancing With The Stars, bigger than the Spice Girls re-union tour, even bigger than the live coverage of the Pope's three-day visit to the International Space Station, which raked in over a half billion dollars for the coffers of the Catholic Church.

Expectations were high. Promoter predictions for its success were in the stratosphere.

Unfortunately, ticket sales were a little slow.

In fact, they were non-existent.

Apparently, even the most dimwitted TV viewers saw the inherent contradiction, if not heavy-handed irony, of paying to watch the end of the world on cable television. Or if indeed the world was ending, the best way to spend the time was not sitting glued to the boob tube.

Or maybe there was just something better on at the same time on another station.

There was this other question surrounding the event.

Why Racine, Wisconsin?

Many news analysts and commentators were asking that very thing.

Was it because of the beautiful scenery, its being a harbor city on the lovely shores of Lake Michigan, earning it the colorful moniker, 'The Belle City of the Lakes'?

Was it the gothic architecture of Racine College, an Episcopal preparatory school for boys founded in 1852?

Was it the fine reporting and journalistic integrity of the hometown newspaper, the Racine Journal-Times?

Was it Racine's maintaining such a strong manufacturing base when so much industry had left America, with the city's factories pumping out everything from farm machinery to floor wax to automobile parts?

Was it the excellent collection of animals at the Racine Zoological Park, one of the finest zoos in the Midwest — perhaps serving as a modern day Noah's ark for the predicted rapture?

Was it the Windpoint Lighthouse, a 112-foot tall structure which had been the object of so many paintings, which on 11-11-11 might act as some sort of cosmological beacon or antenna?

Maybe it was just the aw-shucks friendly-smile good-neighbor Wisconsin hospitality that the city had become known for?

Nope.

None of the above.

Why ... Racine ... Wisconsin?

It was all because of Darin Kendall.

Darin Kendall grew up in Racine, Wisconsin and ...

Darin Kendall wanted to attend his 25-year high school reunion and ...

Darin Kendall's high school reunion was scheduled for Friday November 18th and ...

Before Björn Agynn moved to Sweden and became Björn Agynn ...

World-renowned spiritual guru and cosmic fear-monger ...

Björn Agynn *was* Darin Kendall.

It seemed that Björn was getting a little homesick.

And really looking forward to some rest and relaxation with family and friends.

Björn aka Darin was obviously quite certain the world would *not* be ending on 11-11-11.

Because if it did he wouldn't get to visit his mom and dad and his buddies.

Or spend time with his high school sweetheart, Polly Pfister.

Björn had an endearing nickname for Polly.

He called her Pickles.

Eve of Destruction

Noah's drive from the hospital to Pulnick and back was like being on another planet, or maybe being on this planet countless years sometime in the future.

It had become an increasingly common sight over the past month to see the

177

tin pyramids popping up just about everywhere in and around Monroe County. The billboards had certainly done their job. However, Noah had no way of knowing and frankly didn't care, whether this running joke had gotten legs elsewhere.

On the drive, it became apparent that the madness had swept like wildfire all across Missouri and on at least into the eastern part of Kansas. He hadn't checked the news for so long, who knew? Maybe it was a national or international thing.

This being the 10th of November meant that as the hours ticked off, a final frenzy of pyramid installation was underway. He saw them wherever he looked — in fields, on farms, back yards, front yards, gardens, vacant city lots — erupting like dandelions in spring, or pimples the afternoon of a first date with someone you *really* want to impress.

Someone was really making a killing!

Someone.

Theodore Clemus and Aldous Penthe actually had to open several bank accounts to hold all of the money they were raking in.

They had been smart. Their pyramids were easy to assemble, reasonably light. A strong person could carry one by the handles incorporated in the sturdy box they came in, two persons no problem at all. Plus they were relatively inexpensive to buy and incredibly cheap to manufacture. They even came with a money-back guarantee, whatever that meant. After all, if the world didn't end, they could broadly claim that the pyramids had done their job, and if it did end, good luck finding the Complaint Department.

Unfortunately for the fortunes of the Tin Man Pyramids LLC, their cutting corners by not hiring an attorney to properly fashion the money-back guarantee would ultimately cause them serious problems. They wrote the high-sounding warranty themselves, guaranteeing against defects in workmanship, and included typical reassurances to the effect of: 'If you're not completely satisfied with this product … blah blah blah'. Notwithstanding their best intentions, they would in the not too distant future discover it lacked the convoluted jargon and incomprehensible legalese which would gut it of any meaningful recourse for the customer. Their misplaced frugality would come back to bite them.

The Clemus-Penthe models came in blue and white, which easily represented half of the thousands dotting the countryside, suburbs and even urban neighborhoods which Noah drove through, coming and going to the university hospital where Gretchen was being treated. But he could see there were other players in the pyramid-hawking game. Not only were there slight variations in design, but there was a generous sprinkling of other colors — yellow, green, purple, red and brown — creating the overall impression that a vast fleet of planes in some psychedelic airlift must have dropped thousands of huge sugar-coated candies from the sky.

On his return trip, as he entered the upscale outskirts of suburban Kansas City, Noah even spotted a few of what must be some ultra-deluxe models. They were a little larger, had a burnished platinum finish, were inset with round smoked-glass portholes, and sported satellite TV dishes on top. He wondered what the television reception would be like after the Universe had either been swallowed by a giant black hole, or had trans-dimensionally folded into itself like a piece of rice paper origami tossed into a hydrogen furnace.

As Noah came up within 6 miles of the Missouri-Kansas border, traffic slowed to a crawl. It didn't bother him particularly, since he was in no rush to return to the morbid scene back at the hospital. After twenty or so minutes of incremental progress on the multilane freeway, he took the next exit. He figured he could sit out the traffic for a while, maybe get a cup of coffee, grab a bite to eat.

He saw a few chain restaurants but none that appealed to him, so he kept driving, actually kind of getting lost. Then he stumbled on a sight he would remember for the rest of his life.

Blue Valley Park was just north of the I-70 freeway sitting conveniently mid-way between Independence and Kansas City proper, and was widely regarded as one of the most beautiful parks in the entire region. It was a picnicker's and hiker's paradise with rolling hills and expansive green lawns, the expanse broken and edged by stands of majestic old trees. There was even a well-stocked fishing pond in the middle of its hundreds of acres of verdant tranquility and relative privacy.

But it wasn't very tranquil and private today.

As far as the eye could see stretched a pyramid city, hundreds and hundreds of pyramids and their occupants. Not that anyone was inside the tin can structures.

Rather, they — tens of thousands of them — were out and about, around and between, having themselves one huge boisterous loud crazy outdoor end-of-the-world party.

There were Frisbees and hoola hoops and hackie sacks, shuttlecocks and volley balls, gigantic balloons, inner tubes, and inflatable plastic toys. A lawn sprinkler had created an enormous pool of mud, full of a lot of joyful mud people. There was dancing and singing. There were even two stages set up at opposite ends of the park with local bands pumping out their grindy pounding guitar and synth music at ear-shattering levels. God knows where they got the electricity. It didn't seem likely that this was a properly permitted or city sponsored event.

There was a decent display of indecency. For Kansas, Missouri and the other Bible Belt states, it was a rare and refreshing spectacle, with quite a few nipples perkily perched on bouncing bare breasts, as well as both male and female genitalia being invisibly caressed by the unseasonably warm early afternoon breeze, just like the good old days in the Garden of Eden. The few cops standing around didn't lift a finger to curtail the nudity. They seemed to be enjoying the show.

Noah had to admit. Some of the girls were pretty damn hot. Being from the Kansas City metropolitan area, they were city stock, leaner, more supple, more body and fashion conscious — certainly a pleasing contrast to the genetic mutations which passed for female Pulnick.

A few years ago, he had become familiar and fascinated with Woodstock. He watched clips on YouTube of both the live band performances and the LSD-fueled antics of 400,000 wild hippies. It was his introduction to the summer of love and education in flower power, and their liberating free love ethic, in a time of youthful celebration and hedonistic abandon.

How times change. But maybe not.

What he was seeing today didn't seem that much different. Maybe the idea that the world was going to end had unleashed, if only for a day, a similar liberation and abandonment of business as usual. Or maybe nobody believed that anything was going to happen tomorrow and it was just an excuse to party.

Whatever was going on, Noah was soon having the time of his life! He wandered around, meeting more people in an hour than he had met in the previous twenty three years. Everybody was friendly, full of hugs, glad to share their drugs, and his jaw began to hurt from smiling so much.

He worked his way to the front of one of the stages. The band playing was called Christine Crunk and the Frenetic Funk. They had a bass player and guitarist but were mostly electronic. The music was infectiously danceable and Noah ended up in the middle of more than a hundred writhing, twisting, bouncing, swaying, contorting dancers. He made some moves he had no idea he had in him. He hoped Michael Jackson was watching.

Sweaty and exhausted he worked his way through the crowd, which seemed to be growing by the minute. He ended up by the lawn sprinkler and decided to go for it. Off came all of his clothes and in he went. It was cooler this afternoon than he would have preferred but it still felt good. He took his turn on a mud slide that had been created by laying down a long sheet of plastic and smearing it generously with water and clay, then ended up in a mud throwing contest with a few others, including one girl who seemed to be showing him more than a statistically random amount of attention. She couldn't have been more than 18 or 19 and was a fox!

Unfortunately, it was time for him to go. The celebration would go well on into the night, then continue on into 11-11-11 for whatever that might bring. But even with the high he had gotten from a few tokes along the way, and the nearly irresistible temptation to stick around and see what might evolve with his new mud playmate, Noah knew his evening was already booked.

He rinsed off and started to get dressed. Miss Mud Plaything ran up to him just as he was tying his shoes and planted a life-changing kiss on his slightly blue lips.

"I'm Corrine. You're leaving? I'm sorry. Bye!"

Off she went. The sight of her wonderful naked body running back to play again in the mud would be etched in his mind for the rest of his life — the stuff of dreams and cherished memories recounted in a rocking chair by the pool, in the autumn years of life.

It took him quite a while to find, then extricate his mother's car from the madness. There were cars parked everywhere, often with little regard for letting anyone out, the presumption being that everyone who arrived was there to stay. But by hook, crook, luck and some plain old common courtesy from anonymous but considerate people, he managed to squeeze his vehicle out of the jam, then make it back to the freeway.

Traffic was light now and he would probably pull up to the hospital in about 15 minutes.

Kansas City had a solid reputation for music. It had been mentioned in quite a few songs over the years, not the least being the Lieber-Stoller rhythm and blues classic "Kansas City", made famous in 1959 by Wilbert Harrison. The sprawling metropolis of nearly two million people had over twenty five music stations, playing everything from blues and jazz to all shades of rock, hip hop and R&B.

Noah was bouncing around the radio dial when one particularly maniacal DJ caught his attention. Not that sounding completely insane and jacked up on two grams of coke was that unusual for radio personalities. This one had a special appeal. A demented edge. He had no qualms about totally insulting his audience as he introduced the next song.

> *Jabberwocky! Yo, you low dwellers. Philistines in the cellars. Climb on board! You got the dead end express, the worst of the best goin' nowhere but Route 666. Barry McGuire came alive back in 1965. This is the shite! Yabba dabba doo!*

It was "Eve of Destruction".
What a terrible song!
Decent lyrics but … ugh! It sure sounded bad.

> "Don't you understand what I'm trying to say?
> Can't you see the fears that I'm feeling today?
> If the button is pushed, there's no running away
> There'll be no one to save with the world in a grave"

To make things worse, the DJ kept screaming his incoherent nonsense over the singing.

> *Give me a break, muthah-suckas! We're goin' down alright. No runnin' away. No freakin' way!*

> "My blood's so mad, feels like coagulatin'
> Yeah, I'm sittin' here, just contemplatin'
> I can't twist the truth, it knows no regulation"

> *Yeh! Yell it like it is, Barry. Kaboom! Blam! Tomorrow it's all over, baby!*

"When human respect is disintegratin'
This whole crazy world is just too frustratin'"

When you're sitting in the smoldering ruins, idiots and fools, drones and stooges. Apocalypse apocalypse apocalypse! You heard it first right here! Ha ha ha ha!

"And you tell me over and over and over again my friend
Ah, you don't believe we're on the eve of destruction."

*Apocalypse apocalypse apocalypse! Ha ha ha ha!
AAAAAAAAHHHHHH!!*

"Oh, you tell me over and over and over again my friend,
Yeah, you don't believe we're on the eve of destruction."

America.
Everything was a joke.
And everybody was laughing.
Except for the ones who were crying.
Sometimes the woohoos and the boohoos blended together and there was no way to tell them apart. Tragicomedy? Comitragedy?
Shortly after arriving at the hospital, the beautiful smile that had been affixed to Noah's face as a result of his brief but exhilarating visit to the park, quickly became unglued. Gretchen had plunged into a deep coma, her heartbeat and blood pressure had become erratic, and she was showing early signs of renal failure.
It was no laughing matter.
His mother was crying.
There was nothing he could do but wait and hope for the best.
That seemed to be what a lot of people were doing this eve of November 11th.
Some were also partying. Some like the radio DJ were acting crazy.
But underneath it all, it was wait and hope for the best.
Pretty much like every other day on Earth.
Wait ... and hope for the best.

One Nation Under God

It was the last chance to make a buck and prices had been jacked up.
Jacked up through the ceiling and even the roof.
Regular gas was $8.99 a gallon.
Super was $9.99 a gallon.
A case of PBR $60.
A Swanson's TV dinner $11.

Convenience stores were the worst.

A 40 oz. Slurpy at 7-11 was $11.99 plus tax.

Bottled drinking water, normally $1.59 was an even $10.

A box of six plain unscented regular absorbency Kotex tampons $24.95.

An overcooked leather-nightstick kielbasa and a Pepsi $14.95 — mustard add 2 bucks.

The only bargain was the tin alloy pyramids at Walmart, which in a last ditch-attempt to unload them at their midnight madness sale, had been marked down 70%.

For whatever reason, skepticism had surrendered and rationality had become a murder victim in the tide of hysteria surrounding 11-11-11. A lot of people were taking it very seriously.

Even the White House.

Per a strongly-worded high priority national directive from the President of the United States — purely advisory since the Federal government had no legal authority at state and local levels — all public employees, particularly those involved with law enforcement, fire containment and animal control, were to be called in at midnight and put on emergency duty across the entire country. Mercifully, common sense and properly placed priorities prevailed. 98% of them called in sick, preferring to be with their families, or at their local tavern in the final hours of destiny.

In a perverse way, a country which had been fractured, divided, torn apart, set against one another and against itself over the past twenty or thirty years, in alternating waves of histrionic patriotism and morbid self-loathing, had now come together. To achieve it had taken the odd and unlikely confluence of superstition and rumor, sensationalism and fear-mongering, hypnosis and hysteria, mass manipulation and crass capitulation, spread by a handful of insane people, like a fine dust of PCP over the collective consciousness of the punch-drunk population.

But America was one nation again.

One nation under ... God.

Chapter Eleven

God

Noah was curious.

What was up with God these days?

Noah didn't believe in God. So he was purely asking from the perspective of those around him who did believe — which as far as he could tell was everyone. What did they think?

Was God behind the 11-11-11 thing? Was this really a part of His greater plan?

It's in the Bible!

That's what Noah was constantly hearing.

The Bible is God's own words!

Really?

Had these people actually read the Bible?

Noah had. A lot of it. It didn't paint a very flattering picture of the Creator, that's for sure. There had to be more to Him than what was portrayed in the Holy Book.

Maybe God had this twisted sense of humor. Maybe after creating the Universe, kick starting His little experiment with humans, and watching what a sham it turned out to be, He was bored. So He had resorted to these little pranks. 11-11-11 was like April Fool's Day. Just a little late.

Then again, maybe God was dead serious. Maybe His patience had run out. Maybe He had it up to his God eyebrows, so He was putting on the brakes and ending the whole damn thing. Humans had certainly mucked things up over the years. Wars, genocide, plunder, destruction. Okay, we had done some good constructive things too. But then it seemed like we were always turning around and tearing down what we had painstakingly built, or at least what someone else had built, and killing off a few million along the way.

Or maybe God felt the need to teach us a lesson every now and then. Just scare the bejeezus out of us. That would explain the rumors hovering around all of the time that the world was about to end. A little bogeyman-under-the-bed psychology from the Big Guy in the sky?

But hold on a minute.

This can't be right.

None of it.

Really stopping to think about it, stepping back and getting some perspective, how could anyone actually believe that God gave a flying fuck?

If the Universe was as big as astronomers and astrophysicists claimed, this little wet chunk of dirt in our solar system which we call Earth — but which He may not even have a name for — is one billionth of a trillionth of a quadrillionth of a gazillionth of the whole shebang.

It would be like us obsessing over a piece of lint at the bottom of the ocean.

Yes, if God was indeed *God*, the Guy thought big. Really big! He certainly would not be some sniveling micro-manager. What we mere humans did here on Earth wouldn't even come up on his radar screen. We'd be more like microbes clinging to a worthless piece of space rock — regardless of how many prayers we said, how many candles we burnt, how many hymns we sang, how many services we conducted, how many churches and cathedrals we erected in His honor and to His greater glory.

There was only one conclusion Noah could draw.

God would be sitting out 11-11-11.

Unless He had cable TV.

The Vigil

Many just stayed home.

Stayed home to be close to loved ones. To make love. To make dinner. To watch TV. Taking no precautions or pre-emptives. Hosting no visions or nightmares. No dreams. Harboring no particular expectations or entertaining nebulous hopes.

Que sera, sera.

Then there were thousands who were tucked in their little tin pyramids, eating snack food, playing cards, napping, listening to music on their iPods, generally doing the few things that can be done cramped into a 16 square foot space which required you to be sitting, lying down, or on all fours like a house pet. Most of these pyramid dwellers were in good spirits, implicitly congratulating themselves that they had been smart enough to invest a few dollars to keep themselves safe and avoid whatever horrors might be visited on the rest of the population.

Finally there were the fifty-fivers.

These were the ones gathered here today in a dried patch of marsh land a few miles south of Pulnick, just inside Mark Twain State Park. They not only accepted the idea that the world would end today, but believed that the apocalyptic moment would occur precisely at 11:11 am.

11:11 11-11-11.

There were over two hundred of them. Many brought prayer mats, or what passed for prayer mats, sometimes just the throw rug from the foyer.

A man dressed in an orange monk's robe addressed the crowd.

"10-9-8-7-6-5-4-3-2-1-mark! Watches synchronized. We're all on the same page now."

Thank goodness! Who'd want to risk missing something like this?

People looked about. Eyes shown expectantly.

Smiles were kind and graceful.

It wouldn't be long now.

Tick tick tick.

Suddenly!!!

The seconds ticked away.

The world held its collective breath.

Some sat quietly in their little tin alloy pyramids.

Some sat in lotus position holding hands in giant prayer circles.

Some knelt or bowed before their familiar iconic statues of Jesus or the Virgin Mary.

Some were curled up like fetuses, ready to leave the world much as they entered it.

Some thrust out their chests and threw back their shoulders to open the portals of their seven chakras to the infinite pure Oneness that all of the All would become.

Some cowered and diminished themselves, trying to become tiny and insignificant, hoping their humility would make them immaterial to the catastrophic fate of the rest of the Universe. By being so unworthy, they would avoid being dealt the destruction that should be their due.

Some sat outdoors with the unbounded heavens as their personal cathedral, hands lifted reverently to the sky, reaching high overhead to invite cataclysm or consecration, whichever arrived in a huge cleansing wave, a final tsunami of purifying light.

Some just became inert, hypnotized or rendered comatose by their anticipation of an event that was beyond their comprehension.

Then at precisely 11:11 am, as thousands upon thousands braced for eternity, their bodies resolute in austere asceticism and their hearts stretched wide like vast angelic wings ready to embrace some infinite possibility ... SUDDENLY!!!

!!!!!!!. . .   .   .

Nothing.

Nothing happened.

Nothing happened that wasn't already happening, or typically about to happen, that is. Birds chirped, clouds hovered, sewage made its way sluggishly through pipes buried under city sidewalks, a few remaining dead leaves fell to the ground, babies gurgled or cried or slept, the stock market kept churning out money for rich people, bread was rising on kitchen countertops, fish were jumping, and at least one person was plucking an unsightly hair from a mole.

Which goes to say that there were a few red faces when 11:11 am came and went, and nothing out of the usual happened. And quite a few disappointed faces. And relieved ones. Glassy-eyed ones. Some people cried. Some laughed. Others sang and chanted. Others just looked as they always looked ... confused.

Speaking of confusion.

How could anyone think the world would end at precisely 11:11 am?

What about the different time zones?

Did they picture the annihilation of the world taking place in chunks of disaster which mysteriously respected the artificial bands stretching from pole to pole, set up by the forward looking minds of the 19th Century?

Understandably, it is useful and sensible to have the manmade virtual tracking of time correlate with the movement of the sun across the sky. At 12 noon, the sun is at its highest point no matter where you stand on the planet. Everywhere on Earth, the sun rises in the morning hours and sets in the evening. And so on and so on. It all made sense.

But what sense did it make to predict that the entire Universe would end at 11:11 am?

Which brought up another highly salient point. What was supposed to happen at 11:11? There were certainly widely divergent opinions among the doomsdayers. The Second Coming. Annihilation. Rapture. Destruction. Reincarnation. Judgment Day. Last Train To Clarksville. All of the above. None of the above.

Of course by the end of the day, it all became a moot point. Tick tick tick went the clock, midnight arrived right on time, and the daily calendar flipped over another leaf, offering today's famous fun quote ...

11-11-11

The last thing that caught Noah's eye, as they pulled the bed sheet up to cover Gretchen's lifeless still body, was the tattoo.

11-11-11.

He never found out what her connection was to the metaphysical day of doom, or why she had decided to have it inked across her chest. Now he never would.

While the rest of the world — or more accurately the most recent batch of bananas from the crazy farm which constantly replenished the ranks of the normal-folks-gone-cuckoo — offered alms to amorphous invisible balls of energy, prayed to 1,111 angelic spirit guides, attempted to placate angry ancient gods who were returning for the great day of reckoning, exhorted their fellow man with poems citing quantum and string theory, chanted mantras, clicked their throats and clucked their tongues, twisted their bodies into pretzel-shaped antennas to become mystic receptacles for the beams of enlightenment which would irradiate the entire planet at some point in the course of the epic day, Noah just sat at his sister's bedside.

His mother cowered in one corner of the room sniffling and blowing her nose into a frilly handkerchief, which she repeatedly removed from and then replaced in the clammy cleavage between her saggy breasts. She had an unlit cigarette dangling in the corner of her mouth, was wearing fake Versace sunglasses much too large for her face, looked like she was being strangled by a long string of cheap plastic turquoise, and wore a Betty Davis hat. Her imitation mink half-stole was more in need of a good grooming than ever.

Noah just sat, elbows on knees, head hanging almost between his legs. Occasionally he looked up at the immobile, barely alive body attached to a respirator and a panoply of other miraculous medical devices which were brought in out of desperation, on the outside chance that some amazing turnaround might occur in Gretchen's losing struggle to keep going.

Gretchen died not at 11:11 a.m. or 11:11 p.m. but sometime in the middle of the afternoon. Her death was not heralded by the arrival of any bursts of cosmic energy, no floating apparitions, no signs from God, no disembodied orating anthropomorphic puffs.

The lines on the monitors just went flat. The thump thump of her heart was silenced.

They covered her body and wheeled it out of ICU on a stainless steel gurney.

Noah was left with the haunting afterimage of her tattoo.

11-11-11.

Had she somehow had a precognition of dying today?

A medical examiner came and went. Forms were filled out. Noah would eventually learn that her cause of death was attributed to massive failure of multiple internal organs, dysfunction the result of chronic deterioration over several months, and very recent chemical toxicity. Detected at time of admission were high levels of methamphetamine sulfate and cocaine. Traces of heroin were present, as well as evidence of recent alcohol intake. Superficial burns to 30% of her body placed additional demands on her compromised health. Death was finally caused by systemic failure resulting from gradual decline and the eventual cessation in the minimum functioning of several vital organs.

Systemic failure.

It was systemic failure alright.

A failure of the system.

But not just her system.

The entire system.

A breakdown of the family system. The educational system. The media. TV. Pop music. Everything. The American Way. It was all a fucking sham. A destructive hoax. A charade. A lethal game with only losers.

He hated her. But he had never wanted this. Maybe she was by his measure worthless. But it wasn't for him to measure. Didn't every human life have intrinsic value?

He leaned back and closed his eyes. Trying to grasp what had happened. The absolute finality of death. Gretchen. His little sister. What now?

When he opened them again, a nurse was bent over his mom. Looking very concerned.

"How long has she been like this?"

"Like what?"

The nurse immediately grabbed her intercom.

"Code blue! Burns. Station 4."

"Is there something wrong? I thought—"

"I think it's a stroke. There's sagging … the side of her face."

When the nurse pointed it out, it was obvious. How could he have missed it?

Then again, he hadn't even looked.

Suddenly the room was again full. A doctor and several nurses and attendants. His mom was lifted onto a gurney and rushed out the door before he could even take another breath.

It had indeed been a stroke. First she suffered an intracerebral hemorrhage. The blockage of a massive constellation of capillaries blew a hole in her brain like an erupting volcano.

Seven hours later she died.

Noah's mother had neglected to tell him that during the last month, she had suffered some serious setbacks in terms of her cancer. Her doctors had begun to suspect, then tests confirmed, that it was metastasizing. They had originally been confident they had removed it all in surgery, but these things are never 100%. Until they could determine the extent to which it had spread, then decide what to do, they put her on a new wonder drug that was supposed to help minimize the rate at which cancer cells multiplied. One serious risk — the one that killed her — was the tendency for the drug to cause blood clots. They prescribed an anti-coagulant to offset this, but apparently in this case, it didn't work. Clots eventually worked their way to her brain. Probably the stress of watching her only daughter — her little girl with the sweet tooth — didn't help. Who was to say? And what did it matter?

11-11-11.

Nothing of cosmological, epistemological or historical importance happened that day. No comets crashed into the Earth. No tsunamis swamped any continents. No spirit balls came to collect human souls. The moon remained in orbit as did the Earth itself and all of the other planets. No black holes swallowed the solar system. Jesus stayed home.

What did happen on that day was that some of the very same flesh and blood that Noah himself was made of, became inert and inanimate.

11-11-11.

It was a day that took away those most dear to him.

Who were not very dear to him at all.

It was all so completely ...
Incomprehensible.

The Perfect Blissful Fog of Nothingness

American ingenuity always saves the day.

Everybody got busy and with all due speed readied both Gretchen and Noah's mom so that there could be a double funeral. It was efficient, economical, and packed twice the punch in terms of personal suffering and sense of loss.

Kind of a two-for-one deal.

Serious bang for the buck bereavement.

Noah was so thoroughly staggered he was speechless.

Whatever was suggested he just nodded. Double funeral. Sure. Bronze caskets. Okay. Silk lining. Uh huh. Princess Diana hand corsages. Right. Seal the coffins with epoxy. Yes. Concrete grave liner. Do it. Shared tombstone. Of course. Perpetual gravesite care ...

His head just kept nodding.

Insanity is supposed to be the ultimate anesthetic.

It doesn't have to be taken internally to be 100% effective. It can just be around a person. Like a cloud of erosive numbing invisible gas. It can't be detected and there's no antidote.

Noah didn't cry at the funeral.

Because he couldn't.

He heard nothing of what was said.

He just stood there mute. Dumbfounded. Paralyzed.

Gretchen was buried in a beautiful floral print girly dress, the kind she never would have worn. It billowed about her shoulders and the lace-trimmed collar was tight around her frail, thin neck. They were spared seeing the tattoo. Her makeup was soft and subdued. As they always say, she just looked like she was sleeping.

His mom went out in style. The dresser at the funeral parlor must have had a sixth sense. She was wearing a tiara, black velvet choker, a pearl necklace and matching pearl earrings, a fur stole, and long suede gloves that went up to her elbows. Noah assumed she was wearing a long skirt, hosiery, and dress shoes. But the shiny bronze coffin only allowed her to be viewed from the waist up, so who knew. She might have been wearing a neoprene wet suit and flippers.

Quite a few people came through the doors at Greening Eagan Hayes Funeral Home in Shelbina. Not that he tried very hard, but Noah could only identify a few. A couple neighbors. A few folks he remembered from his two visits to Salem First Baptist Church. There may have been a lot of lookie-loos, or people with nothing else to do. The vast majority were quite old. Maybe they were there for a grim reminder of their own mortality and a preview of coming attractions.

Mercifully, there was only one day of open-casket farewells. Noah could not have handled a single additional minute of pained melancholy faces and weepy cocker spaniel eyes, and doubted if he could ever again smell flowers and not instantly vomit. He certainly never ever wanted to hear again the phrases *"I'm so sorry"*, *"It's part of God's plan"*, *"We're here for you"*, or *"They're in a happier place now"* — not because they weren't heartfelt or well-intended, but because they didn't make a damn bit of difference. Despite the best efforts of many kind individuals, he felt very little condoled and not at all consoled.

Fortunately, none of Gretchen's new dope friends showed up at the funeral parlor or burial. Obviously, his longtime friend Phil Roswell, who had been sweet on her forever, was absent. Noah, of course, knew why.

There were a handful of what he assumed were Gretchen's former classmates — they appeared to be her age. He never knew if she had any real friends. He always had his doubts.

Very sad.

Finally, on a cold windy day with gloomy grey skies that threatened to lash out with bitter icy rains, Noah's sister and his mom were lowered into the ground in nearby Hunnewell. The final service took place Wednesday November 16th at 9:30 am. A semi-retired pastor from Salem First Baptist gave a generic eulogy, then mumbled some brief prayers and routine quotes from the Bible.

People drifted back to their automobiles.

Noah just stood there. He vaguely remembered more than one person coming up to him and saying something. But he was deep within the anechoic chamber of his own perfect isolation. Their voices sounded like grey leaves blowing across a frozen lawn.

He stayed and watched as the cemetery grounds keepers finished filling the graves and tamping down the last few shovelfuls of dirt.

Then he turned and went home.

Magnetic North

Life returned to normal. As normal as it gets in Pulnick anyway.

The tin pyramids started to disappear. Sort of the way Christmas decorations eventually get pulled down and put away. The pyramids weren't good for anything. A few farmers tried to use them to store seeds or tools they might need in the field, but basically they were worthless.

Based on what Gretchen had told Noah, authorities checked dental records against the pile of cinders, bones and teeth stored at the forensics lab in St. Louis.

It was a match. Phil 'Zipper' Roswell, Noah's offbeat and adventurous childhood friend, always looking for something new and crazy and interesting, had bitten off one last chunk of living on the edge which he couldn't chew.

A memorial service was scheduled for Sunday November 27th, to be held at the First Christian Church in Pulnick. It was a rough way to cap off the Thanksgiving holiday weekend. It didn't seem like there was a lot to be thankful for this year.

Noah couldn't believe it. Another wake.

The gathering was small — family and close friends. Jinx was there with his entire horde. It looked like Mrs. Jinx had another one in the oven. Jiffy wandered in late, still on leave and still in full dress uniform. He stood at the rear of the church.

The pastor mounted the pulpit and immediately started to cry.

Noah couldn't listen. He was saturated with death and mourning.

After the official formal piety had run its course — an hour that would remain as a blank silent void in Noah's memory for the rest of his life — there was an informal reception in the church basement. Pretzels and soda pop. Pulnick knew how to pull out all the stops.

Noah got to say a 'hi' and 'good-bye' to Jinx before he and his wife wrestled their whining tantrum-throwing children out the door. He then walked up to Jiff, who appeared to be toasting anyone who came near him with a Dixie cup of Dad's Root Beer. No one came near him.

"Am I supposed to salute?"

"No. But you can kiss my ass."

"Well? How's it been? Being back home, I mean."

"Fucked up. That Margie Guster is all over me, man."

"She's just returning the favor. You were all over her, weren't you?"

"I have been nailed to the fucking cross! That wiggly lump of meat in her fat ass belly? They're sayin' it's mine!"

"What? What are you talking about?"

"Prenatal paternity testing. They can finger the father of the little turd before he even pops out of the pooper. Why me? It was a crowded field, dude. The fucking Boston Marathon."

"Looks like your sperm won the 10 cm dash."

"I wish it hadn't."

"What's next?"

"At a shotgun wedding, can I shoot the bride?"

"You're not going to marry her, are you?"

"No! Of course not. Just joking. I'm counting on its not being human. Then we can just drop it off at the Humane Society and have them put it to sleep."

"I gather you haven't really thought this through."

"But I have! Okay. Not really."

"Dude! It's my turn to say good-bye."

"You're moving to Hannibal."

"A little further. Alaska, my friend. North to Alaska."

"Smart move. Great timing. This time of year I hear it's minus 120 degrees. That's on a warm day."

"Whatever. Sometimes destiny has to wear thermal underwear."

This would be the last time Noah would see Jiff for … well, who knew?

He spontaneously grabbed his lifelong friend and gave him a hug. It was quick. Over in two seconds. Jiff gave Noah a look of mock sternness.

"You're not a homo now, are you?"

They both laughed. Then they high-fived and went their separate ways.

Noah was finally free to leave. Tomorrow was the big day. No more funerals. No more good-byes. No more misery. No more Missouri. It was over.

It seemed ironic or just plain cruel that the price of his freedom was losing both his mom and Gretchen. But that was the ugly fact. The truth isn't always pretty. Maybe it never was.

His bags were still packed from back in June when he was so determined to get out of Pulnick and on with life — actually to get a life. All his worldly possessions — all the ones that didn't end up in the dumpster behind the Buckman's Convenience Store on the main drag into town — were stuffed into a backpack and a carry-on duffel bag.

And so it was.

Please fasten your seatbelts and return your trays to their upright position in preparation for landing. We will be touching down in approximately 15 minutes.

As the plane circled Fairbanks for a landing, welling up in Noah to the point of bursting, was an exhilaration, an elation, a *rapture* — the powerful and nearly overwhelming feeling that he was finally free from the interminable confines of a prison.

It was finally behind him.

When Noah's plane touched down in Fairbanks, after nearly 17 hours of flying a circuitous and environmentally-unfriendly 3,378 miles, he entered the land of grizzly bears and oil pipelines, caribou and women that didn't look much different, steely-armed men with beer in their veins, and glaciers of ice the size of mountains.

His first impulse on deplaning was to kneel down and kiss the good earth of his new home.

Good thing he didn't. His lips would have instantly frozen to the tarmac.

"Holy fuck! Jiff was right. It *is* cold here!"

More Books by John Rachel

If you were dazzled by what you just read, please check out these other fine novels by this author and political blogger.

"The Man Who Loved Too Much"
Trilogy

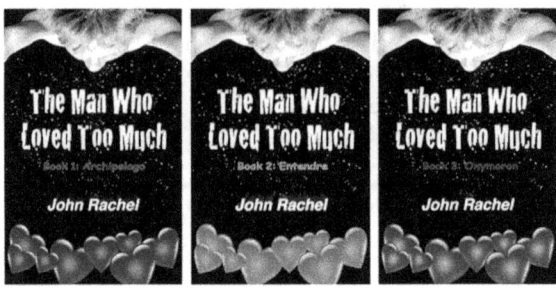

Billy Green is bright, enigmatic, and lost. He spent his first 28 years trying to figure out who he is and where he fits in. His life has been a wild, unpredictable quest to attach himself to some reality he can grasp and live with. He grew up in an abysmal suburb of Detroit, escaped to university life at Cornell, got married and divorced before being thrown headlong and entirely unprepared into the insanity and social chaos of New York City.

Book 1: Archipelago
Amazon (Kindle): amzn.to/1tyIRiw
Amazon (Print): amzn.to/1z8F8aD
Barnes & Noble: bit.ly/ZDnQVO
Apple iBook: bit.ly/1ycltFD
Smashwords: bit.ly/1w62HOX

Book 2: Entendre
Amazon (Kindle): amzn.to/18x1ZnS
Amazon (Print): amzn.to/1xfmjp3
Barnes & Noble: bit.ly/18OGY85
Apple iBook: apple.co/1bkFQe7
Smashwords: bit.ly/1AMUCPz

Book 3: Oxymoron
Amazon (Kindle): amzn.to/1LJnMc
Amazon (Print): amzn.to/1NZPU9Y
Barnes & Noble: bit.ly/1fvzxXD
Apple iBook: apple.co/1DfoG9g
Smashwords: bit.ly/1LJnRgJ

"An Unlikely Truth"

In this political drama, a bright, young, idealistic, Green Party candidate in his bid for the congressional seat of a conservative district in Ohio, teams with a beautiful, fiery African-American intern to combat the slick deceptions and ruthless tactics of a sweet-talking right wing incumbent.

Amazon (Kindle): amzn.to/1jetpiY
Amazon (Print): amzn.to/1lddvsp
Barnes & Noble: bit.ly/1l5FmuG
Apple iBook: bit.ly/1gT2O7w
Smashwords: bit.ly/1fIU3Mq

"Candidate Contracts: Taking Back Our Democracy"

Candidate Contracts: Taking Back Our Democracy

A Step-By-Step Plan for Radical Electoral Reform and 3rd Party Empowerment

by John Rachel

Prepare to understand contemporary politics as never before! Prepare to see the future of American democracy! This manifesto offers a detailed, step-by-step plan for cleaning up the corruption in Washington DC. This is electoral reform so radical that in one master stroke, it puts America on the path to a healthy economy and directly addresses its #1 and #2 challenges: the suicidal march to war and the destructive impact of a historically high level of wealth inequality.

Amazon (Kindle): amzn.to/1QJRiNZ
Amazon (Print): amzn.to/1Cuq0du
Barnes & Noble: bit.ly/1GpTTLq
Apple iBook: apple.co/1BXnPcy
Smashwords: bit.ly/1B4DQCp
Kobo: bit.ly/1QETE64

Coming Soon

[2016 and beyond]

"Sex, Lies and Coffee Beans"

"Love Connection"

"The Last Giraffe"

"13 - 13 - 13"

"Happy Happy Dreaming Girl"

"The Naked American"

"St. Jerome's Home For The Sexually Insane"

About The Author

John Rachel has a B.A. in Philosophy, has traveled extensively, been a songwriter and music producer, and is a bipolar humanist. He has spent his life trying to resolve the intrinsic clash between the metaphysical purity of Buddhism and the overwhelming appeal of narcissism.

Since 2008, when he first embarked on his career as a novelist, he has had eight fiction and two non-fiction books published. These range from three satires and a coming-of-age trilogy, to a political drama and most recently a crime thriller. The two non-fiction works were also political, his attempt to address the crisis of democracy and pandemic corruption in the governing institutions of America.

Never knowing when enough is enough, the hyperthyroid Rachel continues to be very busy. He has three more novels in the pipeline for publication in 2016: *Sex, Lies and Coffee Beans*, a spoof on the self-help crazes of the 80s and 90s; *Love Connection*, a drug-trafficking thriller set in Japan; and finally *The Last Giraffe*, an anthropological drama involving both the worship and devouring of giraffes, which unfolds in 19th Century sub-Saharan Africa. Several major publishers have declared that they will do everything in their power to make sure these books never see the light of day.

Moreover, he recently increased his output of incendiary political blogs, sure to alienate the remaining few remnants of his meager literary following.

John Rachel's last permanent residence in America was Portland, Oregon where he had a state-of-the-art ProTools recording studio, music production house, a radio promotion and music publishing company. He still writes music and, much to the annoyance of his neighbors in the traditional rural Japanese town where he now lives, attempts to sing his original songs.

• • •

You can follow John Rachel's adventures
and developing world view at:
jdrachel.com

• • •

Since the open mind recognizes no borders, you are also
invited to join us in the ongoing dialogue about
literature and the writing arts at:
literaryvagabond.com

Author John Rachel

Legal Notices and Disclaimers

11-11-11 is an original novel which is protected under international copyright law and registered with the U. S. Library of Congress © John D Rachel, 2011 (1st Edition), 2012 (2nd Edition), and 2015 (3rd Edition).

11-11-11 is entirely a work of fiction. Names, characters, places, brands, media, and incidents are either the product of the author's imagination or are used fictitiously. The author acknowledges the trademarked status and trademark owners of various products and services referenced in this work of fiction, which have been used without permission. The publication/use of these trademarks is not authorized, associated with, or sponsored by the trademark owners, but appear as common features in the story as they are common features in modern everyday life. No product endorsements are meant or implied by their use.

The author also quoted song lyrics in the story as follows: "Welcome Home" performed by Metallica, words and music by James Hetfield, published by Creeping Death Music © 1986; "Walk Like An Egyptian" performed by The Bangles, words and music by Liam Sternberg, published by APRS © 1985; "Eve Of Destruction" performed by Barry McGuire, words and music by P. F. Sloan, published by Universal Duchess Music © 1965.

Finally, the sub-chapter "End-of-the-World Sale" appeared as a short story in the June 2011 issue of Down In The Dirt Magazine.

.

www.ingramcontent.com/pod-product-compliance
Lightning Source LLC
Chambersburg PA
CBHW071205260626
47162CB00003B/1176